A Cryptic Clue

Also available by Victoria Gilbert

Booklover's B&B Mystery

A Fatal Booking

Reserved for Murder

Booked for Death

The Blue Ridge Library Mysteries

Death in the Margins

Renewed for Murder

A Deadly Edition

Bound for Murder

Past Due for Murder

Shelved Under Murder

A Murder for the Books

Mirror of Immortality Series

Scepter of Fire

Crown of Ice

A Cryptic Clue

A HUNTER AND CLEWE MYSTERY

Victoria Gilbert

CROOKED LANE

NEW YORK

Published in the United States by Crooked Lane Books, an imprint of The Quick Brown Fox & Company LLC.

Crooked Lane Books and its logo are trademarks of The Quick Brown Fox & Company LLC.

Library of Congress Catalog-in-Publication data available upon request.

ISBN (hardcover): 978-1-63910-252-5
ISBN (ebook): 978-1-63910-253-2

Cover design by Alan Ayers

Printed in the United States.

www.crookedlanebooks.com

Crooked Lane Books
34 West 27th St., 10th Floor
New York, NY 10001

First Edition: July 2023

10 9 8 7 6 5 4 3 2 1

Dedicated, with love, to my mom
Barbara King Lemp
1931–2022

Chapter One

O n the day I met Cameron Clewe, I thought I was simply changing jobs. I had no idea I was also changing my life.

Ushered into a snug but elegant library by a beautiful young woman who informed me she was Lauren Walker, Clewe's personal secretary, I was struck by two things. First, Mr. Clewe, who'd recently hired me, sight unseen, to inventory and catalog his extensive collection of books and related artifacts, was much younger than I'd expected. Given his wealth and interest in rare books and ephemera, I'd assumed he'd be at least forty. But the tall, slim, man standing by a stone fireplace, one fine-boned hand pressed against the rough-hewn wood mantel, looked to be closer to thirty. He was certainly more a contemporary of my daughter than of me.

My second thought was one of aesthetic admiration. With his slightly shaggy auburn hair and aquiline features, Clewe could be mistaken for a model for a prestigious British clothing company. A smattering of freckles sprinkled across his fair skin gave him a boyish quality that was contrasted by the sharp line of his jaw and tightly drawn lips. As my actress daughter would say, he was "leading man material." This impression was enhanced by his tailored wool trousers and the ivory fisherman's knit sweater he wore over a peacock blue button-down shirt. *A definite charmer, I bet*, I thought, as I fiddled with a button on my navy wool jacket.

Then he opened his mouth.

"I didn't realize you were so old," he said, in a voice totally devoid of humor. "And rather heavier than I expected, given that photo on the university website."

I stared into his eyes, gray-green as a cold sea, and took a deep breath. The picture he was referencing had been taken ten years earlier. I'd been scheduled for another photo before everything had fallen apart. A recent reorganization—or *rebranding*, as the new provost put it—at the university where I'd worked as a librarian for over thirty-five years had forced me into retirement.

I considered my next statement. At sixty, I couldn't take early Social Security for another two years, and while my lower-cost group health insurance continued into retirement, my salary did not. This job would allow me to supplement my rather modest pension doing work I loved. It also provided a new challenge. Although the younger generation might see me as over the hill, I still felt the urge to scale new mountains.

All of which meant I had to choose my words with care. I smiled and lifted my hands in a "what-can-you-do" gesture. "That photo is a bit dated. As for my current appearance—years working in academia has taken its toll, it seems. But I'm certain you hired me for my expertise, not my looks."

"I just hope you're up to the challenge. I've stored portions of my latest collection in the attic, so you'll need to carry boxes up and down two flights of stairs on a fairly regular basis." Cameron

Clewe's eyes narrowed. "Please don't expect me to always be available to assist in that endeavor."

I tugged the hem of my jacket over my hips. Maybe I was older, and a little heavier than I used to be, but I still had the use of all my limbs. *And my faculties*, I thought, fixing Clewe with the stare I'd perfected in dealing with students who caused trouble in the library.

"I assure you I'm perfectly capable of any physical exertion required by this position." I kept my tone mild and tried to avoid flinching at the relentless tapping of his fingers against the mantel. "I must say I'm thrilled to be able to work with your materials. In our email exchanges, you mentioned a new acquisition that particularly intrigues me—the collection of books and papers connected to classic mystery and detective authors."

"That's where I want you to start." Clewe, staring at his fingers as if they were something detached from his body, finally stilled their repetitive drumming. "I own several other book collections I'd like you to work on, some of which are stored off site. I kept the mystery-related materials here, as I want you to tackle that first." He cast me a tight-lipped smile. "Mysteries are a particular fascination of mine. I love their logic, and all the clever puzzles. I can usually deduce the culprits before the end, but I still enjoy the mental exercise."

"You said you had materials related to some of the greats, like Christie and Sayers and Rinehart," I said, shifting from foot to foot. The floor of the library, while beautifully finished, was hard beneath the thin soles of the dress pumps I'd worn for the occasion. Not one for heels, I found teetering on them for any length of time uncomfortable.

"Even a few things connected to Poe." Clewe's face brightened. "He was one of the first to write in the genre, you know. He's usually linked to his horror stories, but he also wrote some wonderful detective fiction."

I nodded. "*The Murders in the Rue Morgue*, *The Gold-Bug*, and *The Purloined Letter*. Great stuff."

"Also *The Mystery of Marie Rogêt*. People always forget that one." Clewe's expression and tone grew animated, betraying his deep interest in this subject.

And his need to be right, I thought, studying his angular face with amusement. His enthusiasm reminded me of former library patrons—how their eyes had lit up when discussing any topic they believed they knew more about than I did. I hadn't minded their air of superiority then and didn't mind Clewe's now. It charmed me to see someone so enthused about research and scholarly pursuits.

Lauren Walker entered the library with a pewter tray holding two crystal tumblers. As she passed by, she shot Clewe a sharp look from beneath her thick dark lashes. Setting the tray on a side table, she turned to face him. "Really, Cam, couldn't you at least invite Ms. Hunter to sit down before you launched into one of your dissertations?" She crossed her arms over the bodice of her pale yellow linen dress, Yellow wasn't a color many people could successfully wear, but Lauren, with her dark skin, hair, and eyes, looked quite splendid.

"Besides," she said, wrinkling her brow, "you hired Ms. Hunter because she's a professional. I'm sure she knows as much as you do about literature, not to mention more about how to organize all your books and things."

A Cryptic Clue

Meeting Lauren's implacable gaze, Clewe's face paled, throwing his freckles into high relief. "You're right, of course. Forgive me, Ms. Hunter. Please, take a seat."

"Thank you." I cast Lauren a grateful smile before choosing one of the wing-backed chairs flanking the cherry table holding the tray and glasses. "And please, call me Jane. I know I may be twice your age, but I hope we can be colleagues. At any rate, you don't have to treat me with such formality."

"Of course." Clewe twitched his lips into what he probably thought was a pleasant smile. "And you can call me Cam. Everyone else in the house does," he added, with a glance at Lauren.

She lifted her feathery dark brows before exiting the room, her high heels beating a staccato rhythm against the wide plank floor.

Leaving me alone with the rather intimidating young man who was to be my new employer.

Chapter Two

I studied Clewe after Lauren left, wondering if there was more between them than a boss and employee arrangement. Not that it was any of my business. It was just one of my quirks to be intrigued by human relationships, especially of the romantic variety. *Even though you made a hash of your own*, I thought with a wry smile.

Settling back in my chair, I reached for one of the tumblers. Thankfully, it contained water; just what I needed for my dry throat. Taking a long swallow, I surveyed the library. One wall was dominated by the stone fireplace where Clewe stood, one hand still gripping the rough-hewn mantel, while a bulky antique desk was docked like an old wooden ship on the blue-and-beige patterned rug covering the dark plank floor.

The other walls of the room featured floor-to-ceiling wooden bookshelves, varnished in an ebony finish. Gilt embellishments tooled into the leather spines of many of the books glinted under the soft white lighting hidden beneath the shelves. Setting down my glass, I focused back on Clewe. *No, Cam*, I reminded myself.

He met my inquisitive gaze, his rose-gold lashes fluttering and the knuckles on his hand blanching to bone.

I straightened in my chair as a wave of understanding swept over me. Cameron Clewe's imperious behavior wasn't driven by deliberate rudeness. He was nervous.

Actually, terribly anxious, I realized, *and extremely uncomfortable. One of those people who never knows what to say in social situations and blurts things out without realizing how the words sound to the recipient.* "Wouldn't you like to sit down as well?" I asked gently. "Your secretary left a glass of water for you."

Cam brusquely bobbed his head before striding over and slumping into the chair on the other side of the cherry end table. "I'm not really good with new people," he said without looking at me. He stretched out his long legs and grabbed the second tumbler. After taking one swallow, he plunked down the glass before staring up at the ceiling. "Or people in general, actually."

"I see." I gave him a sidelong glance. With his chin tipped up, his hair spilled over the back of his collar, making him look even younger. He slouched awkwardly in the chair, like a teen who'd grown too fast to arrange his limbs gracefully. "If I can ask without being rude, how old are you, Cam?"

"Thirty-three," he said tonelessly. "Old enough to know how to behave, or so I'm told. But I always seem to put my foot in it, especially when I'm around people I don't know well." He lowered his gaze and shot me a sardonic smile. "You seem to have a way of making me spill my secrets, Ms. Hunter . . . Sorry, Jane."

"Maybe it's all those years working with college students. Or the fact that I've raised an extremely charming but sometimes thoroughly exasperating daughter." I flashed him a warm smile. "She's an actress, you see. Drama is her middle name."

"Ah." Cam's expression grew thoughtful. "She lives with you?"

"No, she's been out on her own for a while. She's thirty, which is difficult for me to believe, but there it is." I pursed my lips, considering the complications that could arise if Bailey met Cam. She was a little too fond of handsome men, especially of the seemingly damaged variety. "Actually, she's off on a national tour for the next year or so. Which is one reason I was happy to find this job, along with an inexpensive apartment in town. It's allowed me to sell our old house and start over without a mortgage. Considering my rent is on the cheaper end, it's definitely a significant savings."

"I hope you'll be comfortable there." Cam sat up and leaned forward, gripping his knees with both hands. "I'm not sure how I'd deal with a small space, especially in terms of proper storage. Of course, Lauren tells me I'm too obsessed with things being . . ." He frowned and gnawed on his lower lip for a second. "A certain way, I guess."

"A place for everything and everything in its place?" I asked. "As a librarian, I can understand that. It helps to be organized, especially when you're undertaking things like this inventory and cataloging project."

"It's a little more than that," Cam said, standing and striding over to one of the bookshelves. "But yes, your work. I hope you plan to start on that by Monday?"

"Happy to," I said, which was a polite lie. I'd rather have waited a few more days so I could unpack all the boxes the movers were scheduled to dump in my apartment tomorrow and still have a day or two of rest before starting my job. But I had the feeling my new boss wouldn't be interested in hearing about, or accommodating, such mundane issues.

"Just so you know, I have some guests staying here right now." Cam ran one hand through his auburn hair, sweeping it away from his forehead. "They shouldn't be a bother. I just don't want you to be surprised by their presence in the house. They're scholars, like me, although somewhat older." He glanced at me. "Closer to your age, I expect."

"Are they here to examine the new collection?"

"No, although at least one of them has a strong interest in such things. She's actually taught courses on the Golden Age mystery authors."

Thinking this offered a good opening to further prove my worth as an employee, I slid to the front edge of my chair. "I know the cataloging comes first, but I'd be happy to help any of your guests with research, since that's another one of my skills."

Cam drummed his fingers again, this time against the other sleeve of his ivory sweater. "Thanks. I'm not sure that will be necessary, but I'll keep it in mind. Anyway, I'm sure you won't get any requests for research assistance this weekend. Everyone's focused on the fundraising gala happening on Sunday evening." Perhaps sensing my surprise, Cam added, "Two friends of mine are actually hosting it. I'm just supplying the space, because their homes aren't big enough. It will be rather a large crowd." Cam grimaced, as if the thought pained him. "Now, if you don't mind, I think I'll have Lauren give you a tour of the house and property."

In other words, I was being dismissed. I rose to my feet and crossed to him, extending my hand. "I really am delighted to be here, Cam. It's a librarian's dream to get to work with such fascinating materials."

Cam examined my outstretched fingers for a moment before placing his own hands behind his back. "I'm just glad you're so enthusiastic about the job. I hope that attitude won't change when you have to dig through stacks of dusty boxes."

"You really think I haven't done that before?" I dropped my hand and offered him a rueful smile. "As I mentioned in my cover letter, we took in a lot of gifts at the library, and one of my duties was to examine and inventory those materials. Trust me, I've dealt with dust. Mold too," I added, wrinkling my nose. "I doubt your collection is in as bad shape as many of those donations."

Cam stared down at his expensive leather loafers. "That's right. It's one reason I put your résumé on top of my consideration pile. Along with your knowledge of cataloging and research, of course."

I tugged down my slightly rumpled jacket. "I hope I can live up to your expectations."

As he raised his head to meet my gaze, the ghost of a smile flickered over Cam's handsome face. "Honestly, that would be a first," he said.

Chapter Three

L auren was waiting for me in the front hall. I noticed she'd changed her heels for flats and had thrown on a sweater.

"I hear you've been given the job of tour guide." I flexed my toes inside my pumps, wishing I could kick them off.

"I have, but perhaps we should stop by the mudroom first, so you can slip on some walking shoes. I think we have something that might fit." Lauren's dark eyes sparkled with humor. "It's not easy to navigate the grounds in heels."

"I would love that." I turned to survey the hall, which had a ceiling that soared up into a complex arrangement of wooden rafters. The lower portions of the walls were paneled in dark wood, with whitewashed plaster above. A grand staircase, its double set of polished wood steps rising on either side in a gentle curve, filled the back of the hall. The arch formed beneath the steps enclosed a marble fireplace. "This is all quite grand, isn't it? I'm surprised the house was built in the twentieth century, to tell you the truth. But I think I read it was constructed around 1920?"

"That's right. It doesn't reflect its actual era much. The original owners, the Airleys, wanted to build their very own old English estate, and imported some of the decorative features from homes and castles in Britain. The even named it Aircroft to evoke an Old World ambience." Lauren cast me a glance. "But you probably researched all that when you were applying for the job."

"I did. They made their money in steel and railroads, if I remember correctly."

"Yes." Lauren gestured toward the tall, iron-strapped wooden front doors. They were set in an arched opening with plaster decorations that included a medallion in the center—a brightly painted shield that looked like it belonged to some British ancestral estate. "As you see, they even had a coat of arms created. I suppose they planned to establish a dynasty, but then their only child died in his late twenties, without any children of his own, so that was the end of that."

"And they continued to live here, just the two of them, even after their son died." I shook my head at the sad image this evoked. "They stayed until their deaths, and then Cam's father bought the place. That was sometime in the early eighties, right?"

"Yes, around eight years before Cam's birth. His mother didn't move in until they married, and Cam was born less than a year later." Lauren took off at a brisk pace, heading down a narrow corridor leading off the main hall. "Cam's dad was twenty years older than his mother, but he still outlived her by many years. So, similar to the Airleys, it was old Mr. Clewe and Cam rattling around here after her death. Along with a housekeeper and chef, of course. Cam's dad, Albert Clewe, started the tradition of having them live in, and Cam has continued that practice."

As I followed Lauren, I noticed that this corridor was much plainer than what I'd seen of the rest of the house. It had unadorned plaster walls, painted a stark white, and tile flooring. We passed by what looked like a storeroom before stepping into a large, airy kitchen.

Unlike the rest of the house, this space made no effort to appear picturesque—white marble countertops, brushed metal racks, and modern appliances sparkled in the light falling from tall windows. The slate floor and white subway-tile walls would be perfectly suited to a commercial restaurant setting. Only the mullions in the windows indicated that this kitchen was located in a vintage home.

Two people standing behind a massive work island looked up at our approach—a short, stocky, middle-aged woman and a man of average height whose muscular arms were at odds with the rest of his wiry build. The woman, who Lauren introduced as Dia Denton, the housekeeper, was tastefully dressed in a crisp white blouse and tailored gray slacks. The man, Mateo Marin, whose dark hair was slicked back from his broad forehead, wore a white coat over black trousers, in keeping with his position as chef.

"Nice to meet you both," I said, after Lauren shared my name and mentioned I'd be working on Cam's book collections. "I guess you're busy preparing for Sunday's gala?"

"Heavens, yes." Dia Denton ran her fingers through her short, toffee-colored hair. "It's always a challenge, especially since we have to bring in extra help for these things."

"Which is why I say we should keep more people on staff permanently. Then we could be better prepared for these special events. But no, we can't do that." Mateo Marin's thin lips tightened into a straight line.

Lauren shrugged. "Cam doesn't believe in paying people who aren't needed most of the time."

"And quite right, too," Dia said. "We don't host parties every night, or even every week. Why should he waste his money?"

"It's not just these fundraising things though, is it?" The chef's dark brows drew together over his hawkish nose. "There are also all those private dinner parties for female guests. Especially that last one. Ungrateful little diva." Grabbing a metal spoon, Mateo spun around to vigorously stir something bubbling in a pot on the eight-burner gas range.

Dia pressed her lips together and cast me a bright, if artificial, smile. "Anyway, Jane, let us know if there's anything you need while you're working here. Food or drink or whatever. We'll be happy to accommodate you."

Mateo's grunt made me question whether he agreed with her gracious offer.

"Thanks," I said, earning another smile from Dia.

Lauren motioned for me to follow her through a side door into a small antechamber filled with coats, sweaters, clogs, and boots. "Take your pick."

Slipping off my pumps, I shoved my stockinged feet into a pair of well-worn loafers. With my dress shoes dangling from one hand, I trailed Lauren out the side door and down a grassy path that led to the home's main entrance. "Just curious, and you can tell me it's none of my business if you want, but you seem very knowledgeable about the estate. How long have you worked here?"

Lauren shot me a quick glance as she led the way onto the flagstone path that ran in front of the house. "Cam hired me after his father died, which was five years ago."

"You must've been right out of college," I said.

"I was twenty-three. Old enough to know better," Lauren said, with a grin. "But I still took the job."

Pausing for a moment, I surveyed the expansive landscape sweeping away from the house. Near the front entrance, a circular cobblestone driveway wrapped around a patch of emerald green grass with a marble fountain set like a jewel in its center. The circle connected to a longer paved drive, lined with maple and pin oak trees, that led to the main gates.

Impressive but not too over-the-top, I thought, glancing up at the home's façade. The central section of the house was taller than the two long wings. They stretched from it, bent at a slight angle like enveloping arms. The entire surface of the house was clad in irregular-shaped stones in tones that ranged from a sandy tan through a charcoal gray, while the trim on the mullioned windows and oak doors was a loam brown. The whole effect was one of earthy elegance, heightened by the dormers that sprang like mushrooms from the slate-tiled roofs of the wings.

"Where did Cam's dad get his money?" I asked as I followed Lauren toward the arched stone entrance to the gardens. "The information I read was a little murky on that point."

"Not surprising, since Cam isn't even sure. Apparently Al wasn't one to talk much about his past. We think he actually started out with nothing and got rich off of his expertise in large-scale construction, then got into real estate and made great investments of various kinds. Some of which Cam still holds, although he did get rid of many of the more questionable ones. You know, those that were environmentally unfriendly or socially irresponsible." Halting in front of the garden entrance, Lauren stared at the adjacent stone and timber building that I guessed to be the estate's garage. Frown lines wrinkled her brow as her gaze flitted over a baby blue sports car parked in front of the closed bay doors. "Oh dear, that doesn't bode well."

"What's that?" I asked, but Lauren brushed off this question by asking about my apartment.

"So your apartment isn't in a complex?" she asked after I told her my address. "I only ask because that's all I could find when I was looking five years ago." Lauren's expression turned thoughtful. "Maybe I should look again. My complex has gotten so noisy."

"Fortunately not. I got lucky. Saw an ad in the paper when I was researching the area, and discovered this little apartment above a garage. My landlord has a lovely brick bungalow in town, just off the main street, so it's quite convenient. He's even allowing me use of one of the garage bays for my car. I'll probably just use it in the winter, though, as there's plenty of space to park outside. The apartment's small, but works perfectly for me, especially since I got rid of most of my furniture when I sold my former home."

Lauren's sidelong look was accompanied by a lift of her dark eyebrows. "You didn't want to buy another house?"

"Not really, mainly because I didn't know how long this job would last." Following her into the gardens, which were enclosed by thick boxwoods interspersed between stone pillars, I wrinkled my nose at the acrid scent of the evergreens. "After my contract is up, I may need to move elsewhere. In the meantime, I can save money and complete my downsizing efforts. Which I really need to do, since the apartment *is* quite small." I shrugged. "But it isn't anything I can't live with. It's functional and, more importantly, relatively cheap."

"That's always a bonus." Lauren paused beside a bed of roses. Since it was early October, the leaves that clung to the dark branches had lost their glossy sheen. "If you find you need something, we can dig through the attic to see if there's any pieces that would work. It's not like any of that furniture is being used otherwise."

"Thanks, but I'll have more than enough with my own stuff." I gazed down the long flagstone path that was bordered on one side by carefully cultivated beds, and on the other by a rectangle of manicured grass. A matching path lined the other side of the garden, both leading to a marble columned, open-sided building with a timber roof. A stepped water feature spilled from a fountain in front of the pavilion to a koi pond. "What a lovely place to walk. I can tell I'll be spending a lot of my free time out here. It's beautiful even this time of year, so I bet it's gorgeous when everything is blooming."

"It's glorious, but takes a lot of work," Lauren said. "Cam has a gardener and crew who come in every other day in season."

We walked on in silence until we reached the pavilion. Through the back columns, I could see that the garden continued, but in a less formal style. This area was wilder, with winding paths and stands of shrubs and small trees. "I bet there are a few hidden benches and grottoes," I said, leaning back against one of the columns.

"There are. It's a good place to get away, if you're ever in need of that." Lauren cast me a smile. "You've met Cam, so you know the urge to escape can happen from time to time."

"I don't doubt that." Sighing, I tightened my grip on my shoes and wondered what sort of hot water I'd gotten myself into this time.

Chapter Four

"So, speaking of Cam," I said, meeting Lauren's steady gaze, "do you mind telling me a little more about him? Nothing salacious, of course," I added, with a wave of my hand. "It's just that . . . Well, I've already guessed he has some type of anxiety."

"Anxiety, OCD, occasional depression, and a general lack of social awareness." Lauren counted off the list with her fingers. "But that's all just a guess. His father refused to have him assessed when he was younger, and Cam always insists there's no need for it at this late date."

"I don't know, therapy has definitely benefited me in the past," I said. "I doubt it's too late for him to get some help."

Lauren's troubled expression told me she concurred, but she simply shook her head. "It's not something Cam is willing to consider, although I agree he should. But he's a fully competent adult, so I don't press the issue. Anyway, aside from that, he's extremely well educated. He's always learning something new, whether it involves languages, history, or some scientific discovery. He surrounds himself with scholars too. He doesn't like to go out much, so he invites them to stay here from time to time.

Which I have to say can sometimes be fascinating, and sometimes . . ." Lauren rolled her eyes.

"I guess it depends upon the guests." I slid one finger up and down the marble column. "He's quite brilliant, it seems."

"Oh yes. A savant, really, especially when it comes to subjects that interest him."

"Like mystery and detective stories?"

"Definitely, and not just the fictional kind. He's obsessed with unsolved real-life mysteries and crimes too. Sometimes I think he imagines himself as one of those amateur detectives he likes to read about."

"I guess he doesn't have to work. I mean, for money. Don't get me wrong, I'm not judging. I assume from your comments that he's constantly studying and engaged in research on top of managing his financial assets."

"And he actually does have a hand in running a couple of the companies his dad set up. He doesn't just sit around doing nothing, that's for sure." Lauren shot me an amused look. "Otherwise, he'd have no use for me."

"You help manage his projects?"

"Most of them. I also deal with the paperwork related to his companies and investments as well as various charitable causes. I also arrange travel for his guests, organize dinner parties, and that sort of thing." As Lauren gazed out over the back garden, the lines bracketing her mouth deepened. "And sometimes I have to deal with the aftermath of his romantic relationships. Not my favorite task."

"Oh dear, is he a playboy?" I examined Lauren's lovely profile with curiosity. Despite Cam's looks, intelligence, and wealth, I couldn't picture this being the case. The man I'd met seemed too socially awkward to possess much game.

Lauren turned her head to meet my gaze. "No. It's more like women chase him, and he allows himself to be caught." Her lips twitched. "For a time, anyway. I mean, he's all in at the beginning. It's just a fleeting enthusiasm, though. He'll be very attentive for several weeks and then some new idea or project captures his fancy and . . ."

"He forgets all about the woman he's been dating?"

"Pretty much." Lauren flicked one of her tight black curls away from her forehead. "Of course, sometimes he doesn't drop them; sometimes they dump him. And with good reason. He's been known to inadvertently insult them, or their friends and families."

Recalling his first words to me, I offered her a wry smile. "No doubt."

Lauren expelled a gusty sigh. "Cam's romantic life is basically a string of disasters, and guess who has to pick up the pieces." She pointed to her chest. "Me, that's who. And I'm afraid it's going to happen again, momentarily."

Pressing a finger to her lips, Lauren tapped her ear with her other hand. Following her lead, I focused on the voices rising from behind a clump of trees in the back garden.

"Is that Cam?"

Lauren nodded. "And Ashley Allen. His latest girlfriend."

Evergreen branches swayed as Cam burst out from behind the shrubbery, followed by a young woman with long chestnut hair. She wore a skin-tight purple dress that perfectly displayed her petite but curvaceous figure, and a pair of lavender shoes whose spiky heels could've doubled as weapons.

"Two weeks!" the young woman shouted. "Fourteen, no, make that fifteen, days!"

I slipped behind the column, knowing it wouldn't completely hide me, but hoping my presence wouldn't be as obvious.

Lauren had no such qualms. She stayed where she was, her gold jewelry and yellow ensemble gleaming in the light. Of course, she was right—Cam and Ashley were too absorbed in their own drama to notice us.

"I told you, I've been busy." The light glinting off Cam's hair tipped the flyaway strands with flame.

"Too busy to make a phone call? Too busy to send a text?" Ashley placed her balled fists on her hips as she faced off with my much taller boss. "I finally stopped trying to get in touch with you after the first few days, not wanting to look too desperate. But then, stupid me, I thought maybe you were ill or injured or something and decided to stop by. And what do I get? Total indifference. It's like you never pursued me, sending all those cards and flowers, and wining and dining me here every night for weeks."

"But that's my point. We spent a lot of time together for a while. Which should've been enough to carry you through when I needed room to pursue other interests."

"That's what you think your girlfriend is supposed to do? Store up your attention like a freaking battery?" Ashley poked Cam's chest with her forefinger. "Listen here, you weirdo. That's not how things work."

"I don't know how *things* are supposed to work. All I know is that this neediness is seriously off-putting." While Cam stood ramrod straight and completely still, his voice vibrated with anger.

"Neediness?" Ashley's voice rose up another octave. "How dare you! Most men would die—die, I tell you—to spend even a minute with me."

Cam looked her over, obvious distaste curling his lips. "Rather short relationship, don't you think?"

Ashley then did something I'd only read about but never seen, except from a toddler—she stamped her foot, sending up a little puff of dust from the well-worn path. "I won't put up with this. Not from you, Mister 'I prefer not to leave the house unless I absolutely have to.' Not from someone who has more odd habits than I have shoes."

"At least my habits don't turn me into a raging wolverine when I don't get what I want the second I want it." Cam looked Ashley over. When he spoke again, his tone was as calm, and cold, as snow. "You aren't that special, you know. Sure, your family money grants you the ability to make the best of what you have. But objectively speaking, you're rather average." He tipped his head. "That's just in the looks department. When I consider your intelligence and personality, well . . . They fall somewhere below the median, I'm afraid." He brushed his hands together, as if dusting off something unpleasant.

I felt a pang of sympathy for the woman confronting him. Even though I guessed her age to be closer to thirty than twenty, Cam's words had to sting, regardless of her level of maturity. *Hell, they'd hurt me, even at my age.* I glanced over at Lauren, who'd crossed her arms over her chest.

"I knew there'd be trouble when I spied that sports car," she said, not bothering to temper her volume.

Cam looked our way, obviously recognizing her voice. "Oh hello," he said. "Sorry for the bother. Ashley was just leaving."

He bounded forward, leaving Ashley standing alone on the path. "Can you escort her back to her car, Lauren? I really need to head inside. Important phone call," he added, speaking directly to me.

"No, I will not do your dirty work, Cam. I've told you that before. I don't pick up your laundry, I don't wash your dishes, and I won't sweep your discarded girlfriends out of sight, or mind." Lauren lifted her chin and stared down her nose at our boss. "And neither will Jane."

Cam's eyelashes fluttered before he dropped his gaze to his feet. "Sorry," he muttered.

I noticed his fingers shaking—whether from the encounter with Ashley or Lauren's stern reprimand, I wasn't sure. He glanced up at me and thrust his hands into his pockets.

Ashley, who'd carefully picked her way over the uneven ground in her high heels, reached the pavilion. She favored Lauren with a sneer before turning to me and sniffing. "Hope you enjoyed the show."

"I regret being here, actually. I don't like to observe other people's meltdowns," I said, before noticing that a clump of her eyeliner had dribbled down her cheek like candle wax. *From tears*, I thought, and softened my tone. "We should've left as soon as we realized you were having a private meeting."

"More like an ambush," Cam said stiffly. "Anyway, it's time Ashley headed home." He turned to face his former girlfriend. "I'll escort you to your car if you want."

Ashley tossed her wavy hair behind her shoulders. "Yes, I want. It's the least you can do."

As they walked off, circling around the pavilion to reach the flagstone path, I heard Ashley tell Cam, "This isn't over. We have a lot more to talk about."

"If you insist. I assume you still plan to attend the fundraiser on Sunday. We can chat then. Briefly." Cam strode down the path, leaving Ashley to stumble after him.

I shared a look with Lauren. "He's really going to see her again?"

She sighed. "That's Cam for you. If he doesn't know how to handle the situation, he just pushes it off."

"But then he has to deal with it all over again."

"I know." Lauren waited until Cam and Ashley had disappeared through the garden arch before adding, "I don't like this, Jane. I'm afraid Cam's in over his head with this one. I think she could turn vindictive."

"But what could she possibly do? Surely she wouldn't try to physically harm him."

Lauren's dark eyes narrowed as the roar of a car engine filled the air. "No, but she knows something . . ." She shook her head. "I shouldn't say more. It's not my information to share."

I mulled over this comment for a second, finally realizing what she meant. "Ashley knows some secret Cam doesn't want to get out?"

"Exactly. He confessed to me that he told her something very personal when they'd both had too much to drink. I don't know what it was, but he was extremely upset about it after the fact." Lauren rolled her shoulders and exhaled. "Anyway, I'm afraid

Ashley may use it against him. Which might force Cam to do something drastic. Honestly, I believe he'd go to any lengths to keep the secret quiet, the way he was fretting over having spilled it."

"You mean, even continue to date her?" I widened my eyes in mock horror.

Lauren's concerned expression brightened. "Yes, even that. A fate worse than death, wouldn't you say?"

Chapter Five

As we strolled toward the main entrance to the garden, Lauren mentioned the fundraising event.

"It's Sunday evening. You don't have to attend, since you aren't officially on the clock until Monday." Lauren's lips twitched. "Wish I didn't."

"Does Cam often host such things?"

Obviously hearing the surprise in my voice, Lauren flashed a sardonic smile. "No, and he's unlikely to make more than a perfunctory appearance at this one. He'll show up at the beginning to thank everyone for their donations, and then disappear to his bedroom suite. Especially since, I bet, despite what he said, he'll be diligently trying to avoid another confrontation with Ashley." Lauren paused and turned to face me. "As he may or may not have told you, the party is actually being hosted by two of Cam's friends, Naomi Wilt and Hannah McKenzie, who are staying with us for a week or so. It benefits one of the local hospitals, so Cam was willing to offer up the space."

"But not his personal involvement?" I asked, with a lift of my eyebrows.

Lauren shook her head. "As you can imagine, he doesn't like crowds. Or talking to people he doesn't know. So while he doesn't mind providing a venue, he isn't going to do much more than that."

"It's still a help, though."

"Oh yes, and Cam's happy to do it. He does have a good heart, underneath all the brusqueness." Lauren resumed walking, but we'd only taken a few strides when a voice rang out, calling out her name.

Dia Denton stood in the doorway to the mudroom, flapping one hand like a flag.

"Please excuse me. This must be something important. Probably concerning the gala. I'd better go and discover what fires I need to put out now." Lauren fished a card out of her pocket and pressed it into my palm. "In case I don't see you again, here's the code to the front gates. We leave them open during major events, but they're locked the rest of the time, so you'll need the code Monday morning. Don't worry about the loafers," she added. "You can wait and bring them back on Monday. No need to return before that, since I'm sure you have a lot of unpacking to do. See you soon." Lauren veered off and hurried to meet Dia, who ushered her into the house with a flurry of muffled comments.

I strolled on, heading for the sidewalk outside of the gardens. But before I could reach the exit, two older women stepped onto the path, blocking my way.

"Hello there," said the taller of the two, a slender woman with a small head perched on a long, graceful neck. With her fine white hair swept back and up into a tight chignon, beaky nose, and vivid pink jacket, she reminded me of a flamingo. "I

28

bet you're Cam's new librarian." She thrust out one bony hand. "I'm Naomi Wilt."

"Jane Hunter." I switched my grip on my pumps to my left hand to give her fingers a quick shake, all the while contemplating the fact that I looked enough like a typical librarian for Naomi to make an accurate guess. "I heard you were staying here for a bit."

"Yes, we're part of Cam's eclectic collection of eccentric scholars." The smile that curled Naomi's thin lips definitely held a hint of sarcasm. "I'm one of the least fascinating ones, I'm afraid."

"Don't you believe her—she's an esteemed professor of English literature and quite interesting in a multitude of ways." The short woman standing next to Naomi was dressed in a beige-and-rust tweed jacket and brown skirt, with well-worn leather boots. She looked as if she'd just strolled in from a hike in the Scottish Highlands. *She's like a plump partridge in contrast to Naomi Wilt's flamingo*, I thought, swallowing a chuckle.

"Retired. A retired professor." Naomi motioned to the woman at her side. "And this is Hannah McKenzie, who's still teaching art history at our local university."

Hannah's smile crinkled the laugh lines around her hazel eyes. "Only part-time now."

Realizing that by "local university," Hannah probably meant Wake Forest University in nearby Winston-Salem, I gave a little nod. "Pretty prestigious. I'm impressed." I turned my attention to Naomi Wilt. "Did you teach at Wake Forest as well?"

"That's where Hannah and I met, eons ago." Naomi's angular face made her appear gaunt, but I had to admit that she had enviable cheekbones.

"How did you meet Cam?" I asked, curious about my boss's connection to these women who were old enough to be his mother. *No, grandmother*, I thought. *I'm old enough to be his mother.*

Naomi narrowed her pale blue eyes. "We actually started out as friends of Al Clewe, Cam's father, who was on the board of the university for a while. Cam basically inherited us."

"Now, Naomi, I wouldn't put it quite like that." Hannah tightened her lips. Her lashes fluttered, making her appear flustered. It was obvious to me that Naomi was the more dominant of the two women.

To a fault, I thought, noticing the sharp glance Naomi cast at her friend before she turned her attention back to me. "Are you working here full-time, Jane?"

"Yes, at least until I fulfill my contract, which I honestly hope will take a year or two." I met her inquiring look with a lift of my eyebrows. "Lauren mentioned that you're hosting a fundraiser Sunday night. How's that shaping up?"

"Very well." Naomi swept one hand through the air, jangling her stack of gold bangle bracelets. "Cam's very generous about allowing his friends to use the estate for such things. It certainly works better than trying to squeeze everyone into my little house in Winston-Salem."

"And it allows all the money raised to go to our selected charity, rather than toward the renting of a hall, which is an added benefit. Although I suspect, despite his avoidance of the actual festivities, it benefits Cam as well." Hannah tipped her head to one side as she studied my face. "Just like inviting a few friends to stay for weeks at a time, you know? I've always assumed this place gets drafty, if not downright spooky, when just Cam and the help are here."

"He does have Lauren," I said, noting Naomi's sniff and Hannah's look of puzzlement at my words. *They consider Lauren "the help," I guess.* I fought the urge to say anything more on that topic. No point in causing friction with my boss's guests at our first meeting.

"Well, we won't keep you. I'm sure you have much to do, having just moved into town." Naomi fixed me with her piercing gaze. "Good luck with that. I despise moving. Which is why I've lived in the same house for decades, even though I probably should've found a new place after my husband passed away. But the thought of packing and all that"—a delicate shudder vibrated her thin shoulders—"I just couldn't face it. You're braver than I am, to uproot your life at our age."

Swallowing back a reply, I simply offered her a smile. Naomi had to be fifteen to twenty years older than me, but common sense dictated that mentioning our age difference was a bad idea. "I don't mind," I said, after a brief pause. "I like new adventures, and anyway, I was ready to downsize. My daughter is on tour with a theater company, so it was the perfect time to find a smaller place. And I just happened to luck into one where I'll be spending much less a month than I did on my mortgage. That allows me to save more toward my actual retirement."

"A definite plus," Hannah said. "Thankfully, my house was paid off a few years ago. I don't know how I'd manage, otherwise. It's not like professors make that much, and with working only part-time . . . Well, thank goodness for Social Security is all I have to say." A bright smile lit up her round face. "Anyway,

I hope you enjoy working here, Jane. I think I would love it, if only for the gardens."

"They are beautiful," I said. "But please, do excuse me. As you suspected, I still have a lot to do. Anyway, I'm sure we'll have a chance to speak again soon." I wished both ladies a good day.

I could hear them talking as I strode off. Sharing their impressions of me, no doubt. Squaring my shoulders, I kept walking. I might not be quite their age, but I really was too old to care what other people thought of me.

Chapter Six

My landlord, Vincent Fisher, a recently retired reporter for a local paper, was obviously still on the hunt for news.

"So you start work on Monday?" he asked, as he handed me the coffee he'd insisted on making for me.

I cradled the mug between my hands, keeping my gaze fixed on the movers as they hauled boxes and furniture up to my apartment. It wasn't an easy task—the outdoor steps that hugged the side of Vince's two-car garage were steep and narrow. A wooden lattice thick with climbing rose vines covered the exterior side of the staircase, creating a thorny barrier quick to snag skin as well as fabric.

I glanced at Vince, who was standing beside me at the railing of his front porch. He was, as he'd told me, sixty-six, although he could pass for someone at least five years younger.

Vince was eyeing me with a searching look that told me he wanted to ask questions. I examined him, tightening my lips. A man of medium height and build, he was attractive in a rough-hewn sort of way, his craggy features set off by the brightness of his hazel eyes and his thick head of gray hair.

"So you'll be working at Aircroft. Do you know much about the estate?" he asked.

"Not much," I replied in a disinterested tone. When we'd first met, Vince had also informed me that he was single, which was why I was careful to remain detached. Not looking for a relationship of any kind, except perhaps a casual friendship, I wanted to set proper boundaries from the start.

"It actually has quite a fascinating history." Vince's eyes glittered behind the lenses of his wire-framed glasses.

Leaning my hip against the white porch railing, I winced when a stream of expletives cascaded from the landing at the top of the garage stairs. I was going to have to give the movers a big tip. "I do know a little about the family who built the place. Samuel Airley was one of those titans of industry types who amassed a fortune in the early twentieth century. His wife, Bridget, was from a poor Irish immigrant family but ended up as a socialite, and they had a son named Calvin, who sadly died before he turned thirty."

"He was only twenty-nine," Vince said. "Know what happened to him?"

"Only that it was some sort of tragic accident." I took a sip of coffee and looked away from Vince's eager face. He appeared strangely energized by this discussion, which raised a red flag in my mind. Had he agreed to rent me the apartment simply because I would soon have access to Aircroft and its library as well as any historical documents kept at the estate?

Vince tapped the white balustrade as if to draw my attention. "That's one theory. But there are rumors that it wasn't as accidental as it seemed. He tumbled off a cliff on the estate, you see."

"Some people believe he was pushed?" I ran one finger around the rim of my mug. "Why would they think that?"

"Because, while it was raining that day, and there was a chance Calvin slipped on the muddy edge of the cliff, there were also reasons for someone, or several someones, to murder him."

"Hold on," I said, as the foreman walked past me, tapping his wristwatch and calling out, "Break." I nodded before turning back to Vince. "You seem unusually well informed about this historical tragedy," I told him. "Did you write an article about it in the past or something?"

Vince took off his glasses and wiped the lenses with the tail of his loose cotton shirt. "I wanted to, but my editor wasn't enthused. She thought it was all hearsay. Which is why I decided to continue my research after I retired. I'm planning to write a full-length exposé on my own time."

"Oh, you're writing a book?" I arched my brows. *Great*, I thought. *Now he'll want you to help him with his research.*

"That's my goal," Vince said, popping the glasses back on. "I'm determined to get to the truth, one way or the other."

"It could be an interesting story, if there's anything to it," I admitted. "But tell me—who would've had a motive to kill Calvin Airley? Surely not his parents."

"No, no, they were devastated by his death. Although to be honest, they may have had some culpability in a roundabout way. Here"—Vince motioned to the two Adirondack chairs that offered the only seating on his wide front porch—"please sit, and I'll explain what I've discovered so far."

Since the movers were on break, and I couldn't do much of anything in the apartment until they finished hauling up my belongings, I crossed to one of the chairs. "Have you been working on this story for a while?" I asked as I sat down.

"A few years," Vince said, settling into the other chair. "I mean, I was always interested. I grew up in the area and heard all the tall tales about Aircroft from the older folks, both in my family and elsewhere. But I didn't really start digging into the story until I was working at the paper."

I plunked my empty coffee mug down on the side table between our chairs. "So what's the scoop?"

Vince cast me an amused glance. "I see what you did there. Anyway, the story is that Samuel and Bridget Airley, having risen from nothing to the pinnacle of, at least, local society, were pretty keen to have their only child marry well. They sent him to the best private schools, then hosted parties at Aircroft to introduce Calvin to well-connected, and wealthy, debutantes."

"But Calvin had other ideas?"

"Exactly. The rumors were that he'd met someone his parents would consider unsuitable. A girl with limited prospects. According to the gossip, they met in secret and fell in love."

"Of course," I said absently, my attention diverted by the movers returning to their truck.

My lack of interest didn't slow Vince's torrent of words. "Unfortunately, the girl ended up 'in the family way,' as they would've said then. Now, to his credit, various sources claimed that Calvin wanted to marry her, and even told his parents as much. Naturally, his mom and dad were opposed to this idea. They forbade the marriage, threatening to cut Calvin off if he carried through with it."

36

I turned to Vince with a frown. "And he backed down?"

"Supposedly. Some fanciful tales I've heard romanticized this a bit, claiming Calvin just wanted to find a way to get hold of some of his inheritance before running off with the girl, but who knows?" Vince shrugged. "Anyway, the upshot was that the girl disappeared."

More intrigued than I wanted to be, I leaned into the arm of my chair. "She was presumed dead?"

Vince shook his head. "No one telling the tale knew for sure what happened to her. To be honest, no one seemed to know exactly who she was. The couple of names bandied about have been proved to be wrong, so even that is a mystery. But when Calvin died not long after . . ."

"Some people thought he might've committed suicide?"

"A few. But there were others who believed it was the girl's family, or a friend, who shoved Calvin off that cliff—an act of revenge for him deserting her." Vince sat back in his chair with a flourish of his hands. "Straight up murder."

I studied his profile for a moment. It was clear that Vince was obsessed with this tale, however apocryphal it might be. "You truly believe that?"

"I think there's a good possibility it could be true." Vince turned his head to meet my incredulous gaze. "I know it sounds far-fetched, especially since it's only based on oral history. Or gossip, if you will. There's no real documentation, or at least none that I've discovered yet." Vince's eyes glittered with excitement. "But that's thrill of it—chasing down all the leads and digging through the dreck to find any diamonds of truth."

"In other words, once a newshound, always a newshound," I said, offering him a slight smile. "But I do understand, in a way. I always felt the same way about library research."

"See, you get it." Vince crossed his arms over his chest. "My former boss thought it was a waste of time, because there was no guarantee I could ever prove anything. I mean, it's all based on stories told by one person to another. Which can certainly jumble things up."

"Hard to get to the actual truth," I agreed, giving a nod to the foreman as the movers resumed hauling my household goods up the unforgiving stairs.

"I know, and it's not like I may be able to absolutely prove anything, one way or the other. I may have to simply take the facts I can gather and extrapolate from there." Vince shot me a quick glance. "Not that I'd make up anything, but I could theorize."

I met his gaze with a lift of my chin. "It is an intriguing premise for a book. I just have one question—do you plan to ask me for help? Getting information from the files and documents that might still be stored at Aircroft, I mean."

To his credit, Vince didn't even blink. "The idea has crossed my mind."

"I thought so," I said, rising to my feet. "I'll have to think about that. And ask my employer if it is okay for me to dig through any papers or other things connected to the Airley family. Deal?"

"Deal," Vince said, standing to face me. "There is one more thing . . ."

A Cryptic Clue

"What's that?" I asked, distracted by one of the movers motioning for me to join him at the truck. Assuming he wanted some instructions on whether to separate the two halves of a bookcase before trying to haul them up to the apartment, I'd taken a few steps toward the porch steps when Vince's words stopped me in my tracks.

"Let me know if you encounter any ghosts," he said.

Chapter Seven

On Monday I rushed through breakfast, pouring my second cup of coffee into a travel mug before grabbing my tote bag. I'd already filled the tote with the loafers I needed to return to the estate, my lunch in a small insulated cooler, my laptop, and a sweater in case the library was cold.

Bailey liked to tease me about the fact that, while I'd never been a Girl Scout, I was always prepared. "One of us needs to be," I'd told her, earning the requisite eyeroll.

Driving to Aircroft took fifteen minutes, five of which were due to traffic. In the few days since moving to Bradfordville, I'd marveled at the steady stream of vehicles filling the small town's main street at almost all hours of the day and night. Where were all of these people going? The town had a few shops and restaurants but didn't offer a significant number of jobs.

But of course, they were commuting to work, like me. Although, unlike me, they were undoubtedly traveling to one of the nearby cities, not driving into the countryside. Aircroft, set back off a side road, was isolated from the bustle of the surrounding towns.

A Cryptic Clue

As I left the other vehicles behind, I encountered a veil of fog that flitted across sections of the narrow road, dissipating or thickening depending on whether I'd topped a rise or descended into a dip. *The perfect morning for cloaking dastardly deeds*, I thought, with a little smile. *And here you are, motoring toward a mansion that wouldn't have seemed out of place in one of Dorothy L. Sayers's Lord Peter Wimsey stories.*

Although my host wasn't exactly suave and urbane. No doubt Lord Peter would've raised his monocle more than once over Cam's rude comments.

This amusing thought almost made me drive past the estate. Fortunately, the gates sat at the summit of a hill and the morning sun glinting off their silver metal gave me enough advance warning to slow down and turn into the driveway.

After punching in the entry code Lauren had provided, I drove through the open gates, glancing over my shoulder as they clanged shut behind me. The driveway was wreathed in fog and I proceeded slowly, low beams on, keeping an eye out for deer or other wild creatures. I also couldn't help but think of Vince's comments about ghosts. Although I wasn't a believer in such things, the view of the mansion, with its rough stones and dark trim slowly unveiled by the fading mist, still gave me a shiver. *Foolishness*, I thought. While I didn't entirely discount the possibility of the rumors Vince had shared being true, I certainly didn't believe that Calvin Airley, or his unknown lover, haunted the halls of Aircroft.

Shaking off any such superstitious nonsense, I parked in the circle, near the front doors of the house. Grabbing my travel mug and canvas tote, I checked my watch as I climbed out of the car. Still fifteen minutes to eight. Good. I strode toward the main entrance, head down to watch my feet and avoid tripping over any cobblestones.

The clatter of footsteps made me lift my gaze to observe a couple of men briskly striding out of the fog from the direction of the gardens. They stopped dead, then began speaking in hushed tones. But there was something about their hunched shoulders and the wild gesticulations of the taller of the two that made me cautious. This wasn't your average low-key discussion. Something seemed to have deeply disturbed both of the men.

Lost in their own conversation, they didn't notice me at first, allowing me time to silently assess them. They were a study in contrasts—one a tall, strikingly handsome man with black hair cropped close to his scalp and dark skin and eyes. I judged him to be in his early forties. The other man, who looked a little older, was much shorter, although well muscled. The wind had whipped a pink tint into his otherwise pale face, and his short, cinnamon-colored beard suggested he'd once had red hair, although all I saw was bald scalp beneath his tweed cap.

"Hello," I said, walking up to them. "I'm Jane Hunter."

Obviously taken aback by my presence, the shorter man blinked and cleared his throat. "Oh, Cam's new librarian. I didn't realize you were already working, although Cam warned us that you were arriving soon."

"Warned you?" I arched my brows. "I promise I'm no Gorgon."

"I assumed as much, since I haven't been turned to stone." The tension I'd notice in the bearded man's face evaporated like the lifting fog as he extended his hand. "I'm Kyle Trent."

I clasped his fingers in a quick handshake. "But to answer your question, yes, I am the newest member of the estate staff."

Kyle looked me over, his blue eyes bright with curiosity. "So you're here to get Cam's collections in order?"

"That's the plan," I said, turning my focus to his companion. "You look familiar, although I don't think we've met. Are you famous in some way?"

The corners of the taller man's deep brown eyes crinkled in amusement. "Not really. I'm Brendan Sloan. Not a household name, but you might've seen some of my work around the area."

"You're the artist who does the amazing glass sculptures?" I pressed my palms together, stilling my first instinct to clap. "My daughter loves your work. She took me to an exhibit at the state museum a few years ago."

"That's me," Brendan said. "Visiting Aircroft due to my partner. In life, not art," he added, draping his arm over the shoulders of his shorter companion. "Kyle's a sociology professor at Wake, and one of Cam's resident scholars."

Kyle Trent rolled his shoulders, forcing Brendan to drop his arm. "Not exactly a resident. I only stay here from time to time, usually during university breaks. Cam is kind enough to invite a few of us for short visits—to use his library and engage in some lively discourse."

"I heard he allowed two other guests to host a party here last night." I glanced around. "Although I see no evidence of such a thing. I would've expected litter or something, if it was a large gathering."

"There was a clean-up crew hired to take care of that immediately after the event. There always is," Kyle said.

"We were at the fundraiser last night, of course," Brendan said, earning a surprisingly sharp glance from his partner. He shrugged this off and focused on me. "It was quite a crowd. Glad that's over, to be honest. I prefer being here with just the smaller group. Not that I contribute much, but I enjoy listening in on the conversations. They're fun."

"Good discussions are always interesting, at least in my opinion," I said.

Kyle tugged on the brim of his hat, pulling it down lower on his forehead. "We do often have a lively time. Sort of a lesser Algonquin Roundtable, I suppose."

"Perhaps not as witty. But certainly entertaining." Brendan flashed me a smile.

"We occasionally stumble into some stimulating discussions," Kyle said dryly.

I smiled, thinking of the pleasure of a conversation with others who enjoyed books and learning. "I'd be interested to hear one of those. And perhaps even join in, from time to time."

"You're certainly welcome," Brendan said.

Kyle said, sharing a cryptic look with his partner, "Well, we should let you go. I assume you're heading in to work, and I'm sure you don't want to be late on your first day."

"Right. Don't let us hold you up." Brendan tapped Kyle's shoulder. "We need to get a move on too, if we're going to get our steps in before breakfast."

I wished them a good day, inwardly marveling at the idea that breakfast at the estate had apparently not yet been served. *How the one percent lives*, I thought, then immediately chided myself. Kyle and Brendan, like Hannah and Naomi, probably didn't live this way most of the time. As Hannah had said, professors didn't make that much money, and certainly artists, even relatively successful ones, didn't either.

Entering the main hall, I once again observed no evidence of the prior evening's festivities. *Cam definitely has a great cleaning crew*, I thought as I crossed to the corridor that led to the library.

This hall, which lacked the windows of the entry, was much dimmer, despite the amber glow from the vintage overhead lights. Strolling more slowly than I had the first time I'd come this way, I took more notice of my surroundings. Above the darkly varnished wainscotting, paintings hung from gilded wires attached to a picture rail that matched the polished wood moldings. I wasn't too interested in most of the paintings, which were primarily still lifes or landscapes executed in oils. They were so heavily varnished that a veil appeared to be drawn over each scene. This made the one exception all the more striking—a vivid depiction of a feral garden created with colored ink, it stood out like a neon sign hung above a cathedral altar.

I leaned in to examine this work, which had been hung just outside the door to the library. The signature, scrawled across one corner in a florid script, was a capital P followed by something like "Benedict" or "Bennett." Stepping back, I recognized pillars and the wooden roof of an outdoor structure and realized the drawing depicted the estate gardens, as seen from the wilder section looking back at the pavilion.

I bet someone created this work on site, I thought. *Perhaps a visiting artist, or maybe a former resident. Certainly not Cam, unless he's using a nom de plume for any artistic endeavors.*

Making a mental note to ask Lauren about the drawing later, I looked up and noticed that the library door, unlike the others along the hall, stood slightly ajar. But despite this invitation, there was no illumination within the room. After pushing the door fully open, I fumbled for the wall switch.

The sudden burst of light made me blink. I squinted as I crossed the room, heading for the desk. Setting my mug and canvas bag down on its pitted and scratched surface, I frowned. *There's something off in here*, I thought, as I looked around.

A slender hand, gleaming white against the patterned rug, added weight to this intuition. Confused, I took a deep breath and stepped around the desk. Crumpled on the floor, with her head turned to one side and her long hair veiling her face, lay a young woman. Her short silver dress glinted under the overhead light, the sequins flashing like fish scales.

And, like a fish beached on the shore, the figure was limp and pale. *That hair and figure—it must be Ashley Allen.* My thoughts skittered as aimlessly as leaves across a frozen pond. *Why is she here? She shouldn't be here, in the library, on the floor.*

I knelt beside her still form. Sweeping the hair away from her chalk-white face revealed a concave divot right above her ear; a depression that exposed bone. As I yanked back my hand, a sticky film coated my fingers. Of course—the dampness streaking her chestnut hair was blood, which had also pooled around her head like a crimson halo.

Fighting an urge to retch, I laid two fingertips on Ashley's neck and clasped her wrist with my other hand. No pulse thumped against my shaking fingers.

My lips formed a scream, but the sound snagged in my throat.

Not that it mattered. Calling for help was futile. Ashley Allen was, unquestionably, irrevocably, dead.

Chapter Eight

I staggered to my feet, using the sturdy desk chair to steady myself. Glancing around the room, my gaze fixed on white shards littering the rug near Ashley's motionless body.

That was odd, but even stranger was my detachment. I'd discovered a dead body, but remained perfectly calm, staring at the shards until I finally made sense of the scene. *There are pieces cracked off that plaster bust*, I realized as my focus shifted to a larger white object that had rolled off the edge of the rug. An empty pedestal next to one of the bookshelves suggested the killer might have grabbed the bust of some random Roman gentleman to use as a murder weapon. *Or maybe not*, I thought, noticing the absence of blood on the scattered pieces. *Perhaps it was just knocked off the pedestal during the attack.*

Realizing the need to alert the police, I grabbed my tote bag off the desk. I thrust my hand inside, searching for my cell phone by touch while my gaze continued to sweep over the room. Nothing else seemed out of place, which suggested that Ashley might've known her killer. *And was struck before perceiving any danger*, I thought. Neither the rug nor any of the furniture had shifted, and even the small knickknacks on the bookshelves hadn't been disturbed. I narrowed my eyes, noticing a ring of brighter wood on the shelf behind the empty pedestal. Crossing to the bookshelf as my fingers clutched the cell phone, I stared at the spot. *The wood shines brighter because there's no dust in the circle. A film covers the rest of the shelf, and even the tops of the books, but not that one spot. Which means something was sitting there.*

Nothing could've fallen from the shelf, as only a few white flakes from the plaster bust marred the dark wood floor. Which meant someone had removed something from the shelf, and that object was no longer in the room.

The murder weapon, I bet, I thought, sliding the phone from my tote bag. My fingers shook as I tried to turn on the device. Like circles radiating out from a stone thrown into a still pond, the tremor spread up my entire arm until I lost my grip on the phone. It fell to the floor with a splintering sound.

I was shaking all over. It was all I could do to scoop up the phone and register the spider web of cracks marring the screen before I stumbled back to the desk. I knew I needed to call 911, but couldn't seem to manipulate the small power button on the side of the phone. I took several deep breaths before the pressure building in my head forced me to flee the room.

Staggering out into the hallway, I slumped against the wall and slid to the floor, the chair rail thumping my waist and ribs before it banged the back of my head.

My thoughts spiraled—*dead body. There's a dead body in the library. The room meant to be my workplace is now a murder scene.*

"Jane? What's wrong?" asked a concerned voice.

I looked up into Lauren's lovely face. "Don't go in there," I said, my voice as ragged as my breathing.

"Why ever not?" Lauren glanced down the hall. "Tell me quick, Cam is coming. If I need to prepare him for a disaster . . ."

"Dead body," I managed to croak out.

Lauren took two steps back. "What?"

I jerked my thumb toward the library door. "There's a dead body in the library."

Opening and closing her mouth without saying anything, Lauren moved to the open doorway and stared into the library as footsteps alerted us to Cam's approach.

"Why are you here so early?" he asked when he reached me.

That was interesting. No mention of me sitting on the floor. I looked up into his face, which had blanched, throwing his freckles into high relief. *Rather like blood splatters.* I instantly banished this thought. There was nothing to suggest that Cam had any involvement in Ashley's death, although I was certain the police would include him in their list of suspects. He was the ex-boyfriend, after all.

And they had argued recently. Perhaps even again last night, who knows?

Clutching my tote bag to my chest like a shield, I met Cam's gaze without flinching. "I like to get to work early, so I can make sure everything's in place. And I like to take a moment to breathe before I start."

"But you're in the hall. That seems rather counterproductive." Cam glanced over at Lauren, who had her back to us. "What is it? Why are you standing in that frozen pose, as if guarding the portal to Hades?"

Lauren kept one hand on the doorjamb as she turned to face him. "Because it's bad. It's really bad, Cam."

"What are you talking about?" Cam strode over to the doorway.

Lauren threw out her other arm and gripped the opposite of the doorjamb, blocking the entrance. "You don't want to go in there."

"Nonsense. This is my house. I'll go wherever I please." Cam's jaw clenched. "Move aside, please."

Lifting her chin, Lauren stared him down. "Not until I tell you"—her dark eyes flashed a warning—"what you'll find."

"Dead body," I said. It seemed to be the only thing I could say.

Cam shot me a fierce look before turning his attention back on Lauren. "Is that right? Did someone collapse and die in the library? Some guest wandering around during the party succumbed to a heart attack, no doubt."

"Yes, someone died. But I don't think it was anything natural," Lauren replied, dropping her arms. "It's Ashley. And it appears she was killed by a blow to the head."

Blinking rapidly, Cam pressed his white-knuckled fists to his chest, as if that motion was a counterbalance to keep him from pitching forward. "You're sure it's Ashley?"

"I can't see her face, but she's wearing that silver sequined dress she had on last night. And her hair . . ." Lauren sucked in an audible breath. "It's her auburn hair."

"I see." Cam's voice was hollow as the echo in a shell. He swayed slightly, then squared his shoulders and stared down at me. "You found her?"

I nodded. "A little while ago, when I first arrived. I meant to call 911, but I couldn't." I swallowed the ball of bile that had risen in my throat. "My hands started shaking and there was this roaring in my ears and I had to get out of there and, well, I just didn't."

"We must do that," Lauren said as she slid a cell phone from the pocket of her simple turquoise dress.

Scrambling to my feet with no assistance from Cam, who'd thrust his clenched hands into the pockets of his brown corduroys, I took a step toward Lauren. "Tell them I didn't move her. I checked for a pulse, but that was all."

"Let me pass, Lauren," Cam said.

Obviously ready to protest, Lauren moved aside as the dispatcher came on the line. Cam disappeared into the library while Lauren spoke with the dispatcher in a clear, if tremulous, voice.

After a minute or two, Cam strode out of the library and crossed to the opposite side of the hall. He stared at the painting hanging just above my head, his eyes glazed over and his mouth a gash against his pale skin. Even though I could see his fingers loosening and tightening against the ribbed fabric of his trouser pockets, his voice was surprisingly calm. "She must've been killed during the party, or soon thereafter, given how she's dressed. There's no sign of her coat," he added, apparently sensing my confusion over this deduction. "And apparently no one checked this room before you arrived this morning, Jane."

"Obviously," I said, finally getting my own voice under control. "I doubt anyone who saw her would've just left her lying there."

Cam didn't appear to be listening to me. "Blow to the head," he added, as if talking to himself. "With a hard object the killer might've found in the room."

Lauren, the phone pressed to her ear, looked over at us. "The broken statue," she said, before responding to another question from the dispatcher.

"I don't think so." Cam's sea-green eyes narrowed. "A silver-plated candlestick is missing."

That was the object that left the circle of clean wood. "From the bookshelf behind the pedestal?"

Cam's gaze snapped to me. "You noticed that as well?"

"Yes. No dust."

"Exactly." Cam looked me up and down—a searching gaze, as if he was truly seeing me for the first time. "Good catch."

"I didn't know what was there before, of course, but a candlestick"—I cleared my throat—"well, if it was heavy enough . . ."

"Could do some damage," Cam said, completing my thought.

Lauren held up the phone. "I'm going to stay on the line, in case they need anything else, but the police are on their way."

"Good." Meeting her concerned gaze, Cam yanked his hands from his pockets and squared his shoulders. "You do realize who will be their number one suspect, of course."

Worry lines creased Lauren's brow. "Someone from the party? But there were over a hundred people in attendance."

"But only one person was Ashley Allen's ex-boyfriend," I said, speaking aloud a thought I'd been trying to suppress.

Lauren's eyes widened but Cam simply shrugged. "Yes, Jane. You've reached the logical conclusion once again. The most likely murderer is me."

Chapter Nine

G iven his issues, I was impressed with Cam's composure, but his analytical attitude quickly evaporated once police and other emergency personnel flooded the halls of Aircroft. As the investigators searched the library, Cam paced the hall like a leopard locked in a cage.

Once we were ushered into separate locations, I didn't see Cam or Lauren again until after I'd spent a grueling hour being questioned by the police. In fact, after receiving stern warnings not to leave town or share information with the media, the first person I encountered after I was released from questioning was Hannah McKenzie. After wandering aimlessly through unrestricted areas of the house, I found her slumped in a chair in one corner of what I assumed to be the ballroom.

I paused in the doorway, examining the room as I composed my thoughts prior to speaking with Hannah. Instead of the dark, polished wood paneling I'd observed elsewhere, this room's wainscotting was painted a gleaming white. Small round tables draped in white linen sat under silver chandeliers dripping with crystals. Board and batten molding, painted a pale ivory, covered the white plaster walls above the wainscotting, and the coffered ceiling was brightened by gilt accents.

Hannah was seated in an ivory-painted chair near a raised platform I assumed was used for live entertainment. Looking up at my approach, she scrubbed the dampness from her round cheeks with the back of one hand.

"Hello, Jane. Please forgive me for looking such a mess. It's just that . . . Well, it's not every day that I'm interrogated by the police."

"You don't have to apologize." I rested my hip against the steps that led up to the low stage. "It's certainly not the most enjoyable activity."

Pulling a handkerchief from her pocket, Hannah dabbed away a few more tears before replying. "It was such a shock. The officers stormed into the breakfast room and forced Naomi, Kyle, and Brendan and me to follow them to separate areas so they could ask us all sorts of intrusive things."

"Not quite as intense as my questioning, I imagine," I said dryly. "After all, I was the one who discovered the body."

Hannah's shoulders jerked. "Sorry, I don't mean to insinuate that I had it the worst. It's just that seeing Ashley Allen at the gala last night, so vibrant and full of life, and then hearing the news this morning . . ." Hannah swiped a tear from her lower lashes with her forefinger. "It's hard to believe."

"Did you speak with Ashley at all?" I asked, keeping my tone light. I was curious about the young woman's activities during the party, but didn't want to further traumatize Hannah, who appeared more upset by this turn of events than I would've expected.

"Only briefly. She was flitting about quite a bit and also disappeared at one point to talk with some skinny, dark-haired young man who I swear must've crashed the party." Hannah met my inquisitive gaze with a shrug. "He was dressed in black, in ripped jeans and a T-shirt. Not what most people would wear to a gala. Anyway, I had a longer conversation with her mother and sister. They are major donors to the hospital. The Allen family owns Alcare Pharmaceuticals, you know."

I stepped closer to her chair. "Wait—Ashley Allen is Gemma Allen's daughter?"

"Yes, do you know her?" Hannah's red-rimmed eyes widened.

"Not well, although we did spend a good deal of time together when we both served on a fundraising committee for my former university library." I drummed my fingers against my hip. "Gemma mentioned having two daughters, but she didn't talk about her family much, so I didn't connect Ashley with those Allens. Was the whole family at your party?"

"No, Stan Allen didn't attend. Gemma came with her younger daughter, Rena. I think Ashley arrived separately."

"Maybe hoping to patch things up with Cam and stay over?"

Hannah's mouth dropped open. "I'm sorry, what? Why do you think Cam and Ashley had broken up prior to the party?"

I couldn't help but note her eagerness to hear my reply. "I caught them arguing when Lauren gave me a tour of the gardens on Friday. It was clear from their attitudes, as well as their words, that they'd recently split up."

"Really?" Hannah buried her face in her handkerchief and blew her nose. "Sorry, but this is all so overwhelming. Anyway, I'm sorry to hear that, especially since I suppose that means the police will be looking at Cam more intensely."

My tense muscles aching from the weight of my tote bag, I shifted it to my other shoulder. "I'm afraid so. Cam even said as much. But honestly, there were a lot of people at the party, which means any number of possible suspects."

"Yes, but"—Hannah straightened in her chair—"not to speak ill of my host, but several people overheard Cam and Ashley fighting at the party. Verbally, of course." She pointed toward the French doors at the other end of the ballroom. "There's a terrace outside that exit. Apparently, Ashley dragged Cam out there and they ended up in an argument. I was standing near the doors, and it was obvious what was going on. I didn't hear what they were saying, exactly, but I certainly noticed their raised voices."

Thinking of Cam's words about being a prime suspect, I frowned. Just my luck to have landed a great job, only to have my employer embroiled in a murder investigation. "I'm sure Ashley interacted with plenty of other people too. She struck me as a real social butterfly."

"Very true. Only, you know, the whole ex thing is always a red flag." Hannah pursed her lips. "I had to mention the argument to the police when they questioned me, which was terribly unpleasant, as you can imagine."

"I'm sure. You being friends with Cam and all." I studied Hannah's face to catch her reaction to this assertion.

Hannah dabbed under her nose with a clean edge of the handkerchief. "I hated doing that. But it was necessary."

"If you hadn't mentioned it, someone else would've, I'm sure."

"Absolutely. Naomi was with me at the time, so she heard the argument as well, and I know she'd tell the police. She's quite a stickler for the truth." Hannah rose to her feet. "Now, if you'll excuse me, I think I'll return to the breakfast room. I don't have any interest in eating, but I'd love another cup of coffee."

"Can't say I blame you." I shifted my weight from foot to foot. "Would it be okay for me to tag along? I could use some caffeine myself."

Hannah, her head lowered, shot me a look from under her damp lashes. "That should be fine. I can introduce you to the other houseguests, if they return to their breakfasts, that is."

"Well, as you know, I've met Naomi. I also ran into the two guys when I arrived this morning. So introductions won't be necessary." I noticed Hannah's lips tightening over this disclosure. *She probably sees me as too forward, as well as rather nosy,* I thought as I followed her out of the ballroom. *But what the heck—if I'd stayed in my supposed place in the past, I'd never have gotten anywhere in life.*

Trailing Hannah down the hall that led to the kitchen, I considered her revelation about Cam's additional argument with Ashley. It didn't look good for him, that was for sure. But somehow, I wasn't convinced that he'd commit murder because of a break-up. For one thing, I couldn't imagine him caring enough about a failed romance to do that.

Although there was that secret Lauren had mentioned—the one she'd worried Cam would do anything to suppress. Perhaps Ashley had threatened to betray his confidence and he'd snapped. It seemed a more likely motive.

I wondered if Lauren had shared that information with the police. Somehow, I doubted it.

Chapter Ten

The breakfast room was larger than most dining rooms in less grand homes. Located close to the kitchen, the floor-to-ceiling windows on two adjacent walls filled the space with light even on a cloudy October day. On the longer solid wall, a small square table held a silver-plated coffee urn and white ceramic mugs as well as all possible coffee accoutrements, while a linen-draped rectangular table offered a bountiful array of breakfast pastries and fruit.

"Mateo will whip you up some eggs and bacon or anything else you want," Hannah said as we walked into the room. "Just let Dia know the next time she pops in."

"Thanks, but I had something earlier." I greeted Kyle, Brendan, and Naomi, who were already seated at the oval oak table that filled the center of the room. A flower arrangement created from chrysanthemums, dried statice, and branches tipped with autumn leaves, decorated the table. "That's lovely," I said as I crossed to the coffee station.

"It's my contribution." Naomi pressed her linen napkin to her lips. "I always think florals add something special to the dining experience."

I turned my back to the table so no one could see the face I made. Having lived alone for a few years, my typical "dining experience" had devolved into a tray on my lap while I was parked on the sofa in front of the television.

"So sorry to hear that you were the one to find Ashley," Kyle said.

"It was a shock," I said, turning to face the table. As I clutched my full mug of coffee and surveyed the houseguests, I couldn't help but notice the strain marking each of their faces. Of course, someone being murdered in the place you were staying had to be worrying. I crossed to the table and sat down. "I suppose all of you were questioned by the police?"

"Yeah, not my favorite activity." Brendan's dark eyes were shadowed under his black lashes. "It always makes me feel guilty, even when I haven't done anything. wrong."

Kyle's grip on his fork tightened. "They wanted us to recount all our movements last night—during the party and after. Hoping we'd seen something, I guess."

"And did you?" I blew across the top of my mug, earning a grimace from Naomi.

"I didn't, and I know Brendan didn't. I don't know about anyone else." Kyle tapped his fork against the rim of his plate, only stopping when Brendan reached over and clasped his hand.

"We went right up to our room after the party ended," Brendan said, lifting his fingers. "Then didn't leave our suite until this morning"

"It was the same for me," Naomi said, emphasizing this statement with a flourish of her hand. "The guest suites are located in a wing of the house that's some distance from the library, so naturally I didn't see or hear anything, at least not during the night. Not anything particularly unusual, anyway."

Hannah pressed her palms together in a prayer-like gesture. "I'm afraid we weren't much help to the authorities, for that reason, among others."

"Sadly, we did overhear an unfortunate fracas, during the party." Naomi cast Hannah a knowing glance. "The argument between Cam and Ashley, remember?"

"Really? I guess I missed that." Kyle scooted his chair back from the table. "Not that I blame Cam. That girl was nothing but trouble from the get-go."

Brendan's dark lashes fluttered. "Kyle, a little sympathy, please."

Sipping my coffee, I studied the two men, interested in this dynamic. It seemed Kyle was untouched by Ashley's death, while Brendan appeared perturbed. "I suppose you, as well as Hannah, shared that with the police? The argument between Cam and the murder victim, I mean."

Naomi arched her thin eyebrows. "Certainly. I'm not saying Cam had anything to do with her death, but the authorities did ask us to recount anything significant we witnessed yesterday evening, and that was definitely one thing that stood out for me." She pressed her lips together as if to smother another comment.

"That isn't going to look too good for Cam," Brendan said, sharing a glance with Kyle.

"Maybe not, but Naomi is right—we simply have to speak the truth as we know it. That's the only way to deal with this sort of situation." Kyle stood and flung his napkin across his empty plate. "Ready to head to the room and pack, Bren? The police did say we could leave, as long as we can be reached at our local address."

"Are you dashing off, then?" The lines bracketing Hannah's mouth deepened as she fidgeted in her chair. "I thought I'd stay for a few more days, if only to show that I don't suspect anyone here of being involved in this dreadful crime."

"I really have no desire to be here while the place is crawling with investigators." Kyle raised one hand in an abbreviated wave before turning on his heel and heading for the door.

Brendan cast Hannah and Naomi an apologetic smile as he rose to his feet. "We'll check in on Cam later in the week—to see how he's doing as well as show our support," he said, following Kyle out of the room.

"Just like men. Jumping ship the minute the waters get rough." Naomi snapped her napkin through the air before dropping it onto her plate. "I, for one, will follow Hannah's example and stay for a little while longer. Never let it be said that I abandoned my friends in their hour of need."

I opened my mouth but closed it again when I realized the words on the tip of my tongue might not endear me to Naomi. Or Hannah, for that matter. The truth was, I found all of Cam's so-called friends rather lacking, except perhaps Brendan. The others seemed more than willing to throw Cam under the bus, especially if that action supported their own image of innocence.

But is that because they don't really care, or perhaps—I finished off my coffee as I mulled over this—*they have something to hide and Cam's the most likely scapegoat?*

"Well, I think I'll go and find Cam or Lauren and see if they want me to do any work today or not." I stood, allowing the empty mug to dangle from my fingers. "I'll just drop this off in the kitchen first."

"That really isn't necessary," Hannah said, her gaze focused on her empty plate.

Naomi waved one bony hand through the air. "Yes, no need to bother with that. Dia will come in and clean up later."

"All the same, I think I'll carry it along. I have to stop by the mudroom to drop off some shoes I borrowed the other day, anyway." I offered Naomi and Hannah a tight smile and headed for the door.

Passing through the kitchen to reach the mudroom, rustling from the adjacent walk-in pantry alerted me to the presence of another person. But, not seeing either Dia or Mateo, I simply set my empty mug on the drainboard next to the sink.

After dropping off the loafers in the mudroom, I was halfway across the kitchen when a querulous woman's voice stopped me in my tracks. Obviously, Dia was working in the pantry.

"It wasn't my responsibility," she said.

"You still should've checked. Can't depend on these flighty rich boys to secure a building," replied a man's voice I identified as belonging to Mateo. "Now we're all being examined like bugs under a magnifying glass because the alarm system wasn't turned back on after that ridiculous party."

"Cam claims he did reactivate the system once all the guests left," Dia said. "At least, that's what I overheard one of the detectives say. But it wasn't engaged this morning when the police checked it out. Which means . . ."

Mateo barked out a laugh. "Cam forgot and was trying to cover his own patrician posterior."

"Or the killer deactivated the system so they could exit the house after the murder," Dia said, with an accompanying rattle of pans. "Although maybe the murderer was one of the guests staying here. I walked in on an argument between Mr. Sloan and the victim during the gala, while I was helping to restock the bar."

I knew I should move but hesitated. Something in this banter sounded off to me. *Almost as if both Dia and Mateo are trying too hard to convince each other of their innocence*, I thought. Walking toward the door to the hall, I heard one more snippet of conversation. It did nothing to lessen the prickle of concern tickling the back of my neck.

"Anyway, it's going to cause no end of problems around here," Dia said in a strained tone. "What with the authorities poking around and digging into all of our lives. I don't like the authorities nosing about, and you should be worried too. Although I suppose that sounds heartless, what with a young woman dead. I guess I should be more sympathetic. It's a young life cut short and all that."

"Ashley Allen?" Mateo's bark of laughter spurred me into dashing into the hall. "No great loss as far as I'm concerned."

Chapter Eleven

I wandered for a while longer, looking for Lauren or Cam, but only running into a bevy of detectives and police personnel. I honestly wanted to return to my apartment, but wasn't sure I should leave without talking to Cam. This was still my first day at a new job, and it was possible Cam would expect me to set up a workspace in another one of Aircroft's many rooms.

It wasn't until I reached a hall that was at the opposite end of the house that I finally heard Lauren's voice.

"But how can that happen?" she asked.

I peeked in the half-open door. Lauren's back was to me, but I could see the person she was speaking to.

"Hello, Jane, please join us," said Cam.

I slipped into the room, noting the elegant grand piano dominating one corner. Polished to a high sheen, its black surface glinted under the lights. "Don't tell me. This must be the music room."

"How did you guess?" Cam's laconic tone offset the tension tightening his shoulders.

"The giant piano, for one thing. And the music stands clustered near shelves filled with vinyl records is a bit of a giveaway too."

"My father bought most of the records." Cam motioned toward a pair of chairs facing an elaborate audio playback system. "Have a seat. You too, Lauren."

"Was your dad a music aficionado?" I asked as I sat down.

A shadow darkened Cam's eyes. "He liked to listen to certain things. But more importantly, he liked to acquire rare or unusual recordings, just so he could show . . ." Cam bit his lower lip and took a breath before continuing. "So he could share them with his guests."

"Ah, more of a collector than a fan, then. Do you play?" I added, indicating the piano.

Cam dragged a wooden chair next to the upholstered armchairs and shook his head. "Sadly, I'm not musically inclined. My mother was supposedly an excellent pianist, but I didn't inherit that gene. I don't sing either. Never had the ear for it."

"I used to play," I said, squarely meeting Cam's speculative stare.

"Feel free to use the piano then. Although it probably needs some maintenance. It hasn't been touched in a while." Cam shifted his gaze to Lauren, who'd just typed something into her cell phone.

Probably a note to have the piano tuned. "It's been a while." I grimaced, thinking of the last time my fingers had danced across piano keys. That wasn't a memory I cherished. "But thanks."

Cam stretched his long legs out over the hardwood floor planks. "Getting back to the topic at hand—I was just telling

Lauren that I intend to do some investigating of my own. It seems I must, since I appear to be the prime suspect in Ashley's murder, at least in the eyes of the police."

"What makes you say that?" I shifted in my chair. "You haven't been charged with anything, have you?"

Cam's lips tightened. "Not yet. But I'm afraid it's only a matter of time."

"Cam's worried that being the ex-boyfriend puts a target on his back," Lauren said, her dark eyes narrowing.

"Not to mention the murder occurring in my house, during a time period when no one can really account for my whereabouts." Cam's rose-gold lashes fluttered as he rapidly blinked. "I was in my bedroom most of the time but have no witnesses to that fact. And of course, having lived here my whole life, I know ways to get around Aircroft without being seen."

"It's all such nonsense. It would be just as likely that I killed her," Lauren said.

Cam tapped the heel of one loafer against the floor. "Perhaps you might be on the list too, if anyone questioned my other houseguests about your feelings concerning Ashley. But fortunately, you weren't here."

I turned to Lauren. "You didn't attend the party last night? I would've thought . . ."

"That I was indispensable?" Lauren said dryly. "Yeah, Hannah and Naomi thought so too. They complained quite vociferously when I left. But a good friend of mine called halfway through the party and asked me to meet her at the hospital. She'd been in a minor car wreck and needed a ride home. After they checked her out, I stayed at her place to keep an eye on her overnight. I left Aircroft while Ashley was still very much alive and didn't return until this morning."

"A fortuitous sequence of events, as it turns out, since it's removed Lauren from the list of possible suspects." Cam pulled his legs in against the wooden legs of his chair. "Although it does make my alibi less convincing."

Obviously sensing my heightened interest, Lauren snapped her fingers. "Not that I could vouch for Cam staying in his bedroom, or anything like that. I do occasionally sleep in one of the guest rooms when we have late night events, but"—she shoved her drooping curls away from her forehead—"I wasn't around long enough last night to notice anyone's movements during or after the gala."

"The upshot is that I feel I must be proactive." Cam leapt to his feet. "I refuse to simply lounge around while the authorities build a case against me."

"You don't actually know that they'll do that," I pointed out as Cam paced from one side of the room to the other.

"I don't want to wait and find out." Cam stopped in midstride and wheeled around to face me. "I'd rather use my wits to keep me from ever being charged, rather than need my money to get me out on bail. To start with, I need to discover who else might've wanted to murder Ashley."

Lauren sighed. "The problem is that there were a lot of guests at the party, and looking into their lives, beyond what can be found online, could be difficult."

"You could ask around town and the surrounding areas. Surely the guests, most of whom, I assume, are prominent in society, would be known by many people in the community."

I lifted my hands. "And I imagine people would be willing to speak with you, if only because of who you are. Wealth does offer many privileges."

Cam turned his back on us and stared at the tower of audio equipment as Lauren leaned across the plush arm of her chair to address me. "That's not as easy as you might think," she said, her voice lowered. "You see, Cam doesn't like to leave the estate."

"Excuse me?" I straightened and scooted to the edge of my chair. "Are you saying you have agoraphobia along with . . ." I cleared my throat after Lauren shot me a warning look. "Sorry, that you suffer from agoraphobia?"

"I don't know if I'd call it that," Cam said, his tone as stiff as his posture. "I do drive out from time to time. But I admit to preferring not to leave Aircroft unless I absolutely have to."

"I see," I said, as another piece of the puzzle that was my new boss snapped into place. "So traveling around a wide area and questioning strangers is off the table, I guess."

"It would be very difficult, I'm afraid," Lauren said.

"Which is why I'd like to have . . ." Cam turned around, his hands clasped behind his back. "I'd like to ask, that is, if you two would be willing to aid my investigation."

"You want us to play Watson to your Sherlock?" Lauren asked.

I pursed my lips. "More like Archie to his Nero Wolfe."

Cam widened his eyes, but a slight twitch of his lips betrayed his amusement at my remark. "Without the fixation on gourmet meals. But yes. I can conduct some online research, and see if any of my legal or business contacts can offer any insights. I can also talk to Dia and Mateo and my houseguests about what they observed last night, and try to discern if they're hiding anything. But I'll need help collecting information from the wider community. Which is what I'd like you two to do. Bring me back any clues you uncover, and I can piece it together, and perhaps solve this case before the authorities start casting about for a scapegoat. Namely me."

Filing away the interesting tidbit that Cam immediately thought the worst about the police, I met his intense gaze with a lift of my chin. "That's assuming Lauren and I can't come to the correct conclusions on our own."

Cam, staring at a point over my shoulder, didn't reply to this sally. "Will you do this? It can be considered part of your assigned duties, if you're worried about taking time out of your actual jobs."

"Well, if you put it that way." I stood, shaking out my foot, which had gone to sleep. "Sure, I don't mind seeing what I can find, although you should know that I don't have many connections in this area."

"I thought you worked at a university not too far from here," Cam said.

"Yes, but I lived on the other side of the county. I could easily commute to the university, but there was no reason for me to travel to Bradfordville. Especially since there were plenty of shops and other conveniences closer to me."

"You never visited this area?" Lauren asked.

"Not really. I drove through once or twice, but that was it. I certainly don't know many people who live here. Sorry, but that's the truth." I suspected I could exploit the curiosity and contacts of my landlord, former investigative reporter Vince, but thought better of dragging his name into the conversation without his permission. "Although I do have a passing acquaintance with Ashley's mother, since we worked on a library fundraising campaign a while back. I suppose I could meet with her to offer my condolences."

Lauren shot me a surprised look. "That seems a little . . ."

"Heartless?" I responded, with a grim smile. "I suppose you could call it that. Although I honestly do feel sympathetic, so it's not like that would be a lie."

"I like that idea," Cam said. "It's not like I can approach the Allens myself. I burned that bridge, I'm afraid."

"Oh right, the dinner party incident," Lauren said, rolling her eyes.

I didn't bother to ask what she meant. I was quickly learning that Cam's capacity to offend people was on par with his intellectual ability. "I'll drop by the Allens' with some flowers one day this week."

"Good," Cam said, casting me an approving glance.

"I guess I can ask around and see if anyone in town's heard any gossip," Lauren said. "My aunt's a hair stylist at one of the bigger salons, so if anyone's spreading rumors, she'll probably know."

Cam surveyed us, a glint of excitement lighting up his eyes. "Right. So I'm headed to my office to start my online research. I suggest you two get busy as well."

After he strode out of the room, I turned to Lauren. "He really expects us to dash off and start playing amateur detective on the day we stumbled over a dead body?"

A Cryptic Clue

"I'm afraid that's very Cam," Lauren replied, running her fingers through her hair. "Once he's on the scent, he's like a bloodhound."

"Bloodhound? More like a nervy Irish setter. And one that needs a handler," I said, earning the first laugh I'd heard that day.

Chapter Twelve

After that conversation, I drove back to my apartment, planning to pursue at least one aspect of my new job. Although I might not be able to work on Cam's collections yet, I could talk with Vince. I hoped he might have contacts who could provide alternative suspects in Ashley's murder.

I thought I'd drop off my tote bag in the apartment first, but as soon as I parked in the driveway, Vince popped out of his front door and flagged me down.

"I guess you've heard the news," I said, joining him on the porch.

"About a murder out at Aircroft?" Vince's eyes sparkled with excitement. "Of course. It's been all over the news."

"Unfortunately for me, I was the first person to stumble over the body."

"Really? Well, come in and tell me all about it." Vince paused, holding the front door ajar. "If you feel like it, I mean."

"It's fine. As a matter of fact, I have a few questions you might be able to answer, seeing as you've covered the news in this area for years."

"Happy to oblige." Vince opened the door wider and motioned for me to walk inside in front of him.

I'd been in the house before, when I'd signed the rental paperwork, but the interior still took me by surprise. Although the exterior of Vince's home was a typical 1920s brick bungalow, inside he'd gone with a totally different style—Scandinavian modern at its most sleek, with blonde wood floors and trim and low-backed ivory sofas. Everything was simple, but still stylish. The bookshelves and cabinets flanking the large-screen television were as snugly fitted as the accoutrements on an expensive yacht. There wasn't a handle in sight, only slight indentations that obviously functioned as pulls.

Sitting in one of the wooden chairs that did double duty as sculptural accents, I set my tote bag on the floor and waited for Vince to take a seat on the sofa facing me.

"I'm sure it was a shock. Sorry that happened to you," he said.

I crossed my ankles and leaned back in the chair. "It certainly put an interesting spin on starting a new job."

"I'll say." Vince looked me over. "Forgive me, I should've asked if you wanted something to drink. Water, coffee, or tea, and I have some of the harder stuff if that would help."

I waved away this offer. "Thanks, but I'm fine. I just wanted to . . . Okay, Cameron Clewe asked me to do a little investigating. It's actually in lieu of me being able to inventory or catalog his collections, at least for now. He thinks finding anyone else in the area who might've had a reason to kill Ashley Allen could be helpful to his own status as a suspect."

Vince raised his bushy brows. "And you believe I might know something?"

"I think you may know some people who might," I replied. "Or at least you could point me in the right direction. Tell me who to talk to, that sort of thing."

Vince settled back and crossed his arms over his chest. "Why are you pursuing this? Don't tell me Cameron Clewe has charmed you into becoming a devoted acolyte already."

I snorted. "Hardly. I'm not sure he's capable of that, and anyway, I'm not that gullible. It's just . . . Honestly, I also feel there's more to this story than the easy answer of a guy killing an ex-lover after an argument."

"I hope so. Sadly, Clewe is an odd duck, which probably doesn't help his cause." Vince dropped his arms to his sides. "Maybe that's unfair. I confess I don't really know him, although I did interview his dad several times in the past."

Leaning forward, I gripped my knees with my hands. "What was Cam's dad like? All I know is that he was quite a bit older than Cam's mom and was some sort of wealthy industrialist."

"You're not wrong on the age part. Albert Clewe probably had a good twenty years on his wife, Patricia." Vince's expression grew thoughtful. "I met her a few times, but only in passing. Never really had a conversation with her. Sadly, they weren't married for very long. She died only a couple of years after Cameron was born. But I remember she was quite the beauty—auburn hair and green eyes and a figure that could stop traffic."

So Cam takes after his mom, at least in his coloring. "How did she die? She couldn't have been very old."

"A rare form of cancer, from what I understand. Apparently she'd had a bout of it when she was just a kid, and went into remission for many years. But it came back after her son was born."

I shook my head. "Shame."

"It was. Albert Clewe, or Al as he liked to be called, was very broken up about it. You could tell. Even though he didn't say much about her death when I interviewed him, the pain was apparent in his eyes. And I guess it must've been tough, raising Cam on his own."

"Although he did have money for nannies and other help." I gnawed on the inside of my cheek, fighting the urge to say more. I'd been a single parent, raising my daughter since she was a baby, without nannies or maids or any other assistance. But that fact wasn't relevant to this discussion. "What sort of man was Al Clewe?"

"Much more social than his son, and certainly not as interested in intellectual pursuits. He was gregarious and good-natured, as far as I could tell. A down-to-earth type of guy. The kind who seems like they'd be more comfortable in overalls and a hard hat than in a suit. He started out with nothing, you know, and built an empire in construction and, eventually, real estate."

"Cam's assistant told me he didn't come from money."

"Heck no. He was one of those self-made millionaires. I think maybe that was one of the problems . . ." Vince cleared his throat. "Well, I always had the impression that he was a little disappointed in his son. He didn't talk about him much, except to say that Cameron was studying this or that. My reporter radar picked up on some tension between them, especially as Al always seemed reluctant to discuss the future of his economic empire, as if he knew it wouldn't last. At least, not in the form he'd created."

"But he left everything to Cam anyway?"

"As far as I know." Vince rose to his feet. "I'm going to grab a beer. Sure you don't want anything?"

"Maybe some water." I actually wouldn't have minded a glass of wine, but a quick peek at my watch told me it was too early to start drinking anything alcoholic. I had hard and fast rules about that, based on past experiences. *You never want to go down that road*, I reminded myself, remembering what could happen when alcohol became a buffer against bad experiences. *Or just life in general.*

I stared across the room at a large painting of a glacier. A study in shades of white, the work's simple lines and chilly ambience lent a bleak beauty to the living room. It made me wonder what had driven Vince to decorate his home in such a minimalistic fashion. My first impression of him had been of a slightly messy, Columbo sort of character, while his surroundings seemed more in keeping with a depressed detective in a Scandinavian noir novel.

Vince returned quickly, handing me a tumbler of water before popping open the tab on his can. Leaning against a streamlined sofa table, he sipped his beer and examined me for a moment. "I'm picking up that you want me to help dig up some information that might help Clewe? I suppose I could ask around. Not that I care much about what happens to the guy, but because I'd hate to see you cheated out of a job."

"I'd appreciate that. Being new to the area, I don't have your connections."

Vince took a swig of his beer before replying. "I guess one line of inquiry might be other boyfriends. I doubt Cameron Clewe was the first guy Ashley Allen ever dated. She was an attractive and wealthy young woman, from what I understand."

"True. I doubt Cam was the only ex. I only met the girl once, but she struck me as the sort who'd collect male admirers like designer shoes."

"And there's the whole heir to a pharmaceutical empire angle," Vince said. "Who's to say some disgruntled patient adversely affected by one of the company's drugs didn't decide to take his or her anger out on the owner's daughter?"

I gave him an approving nod. "Good point. Ashley could've been a target for a number of reasons, none of them connected to Cam."

"On the other hand"—Vince took another long swallow of beer—"Clewe has motive, means, and opportunity, all of which point to him as the killer. But I agree it's not the only option."

"I'd just like to know that all possibilities are being pursued by the authorities," I said. "And since I'm not sure that will happen naturally . . ."

"You want to offer a few jolts to the process?" Vince grinned and squeezed the beer can, crushing it with his fist. "Well, count me in. Never could resist a little detective work."

"Thanks." I stood up to face him. "Maybe start with your former news contacts around town. See if they know of any problems Ashley Allen might've had with any locals."

"Will do. What about you?" Vince looked me over. "After you take the afternoon off to get over your morning shock, I mean."

"I'm going to exploit my past association with Gemma Allen to justify paying a visit to the grieving family." I grimaced. "Sounds horrible, I know."

Vince saluted me with the crumpled beer can. "Nope, sounds like what a good reporter would do."

Chapter Thirteen

L auren called me Monday evening. Given the ongoing police
activity at Aircroft, she suggested that I stay home on Tuesday and Wednesday.

"Cam thinks you could get back to work on Thursday,
although perhaps not in the library. But he plans to have some
other portions of the new book collection brought down from
the attic. If we set up a table in the music room, you could work
in there until the library is cleared for use," she told me.

"That's fine. I can really work anywhere as long as I have my
laptop and a little space to spread out books and notes." I stared at
the photo of Bailey as Nora in *A Doll's House* that I'd hung over
my dresser. "By the way, I've discovered that the Allen family is
opening their home on Wednesday for friends or family to stop
by and offer condolences. Please let Cam know I plan to drop in
on them at some point that day. I'm not sure whether my visit
will uncover any useful information, but I thought it was worth
my time, especially since I can't work at Aircroft at the moment."

"That sound great. Thanks so much. I'm going to be talking
to a few local people over the next few days too." Lauren cleared

her throat. "One thing, Jane—and this is coming from me, not Cam—please don't feel like you have to go overboard playing amateur detective. I know Cam said he'd consider such activities part of our jobs, but that isn't exactly what you signed up for."

"I don't mind. But I'm not sure I'm going to be the best investigator. I'm not someone who finds it easy to make small talk with strangers."

"I'm sure you'll do fine. Cam's already impressed with you." Lauren's voice took on a lilt that told me she was amused by this. "He says you appear to have an unusually logical mind."

"For a woman, you mean?"

"He didn't phrase it that way," Lauren said. "I think he probably meant in general. For all of Cam's faults, he isn't a misogynist."

"It's just that I've received that accolade in the past, but with the 'for a female' caveat obvious even when it was unspoken." I inwardly cursed my tendency to assume the worst when I heard such comments. I didn't want Lauren to think I was always focused on the negative. "Sorry if I came off a bit harsh."

"I think you can be forgiven, especially after the events of today," Lauren said, before wishing me a good evening.

As soon as that call ended, my cell phone chimed again, this time with a snippet from "Children Will Listen" by Sondheim, the ringtone I'd assigned to my daughter.

"Mom!" Bailey's clear voice resonated through the phone's speaker. "I just saw something on the news about a murder at that place where you're working. What's that all about?"

After I reassured her that I was fine and in no danger, I filled her in on the few details I knew about the case. "I didn't really know the girl, but of course it's always a tragedy to lose someone that young. I think she was only twenty-eight or so." My grip on my cell phone tightened. Bailey, who was thirty, was also an attractive, vivacious young woman. The thought of losing her instantly made my feelings for the Allens bloom into more heart-felt sympathy.

"The victim was your new boss's ex-girlfriend? Ouch. I guess the authorities will be looking closely at him, then. You know how it is—the significant other is often the killer. Or at least"—Bailey's throaty laugh reverberated in my ear—" that's what usually happens in all the made-for-TV movies I've been in."

"Only this is real life. So I don't think we can assume anything," I said. "Anyway, enough about murder. How's the tour going?"

"Equal parts exhausting and exhilarating, as usual."

"How's Charlie?" I asked, hoping the answer wasn't the one I was expecting. Bailey had been dating Charlie Hempstead, a fellow actor, for over a year. While they'd been thrilled when they'd been cast in a national touring company of *Les Misérables* as Marius and the grown-up Cosette, I'd been skeptical. *Too close for comfort*, I'd thought at the time, dreading the strain on Bailey when she'd have to travel and perform with Charlie after their inevitable break-up.

"Fine," Bailey said, in a tone that told me things between the couple were definitely not fine.

"You want to talk about it?"

A faint sniffle prefaced Bailey's next words. "Not right now. We aren't speaking, but it's no big thing, just a little misunderstanding. Certainly nothing you should worry about. I mean, really, Mom, you found a dead body today. That trumps any troubles I might have."

"Not in my mind," I said. "But if you aren't ready to talk, that's fine. Just know I'm here if you need me."

"You always are." The quaver in Bailey's voice smoothed out. "I gotta go. We're dark tonight, which means a chance for me to get some much-needed sleep. I just wanted to make sure you were okay."

"I'm fine. You go and get some rest. I suppose you have shows every night this week?"

"Yeah. Best time to call is Saturday or Sunday, late morning or early afternoon, as usual." There was a slight pause before Bailey added, "Bye, Mom. Love you."

"I love you too," I said before we ended the call.

Settling back into the pillows piled up against the headboard of my double bed, I stared up at the beadboard paneling that covered the ceiling of the apartment. Bailey and I had lived together until her acting career had taken off about six years ago. A team of two, always facing our problems together despite occasional disagreements. *Stubborn battling stubborn*, I thought with a smile. We were both strong-willed, which could be challenging. But I was glad Bailey was independent and assertive when needed. It was one thing that had helped her succeed in her career.

It also meant that she didn't put up with much nonsense in her dating life. Despite being drawn to men who were, in my opinion, far too high maintenance, Bailey never allowed any of them to truly take advantage of her.

Which made me wonder whether Charlie's contribution to their "misunderstanding" was brunette, like Bailey, or a blonde or redhead. Regardless, if that was the real issue, Bailey would kick him to the curb soon enough.

I sighed and sat up. No use worrying over Bailey's love life when I knew she was perfectly capable of handling such things on her own. What I needed to focus on was a way to help my new boss, and keep the job I desperately needed. I switched to a search engine on my cell phone and typed in Ashley Allen's name, curious to see what information might pop up.

Although she'd listed her university prominently in her biographical data, Ashley hadn't included any indication of current employment. Which made me wonder what she'd been doing in the six years since she'd graduated. Of course, she had the money to avoid working a full-time job, but in my experience, people usually mentioned some type of work, even if it was volunteer efforts or entrepreneurial projects. I pursed my lips. Whatever Ashley had been doing, she apparently hadn't felt enough pride in it to list it on her social media.

Continuing to scroll through several of her social media accounts, I skipped over the more recent postings to look for any photos or text references to former boyfriends. There were several, but one in particular stood out—a young man whose silky black hair flopped over his forehead, veiling his dark, kohl-rimmed eyes. Slender in a way that reminded me of a high-fashion model, in one picture he cradled an electric guitar. *A musician*, I realized as I peered at the photo. He wore tattered jeans that hung off his hips and a black T-shirt strategically ripped to display the colorful dragon tattoo on his chest. The caption to this photo only said "Tristan," which didn't really tell me much, although it did offer something new to investigate.

Vince might know of him, if he's local, I thought, bookmarking the post. As I climbed off the bed and crossed to the dresser to plug in my phone charger, I recalled something Hannah McKenzie had said earlier in the day.

She'd mentioned a dark-haired young man dressed in black who she thought must've had crashed the gala. Someone who'd pulled Ashley aside for a private conversation.

That could've the same man from Ashley's photos. Maybe he'd been an ex who hadn't been willing to let go. I'd have to show Hannah the bookmarked photo and see if she recognized the guy.

I crossed to the tall bookshelves I'd set up to separate my sleeping space from the rest of the studio apartment. If former boyfriend Tristan had been at the gala, he might've been a stalker as well as an ex, tracking Ashley down to beg her to come back to him. It was possible he was one of those men who wouldn't take *no* for an answer.

At any rate, Tristan now topped my suspect list.

Chapter Fourteen

The fluted white columns that rose up like tree trunks, spanning the three stories of Stan and Gemma Allen's brick Georgian-style mansion, dwarfed me as I stepped onto the porch.

I shifted the basket holding a tasteful arrangement of white flowers and greenery to my left arm and rang the doorbell. When the tall double doors opened, my outstretched right hand was met with indifference by the older woman standing in the doorway.

Of course the Allen family would have a maid. I dropped my hand. "Hello, I'm Jane Hunter, a former work acquaintance of Ms. Allen, here to pay my respects," I said, as the woman looked me up and down.

"Very well, come in. The family are greeting guests in the great room." She ushered me into an entry hall as large as my new apartment. A chandelier illuminated the two-story foyer, its crystals slender and sharp as icicles. "Here, let me take that," the maid added, as she reached for the flower arrangement.

I handed it over, glad I'd tucked a card into the foliage. "I'm sure it's been a difficult time for everyone in the household,"

I told the maid's back as I trailed her down a wide central hallway.

"Quite tragic," she replied, in a tone that did not convey any such emotion. Pausing in a wide arched doorway, she motioned me forward. "Here we are. Go on in—I'll just add these flowers to the display in the dining area."

I stepped into a high-ceilinged room that encompassed the entire depth of the house. At one end an expansive table, piled high with a wide variety of flower arrangements, sat under a unique chandelier. It was composed of an array of illuminated glass globes in colors ranging from pale periwinkle through midnight blue. Suspended from thin silver chains, the light fixture floated like opalescent bubbles.

That's one of Brendan Sloan's pieces. I recall seeing something similar at the art show I attended with Bailey. I also remembered the price tags on similar works, which were for amounts far beyond my means. Of course, Stan or Gemma Allen probably could've written a check on the spot.

At the other end of the room, a whitewashed brick fireplace provided a neutral backdrop to a somber family tableau. Gemma Allen, a petite woman whose strawberry-blonde hair and chic black dress contrasted with the ivory cushions of a curved-back sofa, was seated next to a gaunt man I assumed was her husband, Stan. On her other side sat a young woman with dark auburn hair, wearing a navy blazer over a simple cream dress. I surmised she was the younger daughter, Rena.

As I jostled my way through the cluster of people gathered in front of the sofa, another young woman gripped my arm. "I'd wait a moment," she said, her wide gray eyes blinking as her gaze flitted over my face. "Let this group move aside first. Relatives," she added, dropping her hand and tossing her long dark hair behind her shoulders.

At that moment, a wail rose from one of the older women standing near the sofa. "Thanks," I murmured to the young woman at my side. "I'm not that closely associated with the family and certainly don't want to intrude."

"You're welcome. I just know how dramatic this particular branch of the family can be." The girl tipped her head to one side. "I'm Evie Grayson, by the way. One of Ashley's friends."

"Very sorry for your loss," I said automatically, while registering Evie's lack of tears. "I'm Jane Hunter. I only know the family through Gemma. We worked together on a fundraising project a little while back. Although I did meet Ashley once." *And found her body*, I thought, but decided not to share that detail.

"It's been quite a shock." Evie's gaze was fixed on the sofa. "I'm sure Gemma will appreciate you stopping by."

"I enjoyed working with her and felt I should express my sympathy in person," I said, my eyes narrowing as I studied Gemma and her family. They appeared remarkably calm for people who'd just lost a child and a sibling. "They seem to be holding up well, all things considered. I don't think I could remain so composed if someone had murdered my daughter."

"It comes natural to them. They do have a great deal of experience with being public figures." Evie cast me a thoughtful glance.

"I guess. They've probably expressed their grief privately." I met Evie's clear-eyed gaze. Her lack of emotional distress puzzled me too, especially if she'd been one of Ashley's close friends.

This disconnect spurred me to dig a little deeper. "I suppose I should confess my other tie to the situation. I've actually started a job working for Cameron Clewe, and since he and Ashley were dating . . ."

"They'd broken up. Didn't you know?"

I mumbled something noncommittal. "At any rate, since poor Ashley was killed at Aircroft, I also wanted to acknowledge that connection." I hoped this didn't sound as lame to Evie as it did to me.

Evie's dark lashes fluttered, veiling her gray eyes. "What are you saying? Are you here at Cam's behest?"

"No, not at all. Although I'm sure he wouldn't mind." I took a step back. "Oh, look, an opening."

I hurried forward, leaving Evie behind. Approaching the family, I considered my next words carefully. "Hello, Gemma. I'm not sure if you remember me . . ."

Gemma looked up at me, her eyes widening. "Yes, of course. It's Jane, isn't it? We worked on that fundraising project for the university library not long ago."

"That's right. Jane Hunter," I said, extending my hand, which Gemma briefly clasped. "I heard the terrible news and just wanted to express my deep condolences. To you and your entire family," I added, glancing from Rena to Stan.

"Thank you." Stan Allen, whose thinning chestnut hair was slicked back from his broad forehead, met my gaze with a tight smile. "We appreciate your kind words at this difficult time."

"Yes, thanks so much." Gemma straightened until her back wasn't touching the sofa. "It's very thoughtful of you to take a moment to stop by."

Rena, gripping her left wrist with her right hand as if to hide any trembling, shifted her position on the sofa. She resembled her late sister, but had sharper features and a less voluptuous figure. Her downcast eyes were impossible to read, but were clearly dry of any tears.

"Well, I won't take up too much of your time. I'm sure there are many others who wish to offer their condolences." I swept my gaze over the three figures on the sofa, none of whom looked as devastated as I'd have expected. I was aware that everyone processed grief differently, but the Allen family's seeming detachment from their recent tragedy left me with many questions.

I slipped back through the waiting crowd. As I headed for the hallway, Evie approached me again.

"It was nice to meet you, Jane," she said, briefly clutching my hand but hurrying off before I could reply.

My fingers curled around the note she'd pressed into my palm. Walking outside, I kept my fist tightly closed, only opening it when I was back inside my car.

Meet me at Memorial Park at 3, it said.

I stared at the note for a minute before shoving it into my purse and driving away.

I'd planned to do some grocery shopping later in the afternoon, but that could wait. Evie Grayson obviously had some important information she wanted to share and I wasn't going to miss the opportunity to discover what it was.

Chapter Fifteen

Arriving back at my apartment, I noticed Vince standing on his porch with an attractive older woman at his side.

"Jane, come and meet my friend, Donna Valenti," he said as I approached.

After introductions, Vince suggested that we stay on the porch. "Donna worked as a secretary at the local high school for many years," he said as we sat down. "So she has a lot of connections in the community."

"He means I hear all the gossip." Donna was a plump woman whose short legs barely touched the floor under her Adirondack chair. Her hair, pulled back into a low ponytail, was pewter gray threaded with a few black strands, and laugh lines crinkled the corners of her deep brown eyes, but her bright smile exuded youthful energy. "Which is true. Even though I'm retired now, old acquaintances still tend to spill all the latest and juiciest rumors whenever we meet."

"I suppose Vince told you why I was interested in such news?" I asked, observing the fond gaze Vince had turned on Donna. *They're more than just friends.* I tightened my lips to disguise my smile.

This was a positive development. I'd certainly feel more comfortable spending time with Vince knowing he already had a girlfriend.

"He did." Donna wrinkled her nose at Vince. "The stinker. Here I thought he wanted to see me so urgently for other, more pleasant reasons, but instead he's just fishing for news. Again."

Vince's face flushed as he squirmed in his chair. "Now, Donna, you know I enjoy your company, whatever the reason."

"Don't believe a word of it. He's always seen me as his source for town gossip." Donna caught my eye and winked.

She was simply teasing, of course. Enjoying Vince's obvious discomfort with this conversation. *Probably because he likes to play it cool and pretend he doesn't care for her as much as he actually does.* I was pretty confident in this assessment, especially when Vince crossed his arms over his chest like a belligerent child.

"Getting back to the topic at hand, why don't you share with Jane what you just told me."

Donna leaned forward, pulling the hem of her navy-and-white polka-dotted dress down over her dimpled knees. "Okay, here's the thing—I happen to know that Ashley Allen had a long-running feud with that chef out at Aircroft."

"You mean Mateo Marin?"

"That's the fellow. This all started long before she dated Cameron Clewe, by the way." Donna cast Vince an amused glance. "As I told Mr. Grumpy over there, it began when Ashley offered to back Mr. Marin's restaurant."

"So she had money of her own, not just the family resources?" I asked.

"Oh my, yes. The girl had a pretty sweet little trust fund. I heard plenty about that when I was working. Not that Ashley attended the public high school, but she did have a couple of friends who did, and they were constantly over-sharing." Donna rolled her eyes. "Bragging about trips to Aspen or Honolulu and that sort of thing."

I idly drew figure eights on the arm of my chair with my forefinger. "Paid for by Ashley, I assume."

"Yep. I suppose it was her allowance back then, since she was underage, but she still had access to cash. Used to make some of the less fortunate girls really resentful. There was one incident where a couple of students came to blows after one of Ashley's friends mocked another girl who was casually talking about her family's recent camping trip." Donna shrugged. "I guess Ashley's friend thought sleeping in a tent at the local campground wasn't glamorous enough or something."

I considered this information. I'd known Ashley came from a wealthy family, but it seemed she also had access to substantial personal funds. If she hadn't had to beg her parents for cash, she definitely wasn't dating Cam simply for his money.

"From what I've been told, Ashley never hesitated to spend money on a whole slew of hobbies as well as clothes and vacations. Well, I call them *hobbies*, which isn't entirely fair. The truth is, after she graduated from college, Ashley didn't get a full-time job. I heard she called herself an entrepreneur." Donna wrinkled her nose. "Sorry, but when someone like Ashley uses that term, I always think it means they want to play around and pretend to work, but maybe that isn't entirely fair. Anyway, she seemed eager to invest in various businesses in the area, but only things that interested her, like art galleries and restaurants." Donna shrugged. "I guess she did follow through on some of those projects, but not all of them. Apparently she dropped her support for a few, like Mateo Marin's restaurant."

"What?" I asked, instantly intrigued. "What did Ashley have to do with Mateo?"

"Basically, she promised to fund his start-up, but when the restaurant was about to open, she pulled out. Leaving Marin holding the bag," Vince said.

"And all the debts," Donna added.

"Ouch. That would cause resentment, for sure." I thought of the conversation between Mateo and Dia that I'd overheard. "Did he lose the restaurant?"

"He lost everything," Donna said. "His business, his house, and even his car. I guess that's why he's working at Aircroft now. It gives him a place to live as well as work while he recovers from bankruptcy."

"That's a pretty solid motive for revenge," I said thoughtfully.

"And since Marin does live at Aircroft, he would've been in the house Sunday evening," Vince said, holding up a finger. "Which is opportunity."

Donna rested her chin on her hand. "But what about means?"

"That's easy enough," I replied. "It appears the murder weapon might've been a heavy candlestick—something the killer could've grabbed because it was readily available."

"So not necessarily premeditated murder. More like someone striking in anger, after an argument escalated," Vince said, rubbing his chin with his fingers.

I sat in silence for a moment, considering this theory, as Vince and Donna discussed various murder scenarios.

"It makes a big difference." Donna waved her hands at Vince's attempts to refute her words. "Heat of passion killing versus premeditated murder calls for a very different sentence."

"True, but can it be established? For all we know, Marin lured Ashley Allen into the library with the intent to kill her."

"Honestly, we don't even know if Mateo had anything to do with it," I said at last. "He does have a motive, but why wait until some time after she ruined his life? I mean, I assume it was a little while ago."

"About two years, I think. And you're right, Jane. The timing is odd." Donna swatted away a buzzing bottle fly. *One of the last of the season*, I thought. *Doomed to die soon.*

"Unless this was the first time Marin had seen her since she wrecked things for him," Vince said.

I shook my head. "It wasn't. I overheard something that makes me think Mateo was forced to cook for her when she and Cam were dating. They had private dinners at the estate, from what I understand."

"That could've stoked his anger." Vince jumped to his feet and strode over the porch railing. "Imagine having to create gourmet meals for someone who destroyed your dream of owning your own restaurant. Something like that could've been the trigger."

"You're right, it could've set him off," I said.

Vince spun around to face us. "So who wants to share this with the authorities? It'd probably be best coming from you, Jane."

Donna frowned and swatted the air again, although I didn't see the fly this time. "Really, dear, do you think we should say anything directly to the police? I assume they'll make the connection between Mr. Marin and the victim on their own. I'd hate to get the man in trouble from some story I pieced together based on gossip and rumors. We don't have any real facts to back up our theories, you know."

I rose to my feet. "Why don't I simply share all this with Cam? It's what he asked me to do—gather information he could use as part of his personal investigation. Of course, if any of us were to run across evidence directly connected to the crime, we should take that to the police, but otherwise . . ." I spread wide my hands.

"I suppose that's best," Vince said. He didn't look particularly happy with this decision.

I suspect he's bored with retirement and is eager to be back in the thick of things, investigating and helping solve complicated cases. I brushed some dust off my navy-blue slacks. "I'll talk to Cam as soon as I can." Meeting Donna's bright gaze, I offered her a warm smile. "Thanks for the info, and if you remember anything else related to Ashley Allen, I'd love to hear it."

"I'll be sure to let Vince know if I do. Although"—Donna flashed a brilliant smile—"I could always talk to you directly, if you'll give me your number. I'd like to get to know you better, anyway. I think we could be good friends. One can't have too many of those."

"That's certainly true. Especially female friends." I glanced at Vince, who was looking a little nonplussed. Perhaps he was uncomfortable with the thought that his tenant, who could easily watch all his comings and goings, was planning on getting chummy with his girlfriend.

Which just made me more determined to follow through on Donna's offer of friendship.

Chapter Sixteen

I shared my phone number with Donna before wishing both of them a good afternoon and retreating to my apartment to freshen up before meeting with Evie Grayson.

I also needed to make sure I knew where the park was located. Slumping down on the sofa, I slid around on sueded upholstery, which was slick and shiny from wear. Readjusting my position, I searched my cell phone for directions.

It turned out that Memorial Park was only a few blocks away. Realizing it would be a quick walk, I did a little more scrolling through Ashley's social media before leaving the apartment at two thirty. Fortunately, Vince's porch was empty. When I strolled past the side of the house, I heard voices through the window.

Since I didn't want anyone asking questions about where I was going, I was glad Vince and Donna were inside the house. I didn't mind sharing some of my activities with Vince, but I also knew I needed to keep his inherent curiosity in mind.

Take his help, but don't tell him everything, I reminded myself. Yes, it was self-serving, but over the years I'd learned that keeping certain things to myself was an unfortunate necessity. Gone were the days when I trusted everyone who seemed to be a "nice person." That naïveté had brought me too much grief in the past.

Bradfordville's main street was quaint for about three blocks, with vintage brick buildings converted into trendy shops selling things no one truly needed, and law and real estate offices interspersed between cafes and bakeries. Outside of the central downtown area, any sense of history gave way to nondescript shopping centers and strip malls. It was clear that Bradfordville had originally been a very small town, and had stayed that way for most of its existence, only sprawling in the last fifteen to twenty years.

Crossing one street, I stepped from the old town into the new and encountered a barrier closing the sidewalk. I took a detour through a wide lot filled with used cars and trucks, ignoring the salesperson who rushed out of the glass-fronted salesroom as I walked by. Turning at the next intersection, I spied a stand of trees that bordered a stretch of beaten-down grass that had to be part of Memorial Park.

Evie hadn't actually stated where we were to meet, which was a problem. The park was larger than I'd expected, the grassy section leading to a maple grove that shaded wooden picnic tables. I strode over to the trees, assuming Evie wouldn't want to have a private talk out in the open.

The cool air bit through the light jacket I'd thrown on before leaving my apartment. As I pulled up the hood to shield my face from the wind, I noticed that deeper in the woods, a small bridge arched over a deep ravine I assumed was a channel for a stream. Leaning over the stone railing was a young woman.

Evie, I thought, just as I heard a whistling sound. A thud echoed right before the woman flinched and fell forward, her fingers scrabbling at the stones to keep herself from tumbling into the ravine. Shoving her palms against the bridge wall, she stumbled backward and fell, hidden from my view.

I abandoned the path and ran directly toward the bridge, ignoring the whips of vines slapping my shins through my thin socks. As I drew closer, a dark figure appeared, half hidden by a scraggly evergreen shrub. I shouted "Stop!" at the figure, but they fled before I could discern anything about them other than their dark clothing and the fact that a hood covered their hair and shadowed their face.

At the bridge, I found Evie on the ground. She was sitting up, cradling her right calf, which was exposed through a ragged rip in her well-worn jeans, with both hands. She'd obviously changed clothes since our meeting at the Allen mansion.

I wish I had, I thought, staring down at the snagged material of my dress slacks. But I couldn't dwell on such things when someone might be badly injured.

"Are you alright?" I asked, moving closer.

Evie looked up at me, her eyes like clear pools in her paper-white face. "I think so. My leg hurts, but it doesn't seem to be broken."

I examined her for a moment, glad I didn't see any blood. "What happened?"

"I'm not sure. I was just standing there at the railing, waiting for you, and I felt something hit my leg. Something hard." Evie bit her lip as she met my concerned gaze. "Hard and sharp. It took me by surprise and I jerked and fell."

"You almost went over into the ravine." I glanced over the stone balustrade. "That could've been a nasty accident. There are spiky rocks in the water."

"I know. Which is why I thrust myself away from the railing. Of course, then I fell and ripped my jeans, but it seemed better than tumbling over." Evie held out her hand. "Help me up? I think I can stand."

Pulling her to her feet, I slid my hand up to her forearm to steady her when she wobbled. "Can you put weight on that leg?"

"I think so. Yeah." Evie grimaced as she pressed down with her foot. "It hurts, but I can stand on it."

"That's good, but you should still sit down for a few minutes." I kept my grip on Evie's arm as we shuffled off the bridge and over to one of the picnic tables. After guiding her to a seat on the wooden bench, I released my hold and stepped back. "I saw someone running away at my approach. Do you have any idea who that could've been?"

Evie swept a tangled lock of hair behind her ear. "Not really. I have a few suspicions, but I can't be sure." She looked up at me, teardrops beading her lashes. "It might be connected to the reason I asked you to meet me here today."

"Someone didn't want you talking with me?"

"Yeah, maybe." Evie looked down, fiddling with the ripped fabric of her jeans. "Or maybe it was just a coincidence that you saw someone running off right after something hit my leg. It could be the person was just as startled as I was and took off, thinking there'd been a gunshot or something. Just like it's possible a wind gust tossed a rock that slammed into my leg."

I fixed her with an intense stare. "But you don't believe any of that."

"No, I don't, because . . . Sit down, please. I might as well explain why I asked you to meet me here in the first place."

"That sounds like a good idea," I said, taking a seat beside her.

Evie cast me an abashed look from under her lowered lashes. "Sorry for all the secrecy, but I didn't want to share any of this with people around. Especially not at the Allens' house."

"Is this connected to Ashley's murder somehow?" I asked. "Because if you have real evidence you should go to the police."

"It is, but I don't." Evie leaned back against the top edge of the picnic table. "I just have my suspicions. And when I learned you were working for Cam, I thought maybe you could share my information with him."

"You didn't want to tell him yourself?"

Massaging her calf with one hand, Evie grimaced again. "You don't just drive up to Aircroft and ask to speak to Cameron Clewe. Not if he doesn't know who you are, and while I know stuff about him, we've never met. I didn't think he'd want to see me, or even talk to me on the phone, and I certainly didn't want to share this information over text or email. So I wasn't sure what to do, and then I met you and you told me you work with him . . ."

"Okay, so what's the deal?" I thought about what Lauren had said—something about a secret Cam would do anything to keep hidden. "Did Ashley share information Cam told her in confidence?"

Blinking rapidly, Evie shook her head. "What? No, nothing like that. This is information I know about the Allen family. About who now stands to inherit a substantial sum of money."

"They're rich already," I said, rubbing a bit of grit from the corner of my eye.

Evie audibly sniffed. "That doesn't matter. From what I've seen, wealthy people always want more money, no matter how much they already have."

The bitterness in Evie's tone made me swivel on the bench to face her. "What's this about an inheritance, then?"

"It was all going to Ashley," Evie said, looking away. "I'm talking about her grandmother's estate, which is worth a fortune. You'd have thought the old lady would've left her money to her son and his wife, or at least split it between them and their girls, but she didn't. She wrote a will that left everything to Ashley, and then stupidly told the whole family about it."

I sucked in a ragged breath. "So Stan, Gemma, and Rena were to get nothing when the grandmother passed?"

Evie turned her head to look me in the eye. "Nothing at all. Nada. Not one cent. Unless, of course, Ashley was dead."

Chapter Seventeen

After dropping this bombshell, Evie refused to speculate further about the Allen family, although she did admit that Stan had picked up Gemma and Rena from the gala on Sunday evening.

"So he was there, however briefly. Which means he could've been the killer, as well as Gemma or Rena," I said, talking more to myself than Evie.

She jumped to her feet, shooting me a sharp look. "Only share this with Cam. I wanted him to have the information so he could use it in his own defense, but I don't want it to go beyond him. Which means, don't tell the authorities what I've told you. Please, Jane. I really have no proof that Stan, Gemma, or Rena were involved in Ashley's death. I admit I don't entirely trust them, but if they are innocent, I also don't want to ruin their lives."

"They apparently did have a motive for wanting her dead," I said, rising to face her. "However, you're right—with no actual facts, it's simply a theory. Besides, I'm sure the investigative team will uncover the financial aspect soon enough. They tend to focus on stuff like that."

"I suppose." Evie lips tightened, as if she wanted to say more, but thought better of it. "I'm going to head home now. Did you drive, or would you like a ride?"

"Thanks, but I think I'll just walk. I can use the time to clear my head," I said, managing a faint smile.

Evie didn't smile in return. "If that's what you want." She walked a few steps, slightly favoring her right leg, then paused and tossed a "thank you" over her shoulder.

"No problem," I called back.

Evie didn't respond. She strode across the lawn, heading for a small gravel parking lot at a pace that made me question whether the injury to her leg was as significant as it had first appeared.

* * *

I arrived at Aircroft early on Thursday morning, hoping to get a chance to speak with Cam before any of the detectives returned to the murder scene.

I was in luck. Running into Lauren in the entry hall of the mansion, I learned that Cam had already had breakfast and was in one of the sitting rooms, reading.

"I don't want to disturb him," I told her, "but I do have some information he might find interesting."

"Good, because I haven't discovered anything useful yet." Lauren covered a yawn with her hand. "Sorry, I haven't been sleeping well."

"That's not surprising, given the events of this week. It's been hard for me to sleep as well."

Lauren flashed me a wan smile before providing directions to the sitting room. "I'd escort you, but I really need to confer with Dia about some household issues."

"Don't worry, I'll find it," I said, not entirely sure this was true.

Fortunately, Lauren's directions were clear, and I located the sitting room without too many wrong turns, although I did open one door leading to a storage closet before I discovered the proper room. Not wanting to startle Cam, I knocked and announced myself before stepping inside.

Like the library, this room featured dark wood wainscotting, but this space was filled with leather armchairs, round side tables, and several glass-fronted display cases instead of bookshelves. The plaster walls above the paneling were painted moss green, which made the room appear dark, even with the heavy drapes thrown back from the tall windows.

Cam was seated in a wing-backed chair whose maroon-tinted leather clashed with his bright auburn hair. "I see you're an early riser, like me," he said, carefully placing a bookmark inside the pages before laying aside the thick volume he'd been reading.

No "hello" or "how are you," I thought as I crossed to the chair facing him. I set down my heavy tote bag. "Actually, I wanted to catch up with you before I started working today. You did say that I could use the music room, right?"

"It's all set up." Cam's cool gray-green gaze raked over my face. "Although you may also need to do a little work in the attic. I couldn't bring down as many boxes as I hoped yesterday, what with the cops still stumbling around the place."

I sat down, aware I probably shouldn't wait for an invitation to do so. "Good morning to you too."

If Cam felt that jab, he showed no signs of it. "Have you uncovered anything that could help solve the case?"

"I don't know about solving it, but I've collected a few pieces of information that might prove useful." I dug my heels into the thick wool rug that filled the floor between the two chairs like a deep blue pool. "Did you know that your chef and Ashley had a history? Not romantic," I added, when Cam's red-gold eyebrows lifted.

"I would think not," he said. "Mateo, for all his talent, isn't the sort of man who would attract Ashley."

"Because he didn't have any money? Well, apparently he had even less after Ashley dashed all his dreams." I leaned forward in the chair and shared the details I'd learned from Donna, although I simply mentioned hearing the story from a reputable source rather than providing her name.

"So Ashley broke a promise? Not surprising, I'm afraid. She did tend to harbor what I called 'enthusiasms'—she'd be totally obsessed with some hobby or interior decorating style or whatever for a short time, then lose all interest in it." Cam pressed his elbows against the buttery leather arms of his chair and rested his chin on his intertwined fingers. "Fortunately, I can easily question Mateo. I'll have to work out the best way to phrase things so he doesn't get suspicious, but Lauren can help me with that."

I opened my mouth but snapped it shut again when I realized my comment about the cavalier way he treated his personal assistant might get me fired. "I wouldn't be surprised if the detectives on the case hadn't already uncovered the connection. A restaurant that never opened and a man forced into bankruptcy would be hard to miss."

"Don't overestimate our local police force," Cam said. "They aren't the cleverest, I'm afraid."

You probably think no one is. I pursed my lips. "Be that as it may, they might be asking Mateo similar questions, so I wouldn't feel overly confident. They may get answers out of him before you do. Anyway, that's not the only information I have to share. Do you want to hear more?"

"Of course." Cam dropped his hands and leaned back in his chair, his eyes gleaming, hard and bright as gemstones.

As I launched into the information concerning Ashley's inheritance, and the motive for murder it offered the rest of her family, Cam lowered his lashes, veiling his eyes. It appeared that he was either deep in thought or falling asleep.

"Who told you this?" he asked, when I finished speaking.

I wasn't sure I wanted to bring Evie's name into the conversation. "One of Ashley's friends."

"Ashley had an actual friend?" Cam rose to his feet and crossed to one of the display cases. "I thought she only collected hangers-on, but I could be wrong. I never allowed her to drag her entourage along when she visited Aircroft."

I studied him for a moment, noticing the tension pulling his slender shoulders up closer to his ears. "Did you love her?"

Cam fiddled with a jade dragon figurine sitting on top of the cabinet for a minute before offering any response. "That's a rather personal question."

"But one you might want to answer more quickly, and with more real emotion, if the police ask. If they haven't already, that is."

"They haven't." Cam's fingers tightened around the figurine. "And you shouldn't."

I rose to my feet and strolled over to where he was standing. Staring at his profile, which was as finely etched as the face on an ancient coin, I tapped the glass top of the cabinet to get his attention. "You haven't expressed even a sliver of sadness over Ashley's death. That's not a good method for establishing your innocence."

Cam set the figurine down so hard I was afraid the top of the display cabinet would crack. "So I'm supposed to perform some sort of grieving ritual to prove I have feelings?"

"It might not hurt," I said, keeping my tone mild. "I suggest this not because I care whether you loved Ashley or not, but simply to offer some advice. Your detachment might be your way of handling grief, but I'm afraid the investigators will see it as a lack of emotion. Which could translate, in their minds, to you not giving a rap for Ashley. They could view you as someone who could've easily disposed of her when she proved troublesome."

Cam shot me a sidelong glance. "So if I don't act appropriately heartbroken, I'm more likely to be seen as a murderer?"

"I don't think so," I said, although privately I admitted his lack of grief had stoked my doubts. "But I'm afraid others might."

Cam pressed his palms against the glass cabinet top and bowed his head. In an instant, the haughtiness that typically suffused his face and bearing evaporated, leaving behind trembling limbs and an expression of despair.

"I know you're right," he said, his voice shaking. "I know I should show how saddened I am by Ashley's death, and display my anger over such a senseless loss of life. I should reveal how fiercely I desire the killer to pay for what they've done. But honestly, Jane"—he lifted his head, revealing the pain haunting his eyes—"Truthfully, I don't know how."

Chapter Eighteen

I took a step toward Cam, my mind racing. I wanted to say something helpful—a few words that would provide ideas on how to handle this situation. It was tough. I'd raised a child, but Bailey was the complete opposite of Cam. She'd never had any difficulty expressing her emotions. In fact, I'd had to teach her how to temper her dramatic outbursts. Dealing with someone who was so closed off was new to me.

As I pondered my next words, I stared down into the glass-topped case. A wide variety of objects were on display—porcelain figurines, small statues carved from stone or wood, and a collection of hand-painted silk fans among them. I looked up, realizing I'd hesitated too long.

Cam had straightened to his full height, his posture stiff as the folds in the damask draperies. "Sorry," he said, staring out the window above the display case. "This is my problem, not yours."

"True, but it might help to talk through a few options. There's nothing wrong with a little acting, if it would allow you to present a better face to the investigators."

Cam shook his head. "I'll be fine. I need to focus on uncovering other possible suspects, that's all. You've already provided me with the names of a few individuals with motives. Now I have to do some more research and logically work out how they could've carried out Ashley's murder."

I pressed my forefinger against the glass of the display cabinet, aware my opportunity to provide any sage advice to Cam had passed. "Changing the subject, I'm curious. Did your family travel a lot when you were younger? I'm guessing most of these items were acquired on trips around the world."

Cam's eyes narrowed. "My father traveled a great deal. For business, mostly. And, as I mentioned before, he was a collector."

I examined a Nativity scene that looked like it had been hand-carved in Germany's Black Forest. "That must've been fun, as well as educational. I've always wanted to travel internationally, but it's so expensive."

"I wouldn't know," Cam said shortly. "Dad never took me with him." He strode over to an antique globe balanced on a wooden stand and stared at it for a moment before speaking again. "Apparently, I wasn't a good traveler."

Strolling across the room, I stopped a few feet away from him. "According to your father, I assume."

"Yes. I don't actually remember taking any trips with him, so I must've been fairly young when he made that determination." Cam slid his fingers over the textured surface of the globe.

I shook my head. The fact was, taking any small child on a long trip could be difficult. I doubted that young Cam had cornered the market on bad behavior. "That's a shame."

Cam smacked the globe, sending it into a wobbly spin. "It doesn't matter. Even though my only traveling has been through reading books and watching documentaries on television or online, I have learned a great deal about other nations and cultures."

"Do you have business interests in other countries?"

Cam lifted his head. "Not really. My father owned several resort properties overseas, but I got rid of them as soon as I could. Sold them back at a discount to people from the local communities." He flashed a wan smile. "I had no interest in continuing my dad's ventures into colonialism. It was probably all those books and documentaries that turned me off that sort of business."

"Good for you," I said, earning another faint smile.

"But enough about my unremarkable childhood," Cam said. "I'd rather discuss my new theory about Ashley's murder."

I arched my eyebrows. "Which is?"

"She may have interrupted a robbery." Cam thrust his hands into the pockets of his beige twill trousers. "Remember the missing candlestick? It was only silver plate over iron, but it looked more expensive. I wonder if a thief infiltrated the gala and was sacking the library before he, or she, was discovered by Ashley. The robber could've hit her when she threatened to scream, then fled."

"But why would Ashley have been there, of all places?" I had to admit it was a logical theory, except for the specific victim ending up in that particular room. I had a feeling that libraries were not Ashley Allen's natural habitat.

Cam turned his head to stare at a lithograph of ancient ruins hung above the globe. "I'm not sure. Perhaps she made an assignation and planned to meet someone there. I've heard rumors that some young man was looking for her at the gala."

"Could that have been someone named Tristan? I saw his photo on her older social media posts. A musician, I think."

I couldn't see Cam's face but noticed his shoulders twitch. "Maybe. I really don't know."

"Ashley never talked with you about her old boyfriends?" I was dubious, but then again, perhaps Cam had cut Ashley short when she tried to bring up such topics. I could picture that scenario. Ashley not discussing her former flames, not so much.

"No, she didn't." Cam turned to face me again. "Anyway, that isn't important. For whatever reason, Ashley ended up in the library, and I believe it's possible she walked in on a robbery. Mainly because in searching the house since the murder, I've discovered other things missing."

"I assume you've shared this with the authorities?"

"Of course. I've also admitted the alarm system was disabled during the gala. They chided me over that, but Naomi begged me to turn the thing off. I thought it would be fine. She knew most of the people attending the event, and was checking everyone against the guest list when they entered the house."

"But someone could've still slipped in."

"Unfortunately." Cam pulled his hands from his pockets and entwined his fingers together at his waist. "It was a mistake to leave the system off so long. Of course, I switched the alarms back on once the event was over and everyone had left, but I suppose it was too late."

I bit the inside of my cheek to silence the words about to tumble from my lips. If Cam had reactivated the alarm system, then he hadn't actually stayed in his bedroom after leaving the party. Not the entire evening, anyway. This fact made me hesitate to say anything more about the Allen family or the mysterious Tristan.

I'd been happy to help Cam uncover information as part of my job. *As a way*, I thought, with a frown, *to keep my job*. But what if the person in the room with me—a brilliant and clever young man by all accounts—was simply playing me for a fool?

Perhaps the murderer didn't need to be found. Maybe he was standing right in front of me.

Chapter Nineteen

"That's my latest theory, anyway." Cam shook out his fingers, apparently oblivious to my agitation.

"It's as logical as any other," I replied, modulating my tone to avoid betraying my suspicions. "But perhaps I should get to work? I think I can find the music room again. The attic is another matter. I'd appreciate it if you could show me the way, in case I do need to pull materials or work up there today."

"Of course." Cam turned on his heel and headed out of the room. I grabbed my tote bag and followed, noting as many details of my surroundings as I could. The sooner I could navigate the house's maze-like corridors without getting lost, the better I'd feel.

We stopped at a narrow door not far from the library. Glancing down the hall, I spied the yellow caution tape that had established a perimeter around the murder scene.

"Have the detectives finished their investigation here at Aircroft?" I asked, as Cam fished a single key from his pocket.

"They said they'd be done by the end of the day and would allow us to enter the library by Monday." Cam handed me the key. "Here you go—I had a copy made so you could access the attic at any time. But please keep this door locked when you're not pulling items or working up there."

"Thanks," I said, pocketing the key. "I'll probably wait and look over the items in the music room first, though. There's heat and electricity in the attic, I hope."

Cam looked down his nose at me. "Of course. I'd hardly store valuable materials in a space lacking the proper environment. I actually keep the rest of my major book collections in climate-controlled storage facilities for that very reason."

His haughtiness had definitely returned with a vengeance. "Right." Shifting my tote bag to my other shoulder, I glanced back at the perimeter tape. "Do you think I could slip past those barriers? I'll be careful to duck under and not break the tape. It's just that I'd love to grab a cup of coffee from the kitchen and using this hall seems the most direct route."

"I don't see why not. It's not like you're going to disturb anything in the library, and the detectives are nowhere to be seen. Probably on a coffee break as well." Cam gnawed on his lower lip as he stared toward the library, then wheeled around and strode off in the opposite direction.

Maneuvering my way past the caution tape was a little harder than I'd anticipated, especially since I had to make sure my tote bag didn't snag and snap the yellow plastic. But I was able to get to the other side and reach the main entry vestibule without incident. Taking the hallway to the kitchen, I again mulled over the possibility that Cam had been lying about leaving his room on the night of the gala only long enough to set the alarms. Perhaps he'd been downstairs for a much more significant period of time—long enough to kill Ashley and hide the murder weapon. *He would know all the secret places in this house better than anyone*, I thought, stopping short as someone called out to me.

"Hello, Jane, how are you holding up?" Dia Denton stood in an open doorway next to the entrance to the kitchen.

Glancing over her shoulder, I realized the room was a walk-in pantry. Its metal shelving was filled with dry goods, cans, and bottles, while boxes stacked in one corner held supplies like paper towels.

"I'm okay," I said. "Back to work today, which is actually my first day in terms of getting anything done."

"I haven't been able to accomplish much this week either." Dia tapped her pen against the clipboard she was holding. "I'm behind in putting together our next supply order."

"It looks like you have a good deal of stuff already," I said.

"We have the basics. I always make sure plenty of those are on hand. But the minute I don't check the pantry before making an order, Mateo will need something we don't have, and I'll have to drive to a local store to get it." Dia made a face. "He chooses the fresh fruit and vegetables at various markets, and selects the fish and meat himself, but I have to keep up with everything else."

"Sounds like a big job." I shifted my tote bag from shoulder to shoulder again. "I guess you've been dealing with the police trampling through the house too."

"Unfortunately." Dia tucked the pen behind her ear, her thick hair holding it in place. "They've asked me multiple times about the security system—why it was turned off for the gala. I've told them we always do that for large events, because otherwise the darn thing gets tripped and wails like a banshee."

"I understand why they'd question that choice, but I can also see why it'd be a bother to keep the system activated. You'd have to hand out the code to all the guests ahead of time, then change it immediately after every event. Besides, I heard Naomi Wilt checked everyone at the front door. I guess she and Hannah figured that was good enough."

Dia's lips curled into a sardonic smile. "Is that what they told the police? Sure, Ms. Wilt was there at the beginning, but then I had to step in. She didn't want to miss the festivities once everything got started, so I was forced to hang out in the front hall to check in any latecomers."

"Did anyone not on the guest list try to get in?" I asked, keeping my tone neutral.

Dia dropped her gaze to her clipboard. "Not while I was there, which was pretty much throughout the party."

I thought of the dark-haired young man that Hannah had mentioned. "Not even a younger guy dressed in a very casual black outfit?"

Throwing up her head like a startled deer, Dia blinked rapidly as she met my inquisitive gaze. "No. If someone like that got into the house, Naomi must've cleared them."

I gave a little shrug, hoping she didn't notice how intrigued I was by her obviously anxious response. "I'm sure it was fine then. Hannah McKenzie said something to me about a younger man who was insistent on talking to Ashley Allen, that's all."

Dia's lips thinned into a straight line. She didn't immediately respond to this comment, choosing to yank the pen from her hair instead. "I'm sure that means nothing. A lot of men seemed fascinated by Ms. Allen, for what reason, I could never understand. Anyway, I doubt the alarm system being deactivated all night had anything to do with her death. If you ask me, it's more likely the killer was one of the invited guests."

I jerked my shoulders back, sending my tote bag sliding down my arm. "Wait, the alarm system was off all night?" I asked as I readjusted the bag.

"It must've been. I get up pretty darn early and it was still deactivated when I checked it Monday morning." Dia scribbled something on the paper attached to her clipboard. "I thought it was odd. Mr. Clewe is so obsessed with stuff like that. He usually checks everything two or three times when we lock up at night."

"Did you actually see him set the alarm after the gala was over?"

"No, I sure didn't. But I wouldn't have, since the main panel is located in a spot not far from the library. It used to be a small storage room until Mr. Clewe's father had it converted into a control room for the security system." Dia shrugged. "I was stuck helping the temp staff clean up in the ballroom, so I wasn't close to the library. No way I could've seen Cam turn on the system. Then again, I didn't see him *not* activate it, either."

"Really? That's . . . interesting," I said, changing my choice of word at the last second. No sense in raising any suspicions in Dia's mind, even if there were plenty swirling around in mine. "But I won't keep you. I just wanted to grab a cup of coffee before starting work on the new book collection."

"There should still be some in the percolator," Dia waved her clipboard at me as she backed into the pantry. "If not, ask Mateo for help. I need to get on with my own inventory."

I wished her a good day before heading into the kitchen, my mind consumed with theories on why Cam would've lied about setting the alarm after the gala had concluded. Because if Dia was telling the truth, Cam had to be lying.

Although it seems a stupid mistake for someone so intelligent to make, I thought. *Cam had to know that Dia, and possibly others, would tell the investigators if the alarm was off when they checked it in the morning.*

Unless Dia is the one lying. Or someone else with the codes turned the system off after Cam reactivated it, I reminded myself as I strolled into the kitchen. I had no idea why Dia would lie about the status of the security system, or why anyone trusted with the access codes would want the system turned off again. But I also couldn't dismiss the possibility that she, or others, might have their own reasons to conceal the truth.

You don't really know Cam, or the houseguests, or the staff, I reminded myself. *Any one of them could be lying*

Mateo looked up from the pastry he was rolling out on the center island. "Can I help you, Jane? Cam and the remaining guests have all had breakfast, but if you need something . . ."

"No, no." I set my tote bag down on the opposite end of the island. "I'm just on the hunt for some coffee. Dia said there might still be some in the pot."

Using his elbow, Mateo gestured toward one of the other counters. "Should be plenty. Help yourself. The mugs, spoons, and sugar are there by the percolator, but if you want cream, you'll have to grab it from the fridge."

"Okay, thanks." After I filled a mug with the rich, dark brew, I walked back to stand across the island from Mateo. "Are you making a pie? That's a skill I admire but, alas, can't seem to master."

"Apple, with a lattice crust. Thought I might as well use some of the fruit we had on hand," he said. "We have a small orchard on the estate, and I like using produce in season."

"I'm impressed." I took a sip of my coffee. "By the way, not to speak ill of the dead, but I heard a rumor about Ashley Allen doing you dirty. Pulling her money out of your restaurant project right when it was almost ready to launch. I'm really sorry that happened. It had to be devastating."

Mateo remained focused on cutting strips of the pie crust with a pastry wheel. "Water under the bridge. I was angry at the time, but now I have this position, so . . ." He looked up at me, his dark eyes narrowed into slits. "You shouldn't listen to rumors, Jane. It's true I didn't like Ashley Allen, but I certainly didn't kill her. She wasn't worth the jail time," he added with a bitter smile.

I held up one hand, palm out. "I'm not accusing you of anything."

"I should hope not." A jangling noise sent Mateo scurrying over to an old landline phone mounted on the wall. He dusted his hands on his apron before he answered. After providing the caller with a short series of numbers, he hung up and sauntered back to the island. "Sorry, but I need to go outside for a delivery." He looked me up and down. "You can take the mug with you. Just bring it back later. Dia gets upset if she has to collect cups and mugs from all over the house."

"No problem." I hoisted the strap of my tote bag onto my shoulder and grabbed the mug as Mateo washed and dried his hands.

A Cryptic Clue

I left the kitchen as soon as he disappeared out a side door. Making my way to the music room, I considered the fact that both he and Dia obviously had the codes needed to open the estate gates, as well as the mansion's doors. Which made sense. In order to properly do their jobs, I assumed they'd also have to be kept updated on any changes to the codes.

Which meant either one of them could've been involved in Ashley's murder, if only as an accomplice. They needn't have done the deed themselves—they could simply have provided the killer with access to the house, whether Cam had reactivated the security system or not.

Chapter Twenty

Judging by the single box left in the music room, Cam had definitely underestimated my abilities. Despite my fascination with the materials, I was able to complete an inventory of the box contents in the morning. Not ready to begin the more arduous cataloging process yet, after lunch I slipped my laptop into my tote bag and headed up to the attic.

Climbing two stories on the steep, narrow staircase made me realize that Cam's original concern over my physical fitness was not simply a young person's snide appraisal of my less than toned figure. I paused on a landing, facing a door that I assumed led to the second floor of the house. Leaning back against the beadboard-paneled wall of the stairwell, I took a few deep breaths and reconsidered my plan to haul several boxes down from the attic on my return. I'd be better off looking through some of the other boxes and making inventory lists in the attic. That way, I could save the more detailed analysis of each item for later. Once I had my inventory spreadsheet listing basic information—like author, title, and publication date—on all of the materials, I could pull a few things at a time and complete the cataloging process in the library, which would be available by that point.

At the top of the stairs, another narrow door opened onto the attic, or a portion of it anyway, as the room I stepped into was not large enough to encompass the entire upper level of the mansion. Facing a wall finished with drywall and white paint, I noticed a door nestled between several ranges of metal shelving. *Obviously that wall divides this space from the rest of the attic*, I thought, surveying the shelves. They were filled with books and accordion-pleated standing file folders, as well as several manuscript boxes. As I approached the collection, I was pleased to see that everything had been stored in acid-free boxes and folders. Cam had obviously done his homework and taken the trouble to properly preserve the collection.

The room was clean, too. Traces of lemon-scented furniture polish and other cleaning fluids lingered in the air. I flicked a switch just inside the door. Blinking in the sudden glare, I realized the overhead lights were on a dimmer switch, and turned the knob to lower the level of illumination. Along with the hum of a dedicated HVAC system and the commercial-grade dehumidifier filling one corner, the cleanliness of the space told me it had definitely been designed to house valuable materials.

The other walls were paneled in the same unpainted bead-board as the stairwell, while the ceiling rafters had been covered with painted drywall. Windows set in the dormers at the front and back of the house were fitted with blackout shades to allow for better control of sunlight—another sign that someone had specifically created this storage space to house books and other print materials. The shades were currently pulled down halfway, providing some filtered light to the room.

I strolled over to a wooden table and chair placed in the center of the room. Grateful that the space could function as a second workroom, I pulled my laptop out of my tote bag and set both on the table. I could definitely compile my inventory of the collection in the attic. I'd have to tell Cam my new plan, of course, but I was sure he wouldn't mind, especially since it would save wear and tear on the collection. *As well as my back*, I thought with a smile.

After setting up my laptop, I conducted a visual examination of the collection. Everything had been arranged alphabetically by the authors' last names. Within each author section, the books appeared to be sequenced by the date of publication. Manuscript boxes and pleated file folders were placed at the end of each section, dividing one author's work from the next. Pulling out a file associated with Mary Roberts Rinehart, I peeked inside, confirming my assumption that the boxes and files held magazine and newspaper clippings as well as other ephemera.

Beyond the metal shelving units, the ceiling dropped to meet the low walls flanking the dormers. Cardboard boxes lined these short, beadboard-covered walls, their distressed condition and lack of labeling indicating they were probably not part of the main collection. But I felt I should check before dismissing them as something outside the scope of my job. I decided to investigate a carton whose yellowed cellophane tape had split open and draped the side of the box like a discarded snake skin. It was filled with a variety of old shoeboxes. Intrigued, I gently lifted one and carried it to the table.

A Cryptic Clue

As I crossed the room, the overhead lights flickered and failed, leaving me in semi-darkness. I clutched the shoebox closer to my chest and shuffled over to the light switch, feeling my way with each footstep. But before I could reach the wall, the lights popped back on, even brighter than before.

"Must be a faulty wire in the switch or dimmer," I said aloud, Somehow, hearing my voice resonate throughout the room made me feel less uneasy. I made a mental note to mention the issue to Lauren or Cam. The last thing we needed was an electrical short that could start a fire and destroy such valuable materials. *Not to mention burn the house down*, I thought as I set the shoebox on the table.

Searching the drawer under the table, I found a packet of thin white cotton gloves and pulled on a pair before opening the shoebox. As I'd suspected, the box held loose photographs, most of which were black and white, with a few hand-colored portraits and sepia-tinted landscapes. Examining the clothing in the pictures, I was able to date the photographs to the late 1920s through the early 1940s. It was the right time period for the Golden Age of mystery and detective fiction, but since most of the settings were clearly the Aircroft mansion or its gardens and grounds, I knew that these photos had nothing to do with Cam's newly acquired collection.

Must've belonged to the Airleys. I recalled Vince's comments about the family as I perused the photographs. Since Calvin, the only heir to the estate, had died young, the pictures had probably been abandoned in the attic when Samuel and Bridget Airley had passed away. Cam, or his father Albert, may have recognized the need to at least offer some protection to the photos and had them moved into this more environmentally friendly portion of the attic.

I carefully flipped through the photos, hoping to discover some of the grown-up Calvin, but while there were numerous pictures of a young boy I assumed to be him, I only found one rather blurry snapshot of a young man in his twenties. In the photo a dark-haired, slender man wearing light, high-waisted trousers and a pale sweater tied around the shoulders of his striped shirt stood in front of a flowering tree. *In the garden at Aircroft*, I realized, even though the shrubs and trees were much smaller than they were now. The young man had a bright smile and an open expression that spoke of comfort and ease. A shiver twitched my shoulders. He looked happy and confident—there was no hint of future tragedy reflected in his light eyes.

Of course he couldn't have known about that. We never know when the shadows will fall, I thought, slipping the photo back into the shoebox. *Just like my wedding photos don't display any hint of the hardships to come.*

I frowned as my gloved fingers absently pulled another photograph from the box. I knew I shouldn't waste my time bemoaning my ill-fated marriage. It had been a disaster, but I'd moved on. *Mostly.*

And there was Bailey. I could never completely regret anything that had given me Bailey. When friends asked if I'd go back in time and call off my wedding, I always told them no. Because I would never give up my daughter, no matter the cost.

As I swished the photograph I held through the air, the lights flickered again. Glancing down at the picture, I was surprised to have my gaze met by a pair of striking light-colored eyes framed by lush black lashes.

It was a photo of a young woman, her pale skin luminous against the dark curls framing her round face. She possessed a type of beauty I associated with Pre-Raphaelite portraits— an air of natural wildness and voluptuousness offset by a shy smile.

As I flipped the photo over, searching for any clues to her name or her connection to the Airley family, the black shade on one of the dormer windows rolled up with a bang. I placed the girl's photo back in the box and crossed the room to lower the shade. I knew the damage too much direct sunlight could wreak on old books.

Returning to the table, I pushed the shoebox to one side and turned on my laptop. My curiosity had been piqued by the photographs, but it was time to get to work on the tasks I was being paid to do.

Although, I thought as I carried a stack of materials from the metal shelving to the table, *I don't see the harm in taking the shoebox home, if only for a day or two, and sharing the pictures with Vince. He might have some inkling of the mysterious young woman's identity, and even if not, I'm sure he'll be interested in these family photos.*

After all, he had given me what I suspected was a discount rate on the rent for my apartment. Sharing a little information on the Airley family was the least I could do in return.

Of course, the fact that, having studied his picture, I was now as intrigued as Vince was over the mystery of Calvin Airley's death might also have had something to do with my decision.

Chapter
Twenty-One

I waited until after I'd changed into sweatpants and a long-sleeved T-shirt and eaten a simple dinner before I grabbed the shoebox of photos and hurried down my apartment steps to knock on Vince's door.

He met me with a questioning look. "Hey, Jane, what's up? Something wrong in the apartment?"

"No, nothing like that. I just have some materials"—I held out the shoebox—"I thought might interest you."

Vince ushered me inside. "Never let it be said I turned away a charming woman bearing gifts."

I didn't respond to the flattery, assuming Vince was one of those people who liked to compliment everyone. Not a bad habit, really, but I wasn't necessarily buying the "charming" appellation. "I probably shouldn't have taken this from the house, but I didn't think Cam would mind. It's a collection of photos from the Airley family that was apparently abandoned in the attic, so it's not like it really has anything to do with him."

Vince quirked one eyebrow. "But you didn't ask?"

"No." I set the box on his wood-and-glass coffee table. "Do you want to see the pictures or not?"

"Of course I do. But first, would you like something to drink?" Vince strolled over to a narrow table made of light wood. A collection of bottles, glasses, and other bar essentials filled a pewter tray on top of the table.

"I wouldn't mind a glass of tonic over ice. No alcohol," I said as I sat down on one of the sleek sofas. The back was too short to support my head, so I stretched my arm across the top of the cushions instead. "By the way, I had an interesting encounter with one of the murder victim's friends yesterday." I described my meeting with Evie as Vince fixed our drinks.

"The Allen family sounds like they put the fun in dysfunctional." Vince offered me a sarcastic smile along with the tumbler of tonic water.

"Well, based on my brief observation of them at their house, they didn't appear terribly grief-stricken." I plucked the lime wedge off the rim and squeezed it into my glass before dropping it into the fizzing tonic water. "Although, to be fair, everyone processes grief differently, so perhaps I'm being too harsh."

"Still, we have to consider all the angles." Vince took a seat in the sculptural chair across from me. "That's the reporter in me. I like to compile all possible information and then look for clues and connections."

"Which is not too far off from what a detective might do." I sipped my drink. "Come to think of it, it's pretty similar to what I used to do when I was a reference librarian. I split my time between reference work and cataloging for several years before focusing on the latter."

"There are definite similarities." Vince set his tumbler on a coaster on the coffee table and picked up the shoebox.

"I stuck a pair of cotton gloves in there," I said.

"Right, don't want to smudge the photographs with my fingerprints." Vince cast me a grin. "Especially if your boss ever does confront you about taking the pictures out of the house. Leave no traces," he said, waving the gloves.

I dropped my arm down from the back of the sofa. "I wasn't actually thinking about that, but it is another benefit. Now, if you glance through those photos, you'll see one of Calvin Airley. At least, that was who I assumed was in the picture."

"This one?" Vince held up the photograph of the young man standing in the gardens at Aircroft. "That's him. I think it must've been taken right after he graduated from Harvard."

Given his family's wealth and connections, I wasn't surprised by this revelation. "Do you know what he studied?"

"Honestly, I'm not sure. He got a B.A., so I assume it wasn't anything in the scientific or mathematical fields." Vince flipped through the photos. "I've seen a few of these before, in articles published around the time of Calvin's death. But not this one." He laid the shoebox aside and peered at the picture, his brow furrowing.

"The portrait of a young woman?" I asked, assuming that was the one that might have captured his attention.

"Yes, a pretty girl with lots of wavy hair." He flipped the photo over. "Nothing indicating her name."

"I thought you might know it," I said, fighting to hide my disappointment. "Since you've done a ton of research into the Airley family in the past, I was hoping you'd run across her picture before."

Vince shook his head. "I have no idea who she is. Strange to see her photograph in a box of family pictures, when I doubt she was part of the family. Of course, to be honest, I've only found photos of a few cousins, which isn't surprising. It wasn't a large family. Samuel was the only child of parents who were only children, so his family basically died out with Calvin. Bridget had two sisters, one of whom became a nun. The other one did marry, so there are some cousins on that side, but they didn't stay in touch. The married sister inherited Airley when Samuel and Bridget died in 1974, since there was no other family alive at that point."

"But she didn't live here, did she?" I asked, thinking about the information I'd read about Aircroft. "I thought the estate has only had two residential owners."

"That's true. The sister, whose name was Mary, held onto it for a while, but never moved in. From what I've discovered, talking to some older locals, Mary visited Aircroft once but fled after a few days, claiming the place was haunted. Which was not a smart move, since it made selling the estate difficult. Mary had to use some of the money she inherited to keep up the property, with estate managers and such, until she finally found a buyer in 1981."

"Cam's dad, Albert Clewe."

"Right. He wasn't concerned about ghosts or any other tales told about the estate, he just wanted to buy it for a good price. Which he did." Vince looked up from his study of the photo he was still holding and met my inquisitive gaze with a wry smile. "I actually contacted one of Bridget's grand-nieces a few years ago. She told me her grandmother, Mary, had asked Bridget for some financial help during a particularly tough time. Bridget said *no* and immediately cut off that entire branch of the family. They never spoke again, or so this lady said. According to her, Mary was pretty astonished when she inherited Aircroft."

"Once Bridget made good, she didn't feel inclined to help her sister? Nice." I took a swig of my drink.

Vince's expression grew thoughtful. "Who knows? Maybe Bridget did help them once or twice, and then the family pestered her relentlessly for more money. I only got the information from one side. Not to mention the grand-niece, Linda, was in her mid-seventies, and she'd only managed to piece together the story from things she'd overheard as a child. Not the most reliable source."

"I'm assuming Linda didn't look anything like the young woman in the photo?"

"Not at all, and I did ask to see some of her family photos. No one bore any resemblance to this mystery woman." Vince tapped the edge of the photo against his gloved palm. "I'm afraid I can't be much help in identifying her, at least not now. But if you could leave this one picture with me . . ."

I shifted on the sueded sofa cushions. "I don't know. I was hoping to take the box back tomorrow."

"I tell you what, let me take a picture with my phone. That way you can return it tomorrow and I'll still have a copy. I'll just set it aside for now, but I'll make sure to give it back to you before you leave." Vince laid the picture on a small table beside his chair. "I think pursuing this lead could really help my investigation, and in return I'll continue to help Cam with his.

Without his knowledge, of course." Vince's smile revealed his slightly yellowed teeth.

Former smoker, I thought. It wasn't surprising, given his age and profession. "Speaking of which, have you discovered anything useful?"

"Since yesterday?" Vince crossed his arms over his broad chest. "I'm flattered by your opinion of my investigative abilities, but no."

I considered his information on the Airley family as I finished my drink. "Haunted, huh? Is that why you wanted me to keep an eye out for ghosts?"

"Or ears, if the specters refuse to materialize." Vince grinned. "But yeah, that's part of the reason. Mary had to hold onto Aircroft for seven years, searching for a buyer who wasn't intimidated by the rumors and folktales surrounding the estate. I just find that interesting. I don't suppose you've experienced any unexplained phenomena yet?"

Lights flickering and a shade opening on its own . . . I shook my head. "Nothing I'd consider significant. I mean, it's a large, echoey place, with an overabundance of rooms and corridors. I bet it's pretty easy to get spooked if you have that sort of mindset."

"Which you don't," Vince said.

"Nope. I've always been a pretty pragmatic person. Skeptical of things that can't be proven, at least on a basic level. Not to say I don't think there are inexplicable aspects to the universe, I just don't immediately jump to some paranormal conclusion when I experience something odd."

"That's fine," Vince said. "I think the best investigator for a haunted house is someone who doesn't really believe in ghosts. That way, they're unlikely to imagine stuff happening just because they want it to happen."

I smiled. "You're in luck, then. I've encountered a lot of unusual characters in my library career, but I can definitely say I've never met a ghost."

Chapter
Twenty-Two

O n Friday I decided to work in the music room, cataloging some of the materials Cam had pulled from the attic earlier in the week.

It wasn't that I was afraid to return to the attic, rather that the heating system in that area wasn't working properly, at least according to Lauren.

"I've called the service company and they'll fix it today, but I think you'd better stay out of the attic until they're done," Lauren had told me when she'd met me in the entry hall. "I hope you'll have enough to do, but if not, don't worry—Cam won't dock your pay if you leave early."

"If I get into cataloging the materials in the music room, it will take more than one day," I assured her. "Cataloging is a much more intensive process than making an inventory. I have to examine each item and enter data into an online form, covering a multitude of things like publication location, item format, paper type, subject headings, and a lot of other details that are specified in the cataloging standards. The basic inventory listing of author, title, publisher, and date of publication is just the tip of the iceberg—like the rest of the berg, hidden underwater, the bulk of cataloging work involves data that few people see. But it is essential for maintaining individual records on the very specific items that researchers worldwide might be looking for."

"Goodness, I had no idea how involved it all was. But I suppose that's why Cam wanted to hire a professional. He certainly doesn't like to do things halfway." Lauren, who was wearing a slim turquoise jacket over an ivory sheath dress, pulled a pale yellow knit hat over her black curls. "I have to run an errand, so I'll see you later. If you need anything, check with Dia or Mateo."

"They'll be in the kitchen, I suppose?"

"That's where Mateo should be, but Dia is actually doing some cleaning upstairs in the guest wing. She's tidying up after our recent guests."

"I thought they'd already left a few days ago," I said, recalling the scene from the breakfast room on the morning after the murder.

"Kyle and Brendan did, but Hannah and Naomi are just leaving today." Lauren flashed a bright smile before turning away. "Good luck with your work. I hope that one box in the music room will give you enough to do."

"Since I'll be cataloging, it certainly will," I told her, then wished her a good day as she headed for the front doors.

I set aside the shoebox of photos I'd planned to return. I'd have to carry it up to the attic another time. Following Vince's lead, I'd already taken a photo of the mystery woman's snapshot so I could keep a copy for myself.

A Cryptic Clue

After consulting the inventory list, I opened the cataloging software on my computer and set to work. It was indeed a complicated process, especially since I'd convinced Cam it would be best to use the Library of Congress cataloging system, which had been created to provide access to research materials, rather than the Dewey Decimal system, which was more appropriate for public libraries. Cam, who wanted his materials to be available to scholars, readily agreed to provide me with professional access to the Online Computer Library Center, now known simply as OCLC, which maintained an international database of cataloging records. That had impressed me, especially since the professional cataloging of his collections required a considerable investment up front. But Cam had agreed that it was worth the money. While access to OCLC's records, and the ability to upload my own cataloging records so that they would be available on WorldCat, OCLC's worldwide library catalog, was expensive, it would allow researchers across the globe to readily locate specific items in Cam's personal collections. They could then either ask to visit Aircroft to study the materials or have relevant passages or pictures copied and emailed to them.

The box in the library contained materials related to Marie Belloc Lowndes and her famous story based on Jack the Ripper, *The Lodger*. Not only were there two copies of the first edition of the novel, published by Methuen in 1913, but also one copy of the January 1911 edition of *McClure's Magazine*, where the short story version of the tale was originally published. Stored in acid-free envelopes like the rest of the unbound print materials, I also found the copies of the 1913 *Daily Telegraph*, in which a longer version of the short story had been serialized before Methuen had released it as a full-length novel.

All of which was intensely intriguing. I wanted to sit down in one of the comfortable armchairs and read, but many years of library work had taught me that I couldn't fall victim to that temptation. Despite what people assumed, library staff did little actual reading at work. There was a lot of skimming of texts to glean the necessary information as part of the cataloging process, but if I wanted to actually read a book, I had to check it out and take it home, just like any other library patron.

I'd begun the cataloging process on the first edition bound volumes when a scream, thump, and crash pierced the quiet. Quickly saving my work on the computer, I dashed into the hall and ran in the direction of another shriek.

Reaching the entry hall, I first noticed the leather suitcase. It lay at the foot of one set of the double-sided stairs, its latches sprung open and a colorful riot of clothes spilled onto the floor. I'd barely registered the oddness of this when the sound of voices made me raise my gaze. I gasped. Naomi was clinging to the balustrade near the top of one set of the steps, wobbling precariously until Hannah reached her and wrapped both arms around her slender waist.

"My goodness, what happened?" I asked, shoving my hand into the pocket of my slacks to grab my cell phone. "I can call for help if you need it."

Naomi waved off this suggestion, her blue eyes unnaturally bright in her pale face. "I was lugging my suitcase down the stairs . . ."

"I told you to ask Dia or Mateo for help." Hannah's hectoring tone earned a glare from Naomi. "Now you've gone and slipped and dropped the darn thing and almost tumbled down after it."

Naomi straightened, pulling free of Hannah's hold. "I didn't slip."

"What in the world is going on?" Dia appeared in the open hall at the top of the stairs, clutching a dustcloth against the bodice of her flower-patterned apron.

"Naomi slipped and almost fell," Hannah told her.

Mateo strode out from one the upper hallways and stood next to Dia on the landing. "Ms. Wilt, thank heavens you're okay. But I wish you hadn't attempted to carry your own case down these stairs. As I've told you before, you can always ask me for help with the luggage."

I frowned. I knew that Dia was supposedly cleaning, but what was Mateo doing upstairs? I was further flabbergasted when Kyle and Brendan rushed out onto the landing from the opposite hallway. *This whole thing is beginning to resemble a French farce.*

"I called the kitchen phone but no one answered, and I had no idea you two were here." Naomi cast Kyle and Brendan a sharp look over her shoulder.

"We stopped by because we wanted to see how Cam was doing," Kyle said, while Brendan, speaking at the same time, said, ". . . to pick up a pair of cuff links Kyle left behind."

I studied the tableau of guests and staff, unsure which, if any of them, were telling the truth. "You're certain you're okay, Naomi?"

"I'm perfectly fine." The older woman lifted her sharp chin. "Although I don't think that was the plan."

Hannah sidestepped to reach the other handrail. "Goodness, dear, whatever do you mean?"

"I couldn't locate Mateo, and I knew Dia was busy, so I decided to carry the case down myself. Which would've been fine, except . . ."

"You stepped wrong and almost fell. Which could've been deadly," Hannah said.

Naomi, her fingers curled around the railing next to her, took two steps down. "Quite true, and the reality is, this was no accident. Someone snuck up behind me. Someone I never saw, because they ran off immediately after, but I certainly remember the pressure of their hands on my back." Reaching the bottom of the staircase, Naomi circled around the open suitcase to face me. "I did not slip, nor did I step wrong. I was pushed."

Chapter
Twenty-Three

The outcries following this announcement mingled, as indistinguishable from one another as the screeching of birds I'd once heard in the aviary at the state zoo. But one voice finally cut through.

"Someone explain." Cam, who'd come out of one of the hallways off the entry vestibule, marched over to face off with both Naomi and me. "I was diligently working in my office until I heard this ungodly racket."

"Naomi says that some unknown person tried to push her down the stairs." Hannah grabbed up a handful of loose clothes and tossed them into Naomi's suitcase as she joined her friend.

Cam looked over both women, his freckles blazing against his ivory skin. "That doesn't sound very likely. Who would do such a thing?" He stared at the upper landing. "And why are all of you hanging out up there?"

"So sorry, Cam," Brendan said, descending the stairs with Kyle on his heels. "We came by to retrieve some cuff links Kyle left in one of the guest rooms." He shot Kyle a warning look that

I assumed was connected to his partner's earlier comment about simply stopping by to check on Cam. "Lauren was here when we arrived and told us you were working on some company reports, so we decided not to bother you."

"She also said it was okay for us to go up and search the room," Kyle said. "For the cuff links," he added, after Brendan elbowed him.

"That's fine, I guess." Cam's eyes narrowed as Dia and Mateo joined the rest of us in the vestibule. "And you two?"

Dia held out her dusting cloth. "I was cleaning guest rooms."

"I was . . . looking for something." Mateo shifted his weight from foot to foot. "That vintage cookbook you talked about, Cam. The one you said might be shelved with your mother's other books."

"In her old studio?" Cam thrust his hands into his pockets and rocked back on his heels. "It's been a while since I mentioned that. What brought it to mind?"

Processing the concept of Patricia Clewe having a studio—and wondering if that was connected to the pen-and-ink drawing I'd seen in the hall outside the library—I almost missed Mateo's next words.

"The apples, sir," Mateo said. "We have such a bumper crop this year. I was looking for new ways to use them. Then I remembered you talking about some recipe for apple jelly in one of your mother's old cookbooks."

"Hmm . . ." As Cam's gaze swept the room, the insistent tapping of his right foot created a drumbeat against the marble floor. "Where's Lauren?"

"Running an errand," I said.

Cam's gaze snapped to me. "And where were you, Jane, when this almost-accident occurred?"

"Working in the music room. Downstairs," I said.

"I suppose that knocks you off the suspect list." Cam's lips twitched into a barely perceptible smile.

"Really, Cam," Kyle said, irritation lacing his tone. "I don't see why any of us would be on such a list."

Cam, his expression somber again, looked Naomi up and down. "You're sure you're okay? Do you want to talk to the police about this?"

"No, what could they do? I didn't see anything." No longer appearing shaken, Naomi squared her shoulders. "Dia, would you mind helping me repack?" She gestured toward the suitcase.

"Of course. Just leave it to me. Why don't you and Ms. McKenzie head to the breakfast room and relax. I'm sure Mateo will make you a coffee or tea or whatever you want before you leave."

"Absolutely," Mateo said, his dark eyes brightening. "I have some pastries too. Made fresh this morning."

Hannah patted Naomi's rigid arm. "What do you say? A little sit-down and a snack wouldn't hurt right now, would it?"

"I suppose not." Naomi glanced over at Kyle and Brendan. "Would you like to join us?"

"No thanks, we were just heading out," Kyle replied, before Brendan could even open his mouth. "Good to see you all. Cam, since you're busy, we'll chat some other time." He grabbed Brendan's arm and walked him to the front doors, barely allowing time for Brendan to call out "Goodbye, everyone" as they exited.

Mateo brushed his hands together as if dusting off flour. "Excuse me, I'm going to start that coffee." Glancing at Cam, he bobbed his head in the slightest of acknowledgments before turning on his heels and striding away.

"It seems everything's arranged. I think I'll get back to work." Cam caught my eye and added, "Come by the office when you get a minute, would you, Jane? I'd like an update."

Not sure whether he was talking about my work on his book collection or the amateur sleuthing he'd asked me to do, I simply nodded. "I want a cup of coffee first, if that's alright."

Cam shrugged. "No hurry. I'll be in the office all day."

It wasn't until he'd left the entry room that I realized I had no idea where the office was.

Seeming to sense my concern, Dia paused in her gathering of Naomi's spilled clothing. "I'll show you the way, once you've grabbed your coffee. You just join the other ladies. I'll stop by when I finish with this."

I thanked her and followed Naomi and Hannah to the breakfast room.

"I'm so sorry you had that terrible fright," I told Naomi.

"Thank you, but I'm fine now," Naomi said, not bothering to turn around.

"Still, someone trying to push you down the stairs has to leave you feeling a little rattled. I know it would take me a while to recover from that." I increased my pace until I was walking abreast with the two older women. "I mean, breaking a leg or hip at our age can be quite debilitating."

Naomi side-eyed me. "I think you are a good ten years younger than either Hannah or me. If not more. But yes, it would be dangerous. Although not as deadly as breaking a neck."

"That's true." I paused, allowing Naomi and Hannah to enter the breakfast room in front of me. "You really didn't see the culprit?"

"I did not." Naomi sat down at the far end of the table. "Ah, here's the coffee. Thanks so much," she told Mateo, as he left a carafe next to the mugs and utensils on the buffet table.

"No problem. Let me know if you need anything else," he said before disappearing into the hall that led to the kitchen.

I hung back, allowing Hannah to prepare coffees for Naomi and herself and carry them to the table. "It's strange how most of the household was upstairs when it happened," I said, crossing to the buffet to fill my own mug. "Even Kyle and Brendan. Which means there's a long list of people who could've shoved you, Naomi. Of course, we can eliminate Lauren and Cam as suspects. And me, I hope." I offered both women a wry smile as I sat down near them.

"Lauren was running an errand, as you said. Which I know because I glanced out the bedroom window when we were packing and saw her drive away. But as for Cam"—Naomi shared a look with Hannah—"we actually can't rule him out."

"He was working downstairs," I said.

"True, but there are back stairs. These old mansions had them built in for the servants to use. Cam, who knows Aircroft inside and out, could easily have accessed the upper floor using one of those staircases," Naomi said.

"And no one would've seen him," Hannah added, her gaze fixed on her coffee cup.

Realizing how hot the liquid still was, I pulled my lips back from the rim of the mug. "But why would Cam want to push you down a flight of stairs?"

Hannah and Naomi shared another secretive look. "Because Naomi . . . well, she saw him near the library the night of the murder," Hannah said, her voice trembling slightly. She stared at the open doorway before continuing. "It was right after the gala was over."

My mug thunked the table as I set it down. Cam had said he'd reset the alarm system, so this might mean nothing. On the other hand . . . "Really? Did you speak with him?"

Naomi smoothed a silken strand of her white hair away from her forehead. "I didn't have a chance. I'd just finished helping some guests who'd gotten a little turned around, directing them to the front doors. That's when I saw Cam. He was stepping out of one of the side corridors, one that has a door closing it off so you wouldn't realize it was there unless you truly knew Aircroft's floor plan. I don't know if he saw me, because he didn't appear to be looking my way, but I remember thinking it was strange." She took a deep breath. "Honestly, it seemed to me that he was lurking behind that half-open door until the guests were out of sight. Only then did he exit the corridor and walk toward the library."

"Maybe he was heading in that direction to set the alarms. Dia told me the control room is near the library. And Cam has claimed he reactivated the system after the gala," I said.

"I suppose that's possible." Naomi took a long swallow of her coffee and dabbed her lips with a napkin before continuing her story. "It's true I didn't see him enter the library. Hannah called out to me from the ballroom and I turned around to find out

144

what she needed. But I did see Cam around the time the murder might've happened. And he was definitely walking toward the library when last I observed him."

I slid back in my chair, keeping my gaze locked on Naomi's angular face. "I imagine you shared this information with the police?"

"I felt I must. I hated to target Cam as a possible suspect, but what else could I do?" Naomi lifted her hands in a mea culpa gesture. "Of course, I can't really picture Cam murdering his ex-girlfriend."

"We definitely don't believe that," Hannah echoed, her hazel eyes blinking.

I pushed back my chair and rose to my feet. "I think I'll take my coffee and go meet with Cam now," I said, surveying the faces of the two women before me.

They may not have lied to the police, but I knew they were lying to me now. They both suspected Cam was the killer.

I wished them a good day and left the room, wondering why I was conflicted over this revelation. Naomi and Hannah both knew Cam much better than I did. If they felt he was capable of murder, who was I to dispute their opinions?

Still, despite my own suspicions, I did.

Chapter
Twenty-Four

As I strode away, I realized I'd forgotten to wait for Dia. Fortunately, she was still in the main entry hall.

"You didn't take much of a break," she said as she clicked the final latch on Naomi's suitcase.

"I want to get back to work, but I'm required to talk with Cam first, it seems. So I thought I'd go ahead and get to that." I held up my mug. "Brought my coffee along."

"Good idea," Dia said, setting the leather suitcase up on its side.

Not sure if she meant nothing by that remark, or if she was implying that a conversation with Cam required stimulants, I simply smiled and followed her into one of the hallways leading off the entry vestibule.

We passed the sitting room I'd visited the day before, as well as several closed doors that led to heaven knew where, finally reaching a room that appeared to be located at the back of the mansion. *Rather far from the front hall. How did Cam hear much of anything from here?*

I pushed this thought aside and thanked Dia, who slipped away, claiming she had too much work to do to linger. After she left, I rapped on the door and stepped inside.

And paused just inside the doorjamb, staring. It was like entering a different world. Gone were the polished paneling, plastered walls, and paintings depicting country landscapes. This room had been renovated to reflect a very different sensibility.

It's more Cam, I realized as I surveyed the clean lines of chrome-and-glass furniture and the arrangement of floating glass shelves that covered one gleaming white wall. The room, which was not overly large, was furnished with an L-shaped glass desk set on sleek chrome legs, a brushed metal storage cabinet, and several legal-sized, silver-toned metal file cabinets. Light spilled in from large windows that filled two walls of the room. The mullions on the windows on the back wall had been removed, providing an unobstructed view into a section of the gardens.

As I crossed the pale, wide-planked wooden floor, Cam looked up from the laptop centered on his desk. "And you are, like everyone, surprised," he said, without any trace of rancor.

"Not when I really think about it," I said, sitting in a simple gray armchair, the only seating other than Cam's high-backed, pewter-toned task chair. "I can imagine you enjoying the simplicity of this room."

"It's clean and efficient," he said, rolling his chair away from the desk. "Which offers less distractions when I'm working."

"Is that why your desk is positioned so you're looking away from the view?" I asked, gesturing to the back windows.

"Exactly." Cam swiveled his chair to face me. "I can turn and look outside when I need a break, but if I were gazing at that constantly . . ." He rubbed the side of his nose with one finger. "I'd be lost, counting clouds and trying to identify birds and that sort of thing."

I placed my hands, one over the other, in my lap. "You wanted to talk to me?"

"I thought we could discuss the facts we've already compiled on the Ashley Allen case," he said. "Compare notes, like proper investigators."

Studying Cam's handsome face, I considered the information Naomi and Hannah had just shared with me. There was something about the nervous energy Cam radiated that made me question whether he could have pulled off a murder and then faced me as he did now—so detached from the horror of such an act. Yet perhaps Cam had a talent for compartmentalization. It would certainly match this room, which probably reflected his personality more closely than the rest of the house.

Neat, precise, controlled, yet somehow also edgy, I thought, resting my hands on the arms of my chair. "Someone tried to push Naomi down the stairs, and almost everyone else in the house was in a position to do so," I said.

Cam held up one finger. "To be perfectly clear—Naomi *claims* someone tried to push her down the stairs."

"Why would she say that if it wasn't true?"

"I have no idea. But we have to keep an open mind about it, along with everything else. As all good detectives do," Cam stretched out his long legs. "No one saw what happened, apparently not even Naomi."

"True, but then there's the fact that Mateo was upstairs along with the others, and I find that extremely odd."

"As do I." Cam pulled in his legs and spun the chair. Leaning forward, he typed something into his laptop. "He had a troubled history with Ashley, as you know. But it seems there were some threats of violence. Enough that Ashley took out a restraining order against him." He turned the laptop so I could view the large screen.

"How did you get this?" I asked as I read the document requiring Mateo to stay away from Ashley and refrain from phoning, texting, or emailing her.

Cam lifted his slender shoulders. "I have some connections in the legal system. Mostly old friends of my dad, but they can occasionally be persuaded to come through for me."

"Mateo did offer up a rather feeble excuse as to why he was up on the second floor just now," I said as Cam swiveled the computer and carefully readjusted its position on the desk.

"Exactly. Of course, Dia was working upstairs as well, and Kyle and Brendan just happened to have stopped by, but I haven't come up with any logical theories as to why they'd want to kill Ashley, or harm Naomi." Cam tapped his fingers against the edge of the laptop. "At least not yet."

"Both Dia and Mateo have all the codes needed to allow entry to any part of the estate," I said.

"Yes, I've thought of that. They could've provided someone else easy access."

"Hired a hit man, you mean?"

Cam raised his eyebrows. "Possibly. Or either one of them could've been paid to provide the codes to someone."

"Ah, bribery. I hadn't considered that angle. That might, forgive my pun, open the door to other suspects." I snapped my fingers. "Like someone in the Allen family. They'd inherit a fortune if Ashley was dead."

"Don't forget, two of them were at the gala," With one elbow propped on his chair arm, Cam rested his chin on his hand. "Gemma and Rena could've slipped away from the party at any time."

"And Stan picked them up after the event, so that places him at the scene as well. He could've entered the house and mingled with the crowd, then fled with Gemma and Rena after the fact."

"True. We certainly have no dearth of suspects in this case."

And then there's you, I thought, keeping my expression neutral as I scooted to the front edge of my chair. "There is one puzzle you can solve right now."

"What's that?" Cam's lashes lowered over his sea-green eyes.

"Okay, so several people have mentioned seeing you downstairs after the gala was over. In the hallway, near the library. I know it might be related to reactivating the alarm system, but a few individuals have suggested that you seemed to be trying to hide, or at least moving in a secretive manner."

Cam lifted his head and stared at the opposite wall for a moment before turning to face me. "Who might that be?"

"I'm not sure that's relevant."

Cam leaned forward, gripping his knees with his hands. "I'd say it was extremely relevant. Given that these individuals are basically accusing me of murder."

"Didn't you leave your room and go downstairs after the gala? Because you've admitted you reactivated the alarm system, which would require you to access the control room." I met Cam's intense gaze without faltering. "Honestly, given that fact, it's not that strange that others have mentioned seeing you later, near the library . . ."

Cam leaped to his feet, the sudden motion sending his desk chair sailing across the room. It hit one of the file cabinets with a clang. Cam ignored this, instead stalking over to the back window and staring out into the gardens. "Near the library, yes. But I didn't enter that room. And if anyone says they saw me do so— well, haven't you considered that any of these people might have their own reasons for twisting the truth?"

"I have thought of that," I said, fighting to keep a tremor out of my voice. "And I admit I don't entirely trust their accounts. But even if you didn't enter the library, being in that hallway unfortunately places you near the murder scene."

"Which makes me guilty, I suppose," Cam said.

I stared at his rigid shoulders, angled like the wings of a young bird. This, combined with the slightly too-long auburn hair spilling over his shirt collar, gave me a moment's pause. He looked so much like a teenager standing there, with his back to me and his slender fingers curled into fists. It was the same defiant pose Bailey had often employed when she was furious with me.

"The thing is, if you want me to successfully act as your sleuthing partner, you have to allow me to suspect everyone. Even you," I said in the calm tone I'd used on my daughter after an argument.

Cam's clenched fingers relaxed. "Very well. I suppose, if we are to discover the truth, everyone should be considered a suspect." He spun around, leaning back and gripping the windowsill with both hands. "Even you."

Chapter
Twenty-Five

"So now that we have that settled, who do you want me to speak to next?" I asked.

"Rena Allen," Cam said without missing a beat. "I've done a little digging into her social media and it seems she's carrying on without any weeping and gnashing of teeth. Not exactly what I'd expect, if one's sister were brutally murdered."

"I don't think I can stop by her parents' house again. Do you have any other ideas how I can track her down?"

Cam straightened and strolled over to the file cabinets to retrieve his chair. "I do. Courtesy of her oversharing on social media, I know that Rena has a part-time job at the university library. She even posted her basic work schedule, which is foolish, but useful for us."

"Which university?" I asked. "There are several in the area."

"*The* university," Cam replied, with a sarcastic smile. "You know, the only one Naomi would consider worthy of the title."

"Ah, I get it." I stood just as Cam sat down. "If that's all, text me Rena's library work hours and I'll see if I can find her during her next shift."

"Find who?" Lauren, who was standing in the doorway, pulled the yellow cap off her head. "Sorry for interrupting. I just got back and thought I'd check in to see if you needed anything, Cam."

"Not at the moment," Cam said, his gaze fixed on the glass top of his desk. "And we were talking about Rena Allen."

I looked from Cam to Lauren, noticing how her bright smile faded when Cam didn't make eye contact. "We were actually discussing poor Ashley's murder. Cam thought it might be useful if I met with Rena in private. I mean, without her parents present. She might know some things about Ashley's life that her mom and dad are totally unaware of." I added this last part off the cuff, but it actually made sense. A sister would likely know things about secret relationships or personal demons that parents would know nothing about.

Heaven knows I've been oblivious to some of Bailey's issues over the years, I thought as Lauren nodded.

"Good idea. Mind if I tag along? Depending on when you're going and if I'm free, of course." Lauren shot a quick glance at Cam.

Cam, drumming his fingers against the desktop, still didn't meet her gaze. "You can go whenever and wherever you want. You should know that."

"Sometimes you need me," Lauren said, wringing the knit cap between her hands.

"I'll let you know if something's inconvenient, but at the moment, I don't think there's a problem." Cam finally lifted his head to meet Lauren's questioning gaze. "Besides, the first available time to meet with Rena Allen is tomorrow at ten in the morning, and since that's a Saturday, I certainly won't expect you to be doing anything for me then." He laid his other hand over his fingers to still their movement. "Anyway, you'll actually be helping me if you accompany Jane to interview Rena."

"That's something, I guess." Lauren ran her fingers through her hair, fluffing her curls into an ebony halo. "Why don't we meet at the university library, Jane? I'm assuming it's Naomi and Hannah's old haunt, since otherwise Cam would've specified. In the lobby at ten? That way we can both have the rest of the day to pursue other interests," she added, as she shoved the hat into one of her coat pockets. "I, for one, am meeting friends later in the day for some fun and relaxation."

"Sounds good," I said, casting a sidelong glance at Cam. He appeared to be fixated on something on his computer screen, but the blankness of his stare told me he was simply pretending. "We'll let you get back to your work now, Cam. No more distractions."

If he recognized any subtext in my words, he gave nothing away.

*   *   *

On Saturday, as I waited for Lauren in the university library lobby, I was glad that this was not the institution where I'd worked for many years. Not because this was an inferior institution, far from it. It was simply that I'd never set foot in my former library since I'd been forced to retire, and had no desire to break that trend.

It was childish, perhaps, but the way I'd been tossed aside, despite years of dedicated service, simply due to my age, still rankled. I also had no desire to run into any of my former colleagues—at least, none that I hadn't continued to remain in contact with after my departure. Fortunately, no one at this university knew me. I was just another older woman in gray wool slacks and a black sweater. I wouldn't draw any attention.

Which was the plan, of course.

Lauren had followed suit, showing up in worn jeans and an oversized team jersey celebrating a popular NFL football team. With her hair swept up under a battered cap, she could easily pass for a student.

"Hi there," she said as she approached me. "Ready for the ambush?"

I tugged down the sleeves of my sweater. "I don't want to think of it like that."

Lauren gave me a wink. "Come on, Miss Marple, let's investigate."

Not sure if I should be offended or flattered by this comparison, I simply followed her to the main bank of elevators. Cam had sent us information on Rena's part-time job, indicating that she was working as a shelver in the general collection.

"It's a lot of territory to cover," I told Lauren as we took the elevator to the first level of the stacks. "Rena could be anywhere on one of several floors. Should we split up so we can divide and conquer?"

"I don't think so. I mean, if one of us finds her, then the other will still be wandering around aimlessly."

"Cell phones," I said, flashing mine. "Whoever locates her first can call the other."

Lauren frowned. "But won't that look odd? If I was Rena, and someone came up to talk to me, then wanted to call somebody else to join us, I'd be out of there so fast your head would spin."

"Good point. Okay, we'll stick together," I said, pocketing my phone.

We set off, zigzagging through the first floor of the stacks without any sight of Rena. It took searching two more floors before we found her.

Shelving books from a rolling metal library cart, Rena was doing the head bopping that told me she was listening to music.

"Hello, Rena," I called out, earning a sharp look from a student studying at one of the carrels lining the walls.

Rena spun around, whipping out her earbuds. "What? Who are you?"

"Jane Hunter," I said, extending my hand.

Ignoring this, Rena stuffed the earbuds into the pocket of her jeans. "Am I supposed to know you? Or you?" she added, giving Lauren the once over.

"I suppose not. I stopped by your house the other day to offer my condolences, but I doubt you'd remember me. I'm actually only acquainted with your mother," I replied, dropping my hand.

"Hi, I'm Lauren Walker. I work at Aircroft," Lauren said, as Rena continued to stare at her. "I'm very sorry for your loss."

"Don't think you tracked me down to offer your condolences," Rena said, with a sniff. "What do you want?"

I studied the young woman for a moment. She was wearing tattered jeans and a sweatshirt with a feminist motto. Her long hair, dark brown with red highlights, was pulled back into a tight ponytail and her sharp-featured face was devoid of makeup, but there was still an echo of resemblance to her late sister. "We just wanted to ask you a couple of questions. Simply to ease our own minds, not to share with the police."

Rena narrowed her eyes. "Ease your minds, huh? Make sure you're not living in the same house as a killer, you mean."

"That might be part of it," I said.

Lauren side-eyed me. "There are quite a few people connected to Aircroft that we're concerned about."

"And maybe you should be, although I think . . ." Rena bit her lower lip and glanced up and down the aisle. "We shouldn't talk here. Follow me."

After adjusting the bookends on the cart so the volumes wouldn't topple sideways, Rena pushed the cart to the end of the aisle. "Look for an empty study room," she said, gesturing to a row of glass-enclosed cubicles.

"Here." Lauren dashed forward to claim the only room not already filled with students. "They aren't reserved or anything, are they?"

"Nope. It's first come, first served." Rena abandoned the book cart outside and joined Lauren and me in the small room, which was furnished with a table and four chairs and a large whiteboard. "There are some spaces you can reserve on the reference floor, but not in the stacks. Too hard to manage," she said, dropping down into one of the chairs.

I sat down next to Lauren. With both of us facing Rena, I was afraid it might feel too much like we were double-teaming to interrogate her, but she appeared unfazed. Shoving back her chair, she plopped her sneakers up on the table.

"Sorry, been on my feet all day," she said, her expression daring us to complain.

"No problem," Lauren murmured, while I simply met Rena's challenging stare with a tight smile.

"So, what do you want to know? Who I think murdered my sister?" Rena reached back and yanked free the rubber band holding her ponytail, allowing her chestnut brown hair to tumble over her shoulders. "That's easy—it was that scumbag, Tristan Blair."

Chapter
Twenty-Six

I leaned forward, pressing my arms against the table top. "Do you have any evidence to back that up?"

"Now you sound like the cops," Rena said, rolling her eyes. "No, I don't have any *evidence*. I just know what Tristan was like when he and Ash were dating. One of those possessive types. Always wanted to know where she was and what she was doing." Rena grimaced. "And who she was with."

"He was jealous?" Lauren asked.

"Yeah, and too clingy. At least I thought so." Rena dropped her feet to the floor with a thud. "He used to try to get me to tell him stuff, but I never would. Maybe my sister and I weren't the closest, but I wasn't about to rat her out." She twirled a lock of her hair around one finger. "Especially not to some guy I figured was just after her money."

"Was he ever physical with her?" I asked. "I mean, in an abusive fashion."

"He did manhandle her a couple of times. Nothing extreme, just grabbing her arm and stuff like that. But I didn't like it." Rena placed her elbows on the table and rested her chin on her clasped hands. "But that's just what I saw, you know. Could've been worse when they were alone. Don't know about that. Ash wasn't about to share such things with me. Always wanted me to think her life was perfect. More perfect than mine, anyway."

Lauren delicately cleared her throat. "You really think Tristan was after her money?"

"Of course. The guy was some type of musician. Mostly focused on guitar and songwriting. You know the kind—a lot of attitude and big talk, but only playing a few gigs here and there and no record deals." Rena made a face. "I didn't think he was very good, but Ash had this idea he could be famous. At first, anyway."

"I'm guessing your parents weren't too thrilled with the relationship," I said, thinking of the cocaine-chic look Tristan had projected in the photos on Ashley's social media.

Rena sat back in her chair. "I expect that was part of the attraction. Ash had always been the perfect daughter—dressed classy, made good grades, hung out with the rich and popular kids, and all that. She was even president of her sorority in college. Chi Omega Delta." Rena pursed her lips. "Not my thing, but she was really into it."

"So dating a scruffy musician was out of character for her?" I asked.

"Very. I figured it was a phase. I'd always been the rebellious child in the family, which did get me a lot of attention, so maybe Ash thought she should try it out." Rena lifted her hands. "Who knows? Anyway, it didn't last long. Ash dumped Tristan as soon as she had Cameron Clewe in her sights."

"I didn't realize Ashley was dating someone else when Cam met her. I don't think he knew that either," Lauren said.

I cast her a sidelong glance, noting her troubled expression. It seemed that Cam confided in his personal assistant only up to a point.

Rena's lips curved into a sardonic smile. "Trust me, Cam hadn't even asked her to dinner yet when Ash gave Tristan the old heave-ho. She was making plans as soon as she laid eyes on Cam at that charity event at Aircroft a while back. Rich and handsome? Ash was all in on that."

Lauren shifted in her chair. "She was tired of playing muse to a down-on-his-luck guitarist, I guess."

"I couldn't blame her at that point. Tristan was possessive, like I said, and Ash didn't like anyone giving her orders. Besides, by the time she met Cam, she and Tristan were fighting all the time. I think she was ready to get rid of him, even if she hadn't already lined up her next victim"—Rena covered her mouth with her hand for a second—"sorry, boyfriend."

I examined her face, surprised by her openness. Her obvious lack of affection for her sister explained why she wasn't grieving too deeply. It also raised the question of whether she was capable of killing Ashley for an inheritance. But if she was being truthful about Tristan Blair's character, it further cemented him as a suspect too.

Still, there was that pesky matter of Ashley inheriting a fortune while the rest of her family got nothing. "I did hear something, a rumor," I said in an even tone. "I'm not necessarily giving credence to it, but maybe you should know what people are saying."

"Gossiping about, you mean." Rena crossed her arms over her chest. "I bet it has to do with my grandmother's will."

"It does," I said.

Lauren's dark brows drew together. "What are you talking about?"

So Cam didn't share that information with her either. Interesting. I swiveled on my chair to face Lauren. "Someone told me that Ashley and Rena's grandmother was leaving her entire, not insignificant, estate to Ashley, cutting out her son and daughter-in-law and"—I shifted my position to confront Rena's sardonic gaze—"her other granddaughter."

"Oh." Lauren slumped back in her chair. "I see. I guess people think that might be a motive for murder?"

"Except *people*," Rena said, edging the word with malice, "have no idea. Sure, that's what my grandmother's will says, bless her cold and calculating heart, but that's not how things were going to go down. My sister, for all her faults, had no intention of keeping the entire amount. She told my parents and me that she was just staying quiet so Granny wouldn't fuss, but planned to split the inheritance with us once it was officially hers."

Rena's triumphant expression told me she thought she'd laid the matter to rest, but I wasn't entirely convinced. It was clear that Rena was an intelligent and self-possessed young woman. She could just as easily have come up with this story to divert suspicion from her or her parents. Still, there was no sense challenging her. I'd share her story with Cam and see if he could find a way to either prove or disprove it. In the meantime, I wanted to pursue another angle.

"I imagine you've shared this information about Tristan Blair with the police?" I asked. "Since you believe him to be the most likely suspect in your sister's murder."

"I definitely did, although they didn't seem as interested as I thought they would be. Of course, maybe they were just playing it cool." Rena glanced out the cubicle window as a shadow darkened the glass.

Following her gaze, I noticed several students hovering around the book cart Rena had left outside the study room. "That's probably true. I'm pretty sure they would've questioned him, after what you just told us."

"And I think I saw him at the gala, which I also told the cops. There was definitely a guy that resembled him skulking around. I only got a passing look at him, but I'm pretty sure it was Tristan." Rena pushed back her chair and jumped to her feet. "Sorry, but I'd better get back to work. I need to finish my shift and I also don't want those twerps snitching books off my reshelving cart."

"Sure, go ahead. We don't want to get you in trouble with your boss," I said.

Lauren stood and offered Rena a smile. "Thanks for talking to us. It was very helpful. So nice of you to indulge our curiosity when you're dealing with such a terrible tragedy."

Rena arched her brows but returned Lauren's smile. "No problem. Happy to set the record straight."

"One thing," I said, as Rena headed for the door. "Do you know where we might find Tristan Blair?"

"Sure. He has a studio in a building in downtown Winston." Rena rolled the rubber band off her wrist, swept up her hair, and tied it back into a ponytail. "On Trade Street, near all the other artsy stores and stuff. He should still be using it, since the rent was covered through this year." She cast Lauren and me a wry look over her shoulder as she strolled out of the study room. "And yes, my sister paid for it."

Chapter
Twenty-Seven

B efore we left the library, I obtained a promise from Lauren
to accompany me when I visited Tristan Blair's music studio
on Sunday afternoon. This time we arranged to drive together,
since I wasn't too sure about the best places to park in downtown
Winston-Salem.

Over the last decade or so, Trade Street had been turned into
an area that truly supported the city's claim to be the "City of
the Arts." Craft stores and art galleries, trendy restaurants, music
stores, and shops catering to those interested in organic items
dominated the street and surrounding blocks.

A little searching on the internet had revealed that Tristan's
studio was located in a larger building that housed several other
businesses.

"Surprised they'd allow music studios next door to some of
these offices," I said as Lauren and I walked from the parking
garage to the address I'd located.

"I bet they're all on one floor," Lauren said. "One very well
sound-proofed floor."

"No doubt." I paused in front of a store window that featured hand-crafted bowls and baskets. "I need to come back when I can do a little shopping. My apartment could use a few items to really make it feel like home."

"You don't need to spend any money on that. Just rummage through the attic at Aircroft and borrow whatever you want." Lauren shaded her eyes with her hand as she looked toward a taller building nearby. "I think that's it, on the next block."

"Would Cam really allow that?" I asked as we strolled to the building entrance.

Lauren cast me a glance as she pushed open the main doors. "You've seen his office. Cam would get rid of half the stuff at Aircroft if he had his way. He just feels restrained by the estate's history. He believes he should preserve most of it, for its historical significance if nothing else."

"Because his dad collected most of the furnishings?" I asked as I followed Lauren into the lobby.

"No, because he didn't. Most of the furniture and decorations at Aircroft are leftovers from when the Airley family owned the place." As Lauren squinted at the lobby's directory sign, I wondered if she was one of those people who only occasionally needed glasses and thus didn't bother to wear them. "Looks like the studios are on the top floor."

"I guess that makes sense." As we entered the elevator my thoughts were distracted by this new information about Cam's estate. If the Airley family had simply left everything in the house, no wonder I'd discovered those photos. The question was, what else might I find? "Albert Clewe probably just added a few things from his travels."

"And some of his wife's paintings and drawings." Lauren used her fingers to fluff out her dark hair. "She was an artist, you know."

"I gathered that. Cam mentioned she also played the piano, so she must've been multitalented."

"Too bad Cam didn't inherit any of those skills." Lauren grinned. "Maybe a real avocation, along with his work with the family companies, would keep him busy enough to stop playing armchair detective."

I shook my head. "I think he has the type of mind where he'd always want to solve mysteries, regardless."

"Unfortunately." Lauren's expression sobered as we exited the elevator and stepped into a tiled vestibule. "I'm not sure it's good for him, all the obsessive mulling over clues and tracking down digital footprints."

I pointed toward one of the halls radiating off the vestibule. "That one, I think."

Lauren squinted again. "Yeah, right range of numbers," she said, striding toward the hallway.

Although the suites appeared to be, as Lauren had surmised, well insulated, the faint whine of an electric guitar made us stop in front of one door. I tapped the metal sign holder on the wall next to the door. A rather crumpled label slipped into the holder read "Tristan Blair."

"And he seems to be here," Lauren said. "Unless he's let some other musician use the space."

Thinking of what I'd heard about Tristan, I shook my head. "Doubtful."

Lauren rapped the door with her knuckles, to no avail.

"Sound-proofed," I said, before giving the door a bang with my fist.

The door flew open, accompanied by a string of the kind of swear words I hadn't heard since wandering the student union at my former university. "What is it?" the young man standing in the doorway finally asked. His gaze swiftly switched from me to Lauren.

I recognized that look from my days working with students— I was too old and stodgy to hold his attention. Lauren, on the other hand . . .

"And who are you?" Tristan Blair asked her, his deep brown eyes expressing appreciation and, I was afraid, more than a little lust. "A fan, I hope," he added, pressing one hand against the doorjamb in a posture that showed off his well-muscled arm and slender torso.

I eyed his all-black ensemble, which consisted of jeans and a strategically ripped T-shirt. It was the exact same outfit he'd worn in the photos on Ashley's social media, and I couldn't help wondering if he owned multiple sets of the same clothes. "I'm Jane Hunter and this is Lauren Walker. We both work for Cameron Clewe."

Tristan's friendly gaze hardened into a grim mask. "Not exactly a friend of mine. So why're you here, exactly?" he asked, finally looking me in the eye.

"We've heard things from a few people, in terms of your connection to Ashley Allen," I said, deciding bluntness was my best tactic.

Tristan reared back. Yanking his hand off the doorjamb, he swept his long fingers through his shoulder-length brown hair in

168

a gesture I thought betrayed rattled nerves. "Not out here," he said, under his breath. "Come inside."

Lauren and I followed him into the studio, which was a simple cube with a hardwood floor and walls padded with sound-dampening materials. A single window was set high in the back wall, over a rehearsal setup that included a microphone and an arrangement of high-quality speakers. One adjacent wall held a rack displaying an array of guitars, both electric and acoustic, while a battered futon and a folding metal chair filled the other wall.

Tristan flopped down onto the futon, his lean limbs spread out so there was little room for anyone else. He pointed to the folding chair. "Have a seat."

I could tell from the direction of his gaze that this offer was being made to Lauren, not me.

Lauren grabbed the metal chair and swung it around to face the futon. "Here you go, Jane. I'll just lean against the wall."

Tristan's sooty eyebrows shot up under the long fringe of hair falling over his forehead. He straightened and shifted his position on the futon, patting a cushion next to him. "You can sit here," he told Lauren.

"Thanks, but I'd rather stand," she replied, her tone as cold as her eyes.

Tristan shrugged. "Suit yourself. So what's this all about then? Ashley's murder, I bet. And before you say anything, I know about the Allens trashing my name with the cops. Figures. They never liked me. Not good enough for their precious princess," he added, his lips curling into a snarl.

"But that's exactly why we wanted to talk to you," I said, sitting down in the folding chair. "To get your side of the story."

"Told that to the cops, not that they seemed interested. Too busy grilling me about where I was that Sunday night."

"You were at the gala. I saw you there," Lauren said, causing Tristan to fix her with a glare.

"Yeah, maybe I was. I already told the cops that, in case anyone gives a crap." As Tristan placed his arms behind his head and leaned back against his cupped hands, a good expanse of his toned midriff was exposed. "Bet your sources didn't know that, did they?"

"They did not," I admitted, studying his face. He looked ticked off, but not frightened. "Why were you there? I can't exactly picture you buying a ticket to a gala. No offense."

"None taken," Tristan said, meeting my inquisitive gaze with a tight smile. "Yeah, normally I wouldn't get within ten miles of a snooty event like that, but a colleague of mine was playing in the little ensemble they put together for the thing. Great rock keyboardist and he gets stuck playing piano for that lame gig. But whatcha gonna do? Money is money."

I widened my eyes. "So you just popped in to visit a fellow musician?"

Tristan scraped the heel of one of his black leather boots against the floor. "Not totally. I mean, it was a good way to get into the event, but I really wanted to talk to Ash. Knew she'd be there from her social media." Tristan grimaced. "She made herself pretty easy to find. Not too smart, like I always told her."

"Because you loved her?" Lauren asked, in a gentle tone.

The sneer disappeared from Tristan's face as quickly as ice melting under a summer sun. It was replaced with an expression that mingled pain and anger. "Yeah, I did. Nobody believed

170

that. They thought all I cared about was her money, but that wasn't right. We might've argued a lot, but I loved her. A lot more than any of those other dudes she went out with."

"Like Cameron Clewe?" I asked.

Tristan snorted in derision. "That guy. Don't think he knows how to love a woman. Or maybe even what love is." He fixed Lauren with an intense stare. "You know him pretty well, right? I remember Ash mentioning some young woman who worked as his personal assistant. She said she was really pretty and smart. Ash couldn't figure out why a girl like that would stick with the job."

"But Ashley dated Cam. Didn't she like him?" I asked, as Lauren exhaled audibly behind me.

Tristan dropped his arms and leaned forward. "She liked his money. Yeah, yeah, she had plenty of her own. And was supposed to come into more eventually."

So he knows about the inheritance. I filed this information away for later. "She still wanted more?"

"I dunno if it was that," Tristan said with a shrug, "or if she just liked being with a guy who could match her lifestyle. Had the same vocabulary, I mean. I didn't know the names of fancy wines or cheeses or what designer shoes she was wearing and things like that. I think she got tired of trying to teach me stuff."

"I heard you were extremely upset when she dumped you," I said.

"Sure, why wouldn't I be? And I was willing to fight to get her back. That's why I slipped into that gala and tried to talk to her. But she wasn't having it." Tristan's eyes narrowed, and again I couldn't tell if it was due to anger or sorrow. He looked over my shoulder, toward Lauren. "I was there, like you said. And I did try to track Ash down to have a conversation with her. But she refused to talk to me, other than a hello and goodbye, so I left." His gaze shifted back to me. "Without killing her."

"Okay." I rose to my feet. "I think we've gotten your side of the story. It does clear some things up."

"It sure should," Tristan said. "You can take all that back to whoever's been bad-mouthing me too. Like I said, the cops already have my statement. And they haven't been pestering me lately, so I think that's enough to clear me."

It wasn't, but I didn't intend to get in an argument with him. "Alright, we'll let you get back to your rehearsing." I crossed to the door and opened it as Lauren strolled to the center of the room.

"Good idea," Tristan said. "Although *you* don't have to go," he told Lauren, who simply shook her head.

"I wouldn't want to take advantage of your grief," she said sweetly as she sailed out the door.

Chapter
Twenty-Eight

On the car ride home, Lauren raised the question I'd been thinking about ever since we left Tristan Blair's studio.

"Do you think he was telling the truth?" she asked, as she maneuvered the car around a double-trailer semitruck on Interstate 40.

"Honestly, I'm not sure. I believe the things he said about his relationship with Ashley were true, and probably his assessment of her reason for getting involved with Cam too. But that story about how he got into the gala . . ."

Lauren shot me a sidelong look. "Yeah, I didn't buy it either. Some friend let him in? Unlikely. That could've cost the friend future gigs, and no struggling musician is going to risk that."

"We do know he was there, from his own account as well as other people claiming to see him there. We just aren't sure how he got in."

Lauren tightened her grip on the steering wheel. "I did have one thought. It may sound far-fetched, but I know for a fact that Cam gave Ashley the access codes to the estate while they were dating. And they hadn't been changed before the gala, or I'd have been informed."

"But how does that help Tristan?" I asked.

"Okay, hear me out. What if Ashley and Tristan had actually reconnected right after Cam broke up with her?" Lauren cast me another glance before shifting her gaze back to the busy road. "From that little scene in the garden, we know Ashley was really angry with Cam. What if she decided to get back at him by giving her old boyfriend access to the estate?"

I turned my head to study Lauren's lovely profile. Her clenched jaw told me she was truly invested in this hypothesis. *Because it might clear Cam of any suspicion?* "For what purpose?"

Lauren rolled her taut shoulders. "To disrupt the gala? Cause a scene that would embarrass Cam? I could imagine her wanting Tristan to confront Cam, but then he arrived too late and Cam had already gone up to his suite. Tristan could've asked Ashley to meet him somewhere to talk, and she could've suggested the library. Then they got into another argument and Tristan struck her down in the heat of passion or something." Lauren lifted one hand off the wheel and pressed her fingers to her forehead. "I don't know. It made more sense to me before I said it aloud."

"Actually, it does make sense. You should share that theory with Cam and see what he thinks. Maybe he can question Mateo and Dia again and see if they noticed Tristan roaming the mansion during the gala. Dia told me that she didn't see anyone that matched his description, but I'm not sure I believe her." I gazed out the side window as we turned off the highway and headed into Bradfordville. "She seemed nervous when I asked about it."

"Sure, I'll tell him." Lauren frowned. "Should we tell the police as well?"

"I don't think so, since it's really just a theory. I'm sure they've been drawing their own conclusions anyway, after questioning Tristan and the others." I unfastened my seat belt as Lauren pulled into the driveway beside Vince's house, but didn't immediately get out of the car. "There is one thing I've been meaning to ask you."

"What's that?" Lauren asked, her expression growing wary.

"Why in the world was Cam dating Ashley?" I asked, resting my hand on the door latch. "I can understand her reasons for dating him, especially after hearing Tristan's comments on the situation, but I really don't see why Cam was attracted to her in the first place. I mean, in spite of her beauty and vivaciousness, she doesn't seem like his type."

"It's like I told you before—Cam's really clueless about relationship stuff. Ashley met him at some charity event at Aircroft and pursued him. She was attractive, around the same age as he was, and actually not unintelligent, so when she sought him out and got him to talk about his various passions, well"—Lauren sighed—"that's all it takes, sometimes."

"I see. He'll reciprocate if he's pursued by someone, but he isn't going to make the effort on his own." I noticed a compact hybrid vehicle parked next to Vince's older model sedan. *Ah, Donna's here.*

"That pretty much covers it. He has no game, and he's afraid to take any chances. He won't interact with a woman unless she makes the first move." Lauren tapped her rose-petal pink polished fingernails against the steering wheel. "That's my assessment, anyway. For what it's worth."

"A lot, I think," I said, offering Lauren a smile as I opened the door. "Thanks for accompanying me today. And for driving," I said, climbing out of the car.

"No problem. Happy to help," Lauren said in a distracted tone that made me think she was still mulling over our last conversation.

After Lauren drove away, I decided to visit Vince and Donna before heading up to my apartment. Since they were both tied to the local community, I wanted to share some of my recent discoveries and see if they had anything they could add to the information I'd gathered.

Vince welcomed me in without hesitation, but once I was inside, I noticed Donna preparing something on the kitchen island. "Sorry, I didn't mean to interrupt your dinner plans," I said.

"Heavens, don't worry about that." Donna waved a paring knife like a baton. "We're just preparing some sauce for pasta night."

"And you're welcome to stay for dinner, especially if you help chop," Vince said.

I followed him across the living room. "I really don't want to crash your meal, but I won't refuse to help in the kitchen, if you don't mind me picking your brains while we work."

"Slim pickings, sometimes," Donna said, with a grin.

Vince, reaching her, wrapped his arm around her waist. "What are you talking about, woman? We're both brilliant."

"Sure, sure. Total geniuses." Donna rolled her eyes. "Here, Jane, take over that other cutting board and chop some peppers, would you?"

I joined them behind the island. "As long as you don't criticize my dicing skills. I'm afraid I'm no master chef."

"You'll fit right in, then." Vince dropped his arm to grab a knife and pluck an onion from a wire basket set on the white quartz countertop. "So what do you want to know, Jane? I'm glad to help, although I admit I haven't discovered any new information concerning the murder."

"I haven't either." Donna, who'd been busy cutting up tomatoes, laid down her knife and wiped her hands on a kitchen towel.

"I'm really more interested in what you might know about certain individuals," I said, before launching into descriptions of my recent interactions with Evie, Rena, Tristan, and Naomi and Hannah.

Vince looked over at Donna. "There was some tragedy associated with the Wilt family, wasn't there? It's been several years, but I think I remember it was related to an incident at school?"

"There was something, but I only remember it vaguely." Donna tipped up her cutting board and scraped the chopped tomatoes into a large ceramic bowl. "It wasn't anything local, so it didn't make the news here."

"No, but I remember some colleague discussing the story at a conference." Vince peeled the outer skin off the onion. "She thought I'd be interested because the extended family lived around here, but I really wasn't, so I'm afraid I didn't listen too closely."

"It was probably after happy hour too." Donna cast him a smile.

"Could've been," Vince replied with a shrug. "Anyway, I doubt that story has any relevance to the murder case. Now, some of the others Jane talked to could be more involved, I think." He glanced at Donna. "Do you have any scoop on the younger Allen girl from your time at the high school?"

"Not really," Donna said. "She's a good seven years or so younger than Ashley, and by the time she was in high school the culture had changed. It seemed like the kids weren't into money and status quite so much. Of course, neither girl attended the public high school, but the younger one—Rena, right?—didn't have any friends at my school. Or at least, I never heard anyone talk about her."

Vince tossed the top, papery layers of the onion into a ceramic crock obviously used for compost. "The only thing I've heard is that she's always been a bit wild. Got into trouble with the law once or twice for underage drinking and that sort of thing." He met my interested gaze with a shrug. "I still follow the local police beat, and I have a few friends on the force."

"Useful," I said, lining up my sliced peppers so I could chop them into smaller bits. "What about Tristan Blair? He's a local musician who does gigs around town, so I thought you might know something about him."

"He doesn't play anywhere I'd frequent," Vince said.

"Me either." Donna turned to the cabinets lining the wall behind us. "I remember him from my work at the high school, though. He hung out with an outsider type of crew, but never actually got into any serious trouble. Although we saw him in the principal's office a few times, mostly because he'd mouthed off to a teacher." She grabbed a small wire tote that held spices and carried it back to the island. "He did have quite a way with words."

Imagining the kind of words those must've been, I smiled. "That doesn't surprise me. He wasn't violent?"

"Not when I knew him. I did hear rumors that his home life wasn't the best, though." Donna fiddled with the setting on a pepper grinder. "There were a lot of kids in that family, many of whom had left home before I knew anything about Tristan. Anyway, I heard stories about his dad being physically abusive with the children. Tristan's mom finally left the guy, but that was after Tristan graduated."

"Good for her, but too bad for Tristan." Realizing I was gripping my knife so tightly that my knuckles had turned white, I laid it down and shook out my fingers. "Do you want these peppers dumped in the bowl with the tomatoes?"

"No, scrape them into that metal bowl. It already has the garlic in it." Donna was studying me in a way that told me she had observed my reaction to her recent words. "It's a terrible thing, domestic violence," she said gently.

"Yes, it is. Even if it's only emotional abuse. I mean, the physical kind is worse, but . . ."

Donna laid her hand over mine. "There are no *buts*. It's all destructive, and I'm sorry."

"What's this?" Vince asked, looking up from his careful dissection of the onion.

Donna flashed him a sweet smile. "Oh nothing, dear. Girl talk."

"Woman talk," I said under my breath, earning a hand squeeze from Donna.

"You know who else has a rather sketchy background?" Vince said, obviously oblivious to any undercurrents in the conversation, as he reached over to grab the metal bowl. "That artist you mentioned, Jane. The one who was staying at Aircroft when you arrived."

"Brendan Sloan?" I slid my hand out from under Donna's fingers. "I find that hard to believe."

"It was years ago, before he got into art, but yeah, Sloan has a record." Vince dumped the diced onion into the bowl. Wiping his hands on the kitchen towel, he leaned his hip against the side of the island as he surveyed Donna and me. "He was just a kid, although unfortunately not a minor. One of my reporters at the paper worked the story when I was a local news editor. Apparently, Sloan developed a cocaine problem and joined a few other guys in a robbery. Needed some quick cash for his blow, I guess. The guys roughed up a storekeeper pretty good. They were all arrested and charged, but Sloan ended up on probation instead of in jail because he was barely over eighteen and hadn't instigated the violence. Apparently, he hadn't really done much more than watch without stopping it, from what was finally revealed."

"You never mentioned this before." My thoughts circled around this new information. I'd overheard Dia telling Mateo that she'd observed Brendan having words with Ashley at the gala, which made me wonder if I really should consider Brendan as a more viable suspect.

"Didn't think it was that important. And I figured the police had probably already listed Sloan as a major suspect just based on his record." Vince's lips twisted. "As far as I know, Sloan has been clean for over two decades and hasn't been in any trouble with the law since that original incident. Knowing how he was likely to be targeted, I didn't want to pile more suspicion on the guy."

"That's good of you," I said. "Honestly, I'd like to talk to him. Just to allow him to tell his story directly." I strolled over to the sink and washed my hands. "You wouldn't happen to know where I could find him, would you?"

"I might," Vince said. "I know he used to have a studio in a building just outside of Bradfordville."

"He still does, it's in the arts collective where I take watercolor lessons," Donna said. "I've peeked into his studio from time to time. It's so fascinating, how he works with glass." She turned to me. "If you want to talk to him, he's usually in the studio until seven or eight o'clock on weekdays."

"I could stop by there tomorrow after work," I said, more to myself than the others.

Vince cleared his throat. "If you plan to talk to him, I'd like to be there, Jane. Not that I don't trust you, but I feel a sort of . . . well, responsibility in terms of Sloan's reputation. You see, when my colleague was covering his case, she was too hard on the guy. I was her editor and should've forced her to temper her words, but"—Vince lifted his hands—"I didn't. I wanted to sell more papers and knew a more sensationalized story would do that. I've regretted that choice for years."

"Alright, happy to have you tag along," I said. "You too," I told Donna, who nodded in agreement. "Tomorrow then? If you text me the directions, I can leave Aircroft a little early and meet you at the studio around six."

"It's a date," Vince said.

"Well, not exactly a date." I smiled and motioned toward Donna. "You'll already have one of those with you."

Donna gave me a wink. "It's fine. We can share."

Vince, whose cheeks were suddenly flushed with color, fell into a coughing fit he blamed on the onions.

Chapter
Twenty-Nine

I spent Monday cataloging the rest of the Marie Belloc Lowndes materials in the music room. Although the library was now available, I didn't see any sense in transferring the books and other items to another location before I returned them to the attic. As I told Cam when I spoke to him briefly on Monday morning, I'd pull a new set of materials and start working on them in the library on Tuesday.

I'd planned to fill him in on my recent information gathering sessions, but after I'd mentioned my work plans and my need to leave a little early, he'd informed me that he was waiting on the imminent arrival of a couple of detectives.

"Apparently I'm still at the top of the suspect list," he'd said, in a perfectly equable tone undercut by the nervous wringing of his hands.

"I have some information to share with you, but I guess we'll have to talk at another time."

"Tomorrow morning, before you start work." Cam had then tapped something into his phone. "There, I've got it scheduled.

Today is out since I have the interrogators plus a long conference call with some business partners."

"Good luck with all of that." I'd also wished him a good day, which had earned me a sarcastic smile.

"Yours will be better, no doubt," he'd told me as I'd exited his office.

After work, I set my GPS to map out directions to the address Vince and Donna had provided the day before. They were already waiting when I arrived at a long, one-story brick building that resembled a warehouse more than any type of artistic establishment.

"I know, it doesn't look like much," Donna said, when I joined them at the front doors. "But it really is a wonderful place. My art teacher always says she couldn't afford the same space anywhere else in the area."

"I'm sure eschewing the bells and whistles does lower the rent," I said, as we entered the plain, cement-floored lobby. Surprisingly, there was no artwork hung in the lobby, although one of Brendan Sloan's gorgeous glass bubble chandeliers floated above our heads. "Where to now, Donna?"

"Right hall, all the way down to the end," she said.

We set off in that direction, occasionally pausing to glance into other studios through the large plate-glass windows that faced the hall.

"I guess it makes sense for Sloan to have his studio on an outside wall, since his work probably requires a furnace and extra ventilation," Vince said.

Unfortunately, when we reached the door at the end of the hall, it was locked. I peered through the window. The lights were off, allowing me to only make out large tables, shadowy forms that looked like metal skeletons, and a faint glow from a dark object in the far corner.

"Darn, he's always been here at this time before," Donna said.

A heavyset young man popped his head out of an adjacent doorway. "You folks looking for Brendan?"

"Yes, we were hoping to talk to him about some artwork." My lie was smooth enough to earn an eyebrow quirk from Vince.

"If you can just hang out for a few minutes, he should be back," the young man said. He held out one beefy hand. "I'm Clay Abbott. I work in wood." He gestured toward the window fronting his studio, where several sleek, abstract sculptures rose up like a leafless forest.

Vince's eyes widened as he examined the artwork. "Those are gorgeous,"

Donna elbowed me. "Uh-oh, I see a sculpture in Vince's future."

"I sure wouldn't mind that," Clay said. "You want to take a closer look? Come on in." He bobbed his head toward the open door to his studio.

"Resist temptation," Donna told Vince in a mock dramatic tone.

"Nope, no can do," Vince replied as he followed Clay into the studio.

I trailed Donna, waiting in the open doorway so I could keep a lookout for Brendan while Clay discussed the finer points of his sculptures with Vince.

"Where is Brendan anyway? Do you know?" I asked when there was a slight lull in the conversation.

Clay shoved back his faded baseball cap, ruffling his straw-colored hair. "Poor guy, he's being hounded by the police over the murder that happened out at that estate. The Ashley Allen thing," Clay added, his light brown eyes filled with derision. "Just because they had some history, the cops have been all over Bren. They're questioning him every other minute, it seems like."

Donna was the first to jump on this new revelation. "There was bad blood between them or something?"

"Yep. Justified, in my opinion. On Bren's part, I mean." Clay yanked off his cap and clutched it with both hands. "That Allen chick was bad news. Her family commissioned one of Bren's lighting pieces for their house, which was fine, but then she gets a notion that she'd like to be an art patroness or something." Clay snorted. "Wanted to be seen as a big wheel in the art world, I guess. From what I've heard, she loved to mingle with artists and musicians and wanted to be accepted as a real member of that crowd, even though she had no talent herself."

"You seem to dislike her pretty intensely. What did she do to cause that reaction?" I asked, glancing down the hall to make sure Brendan wasn't approaching.

Clay twisted the cap between his fingers. "She promised to fund an art gallery that would feature Brendan's works, along with the art of some of his colleagues."

"Including you?" Vince asked, turning away from his examination of one of the wooden sculptures.

"Yeah, I was part of the group. It was going to be a high-class gallery in Winston-Salem. Downtown, in the middle of all the action. I mean, this place is fine"—Clay waved his cap through the air—"as a worksite. But it's not really a gallery where you get a lot of walk-in traffic. Most of us here, we have to cart our stuff out to shows or arts festivals and that sort of thing."

"That must be especially difficult for artists like you and Brendan Sloan." Vince touched one of the sculptures with his fingertip. "Moving something like this, or a piece made of glass, would be tricky."

"It sure is. Which is why Brendan was so thrilled with Ashley Allen's offer to back a gallery. He could still work here, but his pieces would be on display in one location. He could avoid all the hassle of moving them from place to place." Clay slapped the cap back over his rumpled hair. "And there was supposed to be gallery staff, which meant someone else would be dealing with details like promotion, sales, and shipping. That was the dream, ya know? Bren and the rest of us could focus on making art, not marketing it."

"Sounds pretty perfect," Donna said. "I can see why you'd be upset when Ms. Allen reneged on her promise."

"We were all pretty bummed out. But Brendan was really angry. He felt especially bad because when Ashley promised him the gallery, he'd pulled the rest of us into the process. We all spent a lot of time working with architects and that sort of thing. Then Ashley says 'Oops, sorry to disappoint,' and disappears, taking her money with her." Clay made a face. "She even stuck Bren with part of the architect fees, claiming he was a partner in the project."

"Wow, that was heartless," I said.

"It sure was." Clay's expression grew troubled. "Do you think I should talk to the police about all this? I don't want to toss Bren into any more trouble than he's already in, but it might, I dunno, also alert the police to other possible suspects. Like other artists involved in the gallery project."

I met his concerned gaze. "But that might make you a suspect."

"It could, if I didn't have a solid alibi." Clay said. "I can't make enough off my artwork, so I DJ on the side. I had a gig the night Ashley Allen was killed that went on until early morning. Tons of people can vouch for me being nowhere near Aircroft that night."

"That's good." I noticed movement in the hallway and waved my hand. "Someone's coming. Maybe we should step out."

Donna linked her arm through Vince's and pulled him toward the door. "Come on, dear, let's not waste any more of this gentleman's time. We're supposed to be here to speak with Mr. Sloan, remember?"

Vince grumbled something but walked with her, grabbing Clay's business card out of a hand-carved wooden bowl as he passed a retail counter. "I'll be back," he told Clay, holding up the card before pocketing it.

Backing into the hall, I turned to face the approaching figure. It wasn't Brendan.

"It's Kyle Trent," I told Vince and Donna.

Clay Abbott closed his studio door after the three of us stepped into the hallway, which I found a little curious. Since he was friends with Brendan, I assumed he would at least greet Brendan's partner.

"What are you doing here?" Kyle strode up to us, his light eyes flashing with anger. "Isn't it bad enough that Brendan is relentlessly hounded by the police. Do you have to drag reporters into it too?"

Vince threw up his hands, palms out. "I'm no longer working for the paper."

"Really?" Kyle looked him up and down, derision curling his lips. "You're that Vincent Fisher fellow, aren't you? Part of the cabal that dragged Brendan through the mud when he was just a kid."

"He was eighteen, actually," I said without thinking, garnering a furious glare from Kyle.

"No, no, Mr. Trent is right. I was part of a team that was rather unfair to Mr. Sloan back in the day," Vince said.

Donna, still clinging to Vince's arm, shook her head. "He's very sorry about that, believe me."

"Sorry or not, it's still the reason why Brendan keeps being ordered to the police station for more questioning. That old record, exaggerated as it was, has dogged his steps ever since your paper made such a big deal out of a rather ordinary crime." Kyle took a deep breath. "I'm not saying it wasn't wrong, or that Brendan didn't need to pay for what he did. He'll tell you the same. But this reputation for violence that has followed him ever since is unfair and unfounded. He didn't actually participate in the beating, yet the news made it seem like he did." Kyle grimaced. "It felt like we had gotten past it, but then this murder happens and he's right back in the cops' crosshairs."

"I'm really sorry about that," I said. "It's just . . ."

"I know, I know. The whole Ashley Allen breaking her promise over the art gallery motive." Kyle rubbed his bare scalp with one hand. "Yes, she treated Brendan like dirt, but that doesn't mean he'd kill her. Brendan's grown tremendously over the years. He may have had troubles in his youth, but now he's the kindest, most forgiving man on the face of the planet."

"I only met him a couple of times, but he did strike me as a gentle soul," I admitted. It was the truth, but also a way to dial down the temperature in the conversation.

"The fact is, I'd be more likely to kill someone than Brendan would ever be," Kyle said.

Staring into his face, with his expression aflame with repressed rage, I was inclined to believe him.

Which just added another suspect to my list.

Chapter Thirty

After assuring Kyle that we had no intention of causing more problems for his partner, Vince and Donna and I agreed to leave the arts collective without bothering to wait for Brendan. With Kyle standing guard, it was doubtful we could get any useful information out of Brendan anyway.

Driving home, I noticed a small, nondescript beige sedan following me. Seeing such a vehicle on the road behind me wouldn't normally have made me think twice, except that I took a wrong turn on my way back into town. Strangely, the beige car took the same turn, which actually led into a small subdivision. I expected the vehicle to pull into one of the driveways that lined the street, but when I hit a cul-de-sac and had to turn around and head back the way I'd come, the beige car continued to match my moves.

I frowned, staring into my rearview mirror to see if I could catch a glimpse of the driver. But it was already too dark out to get a clear view of the person behind the wheel.

Speeding up slightly, I turned on my GPS to help guide me to the proper streets to lead me home. I should've used it from the beginning, but being somewhat old school about such devices, I tended to only activate the thing when absolutely necessary.

The soothing voice of the GPS narrator filled my car, directing me onto a few back streets in order to get me back to my desired route. It wasn't entirely straightforward, which meant my anxiety flared as I noticed the beige car executing the exact same turns.

What were the odds that someone would get lost the exact way I had, then need to follow precisely the same path? I reached over, fumbling for my cell phone, which I'd set in a holder on the dashboard.

The vehicle behind me flashed its brights, almost blinding me as I glanced in the mirror again. I sped up, hoping to lose them before I reached my apartment. I'd certainly prefer that the driver, whoever they were, didn't know where I lived.

The car increased its speed as well, coming uncomfortably close to my bumper. The glare from its headlights, now at least turned down to low, filled my back seat.

Suddenly, despite this being a two-lane road, the vehicle pulled up beside me. I shrieked, staring through my front windshield, terrified that someone coming from the other direction would plow into my pursuer, creating an accident that could kill us all. Fortunately, the road was empty. Just as I exhaled, a thunderous crash exploded the side window behind me. I gripped the steering wheel so hard I thought my fingers would break, forcing myself to keep steady and prevent my car from rolling into the ditch.

The beige car swept past me, flying down the pavement as if they were preparing to take off into the sky. The red glow of their taillights, burning like the tips of cigarettes, disappeared as they turned off on a side road.

I drove on, my fingers still clutching the wheel in a death grip. When I reached Vince's house, I pulled into the driveway, parked, and turned off my car with detached precision, my mind swept clean of all thought.

It was only when I reached up and felt the bite of the glass shards in my hair that I started to shake. I then remained in my car for some time, finally crawling out only after I felt I could stand up without my legs collapsing under me.

Bracing myself with one palm pressed against the roof of my car, I examined my shattered side window. *The entire thing will need to be replaced*, I thought, immediately fearing what this would do to the cost of my auto insurance. Peering inside, I noticed an odd object on the back seat. As I carefully opened the door, more glass slivers showered down the side of the car.

The missile that had broken my window was actually a rock, wrapped in paper. I reached in, avoiding the larger pieces of glass, and plucked it off the seat.

Peeling the paper off the rock revealed the message someone had obviously decided I needed to hear:

Stop digging into the murder or you'll be hit with something more deadly.

*   *   *

Vince's car wasn't in the driveway. Of course, he and Donna had probably gone out to dinner following our excursion today.

I grabbed my cell phone and dialed 911. After explaining my situation, and being reassured by the dispatcher that a police patrol was on its way, I leaned back against my car and stared up into the sky. Wispy clouds, gray as ash, skittered through the growing darkness. *Shouldn't have touched that note*, I realized, internally kicking myself for my stupidity.

The police arrived, sirens blazing. As I gave my statement to one officer, the other examined my car, along with the rock and the note.

"Sorry I touched that," I told them. "I wasn't exactly thinking clearly."

"It's alright. I'm sure we've got your prints on file from our investigation out at Aircroft. We can eliminate your fingerprints when this is examined more thoroughly." The officer stared at the note, now encased in an evidence bag, creases lining her brow. "Exactly who would you say is your enemy, Ms. Hunter?"

"There actually might be a list," I replied, earning sharp looks from both officers.

Once they'd concluded their interview and bagged all the evidence, the female officer walked me up to my apartment. "Stay inside and lock the door," she told me, after making a quick sweep of the small space. "Call us immediately if anything else happens."

"Oh, I will," I said fervently.

I brushed the glass from my hair and checked the deadbolt several times before I felt comfortable enough to change into my pajamas and pour myself a large glass of wine. Settling onto my couch with my drink and a large bag of prepopped popcorn, I turned the television to HGTV. I was happy to allow the chatter of would-be homeowners searching for dream houses to fill the background as I called my insurance company's twenty-four-hour help line to arrange for a rental while my car was being repaired.

Then I texted Cam.

Sorry, may be a little late tomorrow, I said. *I'll explain when we talk.*

Amazingly, I received a text in response.

Are you okay? Let me know.

I stared at the screen for a moment, bemused by this show of concern. Yes, it was the minimum one would expect, but from what I knew about Cameron Clewe, it was a giant leap of social awareness.

Yes, I replied. *Just a little shaken by something. Will give you all the details in the morning.*

I didn't get another text, but I was satisfied nonetheless.

Maybe Cam wasn't quite as clueless as everyone seemed to think.

Chapter Thirty-One

The next morning, Vince was kind enough to take me to pick up my rental car. Even though my insurance company had scheduled the glass replacement for Wednesday afternoon, I didn't want to be without a vehicle, even for a few days. Living alone, with no family nearby, I felt vulnerable. Especially after the events of Monday evening.

When I arrived at Aircroft later that morning, I immediately headed to Cam's office.

"I have a lot to tell you," I said, when I took a seat in the gray armchair near his desk.

"I guessed that." Cam rolled his chair away from his desk so he could face me. "When I got your text last night, I assumed something had happened."

I nodded and shared my harrowing adventure involving the beige sedan.

"Must've been at least two people in the other car," Cam said when I concluded my story.

"What makes you say that?" I asked.

Cam rolled a pen between his fingers. "Think about it. If someone's driving, especially taking risks like passing cars and breaking the speed limit, how could they throw a rock through the side window? Even if they could steer with one hand, they couldn't achieve the proper aim or velocity."

I stared at him for a second before slapping my forehead. "Of course, you're right. The only way that rock could've been hurled through my window was if someone was sitting on the passenger side of the car."

"Which means whoever wanted to warn you has at least one accomplice." Cam absently chewed on the end of his pen for a moment. "That puts a new spin on any theories about Ashley's killer."

"There's more than one person involved," I said, my mind processing this turn of events. "Or at least someone knows the murderer and is willing to protect them."

"Right." Cam tossed the pen onto his desk. "It makes me wonder if our theory concerning the Allen family might be correct."

I almost objected to the idea that it was "our theory," but decided to let that go. "If either Stan, Gemma, or Rena killed Ashley, it would make sense that the others would help cover up the crime." I straightened in my chair. "I'm favoring Rena as the most likely suspect. She seemed to be harboring a good deal of animosity toward her sister. And if she was the one to kill Ashley, whether it was a premeditated murder or an accidental killing arising out of an argument, I bet Stan and Gemma would be willing to help her escape justice."

Cam tucked a few errant strands of his auburn hair behind his ear. "Even though she killed their other daughter?"

"Well, that's the thing. They've already lost one child. They might not want to lose the other, even if it did circumvent justice." I shrugged. "I know it doesn't sound logical, but I think it's something a parent would do."

"Would you conceal a murder for your daughter's sake?" Cam asked, his feathery eyebrows drawing together.

"I honestly don't know. I might." I offered him a wry smile. "Never underestimate the lengths a parent will go to in order to protect their child."

"Is that so?" Cam's expression told me he would never have expected such treatment from his own father. "Anyway, I'm going to do a little more digging into the Allens. I have some acquaintances who might be able to give me a better picture of their family dynamic."

"I take it Ashley didn't share much about her family."

"She did not." A faint smile curled Cam's lips. "I invited them all here once, for a dinner party. It did not go particularly well."

"I gathered that, from something Lauren said." I leaned forward, resting my palms on my knees. "But leaving the Allen family aside for a moment, there are others you should add to your suspect list." I launched into a detailed description of my encounters with Rena, Tristan, and Kyle, including the information Clay Abbott had shared about Ashley reneging on her promise to Brendan. "Just like with Mateo and Tristan," I said. "It seems it was a habit with her, one which unfortunately could've set her up for murder."

A Cryptic Clue

"There's certainly no shortage of people with motive," Cam said. "And most had opportunity as well, since they all attended the gala, or at least were present in the house while it was going on." Cam leaned back in his chair, staring up at the high ceiling. "What was that thing Rena said about Ashley's sorority?"

Thrown off by this change of subject, I sat back, gripping the arms of the chair. "She claimed Ashley was very involved in one. Chi Omega Delta, I think. She was even president of her chapter, from what Rena told me. Why do you ask? That surely wouldn't have anything to do with her murder."

"Oh, it's not that important," Cam said, his gaze still focused on the ceiling. "It was one of the few things Ashley mentioned from her past when we were dating, that's all."

"She actually talked about that?" I shrugged when Cam snapped his attention onto me. "Sorry, but I had the impression that you and Ashley didn't share much personal information, like family history or your past activities or things like that."

"She did want to live in the moment," Cam said, his expression growing distant. He wheeled his chair around and pulled up to his desk. Leaning forward, he propped his elbows on the desk and rested his forehead on his hands. "Thanks so much for everything you've told me, Jane. It's extremely helpful."

I stared at his profile, noticing the prominence of the freckles splashed across his high cheekbones. *He's pondering a piece of information that has excited him,* I thought. *Something I told him this morning has clicked a puzzle piece into place. But it seems he's not sharing his thoughts, despite my efforts on his behalf.*

Standing, I brushed a piece of lint off my light blue wool sweater. "I suppose I'll go, then. Except, one more thing—did you ever look to see if Mateo was telling the truth about that recipe he was searching for the other day, when Naomi claimed someone tried to push her down the stairs? His excuse for being upstairs was trying to find some cookbook shelved in your mother's old studio."

"No, I haven't." Cam lifted his head and glanced over at me. "Would you mind checking on that? The studio is right above us, on the second floor. You can use the back stairs outside the office. Go up one flight and it's the first door on the right."

"It's unlocked?"

"No. Wait." Cam sat back and fished a set of keys out the pocket of his chino slacks. He tossed them to me. "It's the key with the blue dot. Just drop those off when you're done."

Clutching the keys so tightly that one dug into my palm, I muttered "See you later," and left the office.

Throwing his keys at me like I'm his servant, I thought, anger flushing my face. *No wonder the dinner party with the Allen family didn't turn out so well, if he was that high-handed with them.* Muttering to myself, I left the room, not worrying when the door slammed behind me.

Chapter
Thirty-Two

Still muttering, I climbed the back steps with Cam's set of keys dangling from my fingers. In the hallway at the top of the stairs, I paused to search for the blue dot supposedly painted on one of the keys. Finding it, I unlocked the door and stuffed the keys into my pocket before stepping into the studio.

As in Cam's office, some of the mansion's typical mullioned windows had been replaced, but in this case with a plain sheet of glass that spanned most of the back wall. Light poured in, illuminating a few dust motes that danced in the air.

It was a perfect studio, complete with a standing wooden easel and a porcelain work sink for cleaning brushes and other tools. One wall was filled with built-in shelves designed to hold art supplies, as well as vertical racks for storing stretched canvases. On the opposite wall, a low bookcase sat under another, smaller, window.

As I crossed to the bookcase, I had the strange sensation that the artist who'd abandoned a paint-encrusted palette and a glass jar stuffed with brushes on a small table next to the easel would return at any moment.

It's like a time capsule, I thought. *Left just as it was the last day Patricia Clewe plied her craft in here.*

Despite the dust motes, the room had obviously been cleaned recently. Just like the attic, the studio held traces of scent—lemon polish and the acrid bite of a vinegar-based window cleaner. I suspected that this room, as well as the memory of its former occupant, had been carefully, and lovingly, maintained over the years.

I knelt down in front of the bookcase, looking for anything resembling a cookbook. If Mateo had told the truth about looking for one, there should be at least one shelved with the other books.

But does Mateo even have access to this room? I wondered, as the cluster of keys in my pocket jabbed into my thigh through the thin material of my pocket. *And is that one of the puzzle pieces I suspect Cam is already piecing together without my knowledge?*

I frowned, sliding the thick coffee table art books and thinner, more well-worn books on artistic craft to one side as I searched. I was convinced that Cam had some ideas about the murder he was not sharing with me, despite the significant efforts I'd made to gather information on his behalf.

And the fact that I'd actually put myself in danger. Which, despite the modicum of concern he'd displayed in his text last night, seemed to have made little impression on him.

I'd made my way down the entire bookcase without discovering any cookbooks. This made me question Mateo's excuse for being upstairs on the day Naomi almost fell, especially since I didn't recall him holding a book when he'd appeared at the top of the stairs.

Although, I reminded myself, *it isn't absolute proof that Mateo was lying that day.* There were a couple of spaces where one book had tipped over into another, indicating that perhaps another book had once been shelved between them. *Mateo could've come back at another time to grab a cookbook, if one was ever here.*

I braced my hand against the top of the bookcase as I rose to my feet. Only I found my fingers weren't pressed against the top of the shelving unit, but rather the suede surface of a large, wire-bound sketchbook. I picked up the sketchbook and carried it over to a schoolhouse-style wooden chair placed near the plate glass window.

My curiosity piqued, I sat down and flipped open the sketchbook. As I suspected, it had once belonged to Patricia Clewe—her elegant signature swept across the inside cover. Most of the sketches were simple studies of flowers or landscapes, many of which looked as if they could've been done in the gardens at Aircroft. It was only when I reached the middle of the sketchbook that the artist's true talent emerged.

From that point on, there were numerous drawings, some in pencil and some in colored inks, of a child I immediately identified as Cam. The red hair and the shape of his sea-green eyes were unmistakable. As I flipped the pages, the infant grew into a toddler—a wiry child taking his first steps, his still chubby face filled with both fear and determination. I brushed the surface of the thick paper with the tips of my fingers. The love infused into the drawings was palpable.

After the set of pictures of Cam as a toddler, the pages were blank. *She died*, I thought. *She died far too young, and left behind a boy she obviously loved dearly.*

I rubbed away the tears that had beaded on my lashes, drying my damp fingers on my slacks before touching the sketchbook again. But as I closed the book, something slipped out from between the empty back pages and fluttered to the floor.

Now what's this? I asked myself as I retrieved what looked like another drawing.

This piece had been created on a lighter-weight paper than the pages in the sketchbook, but it was unmistakably one of Patricia Clewe's drawings. I laid it on top of the closed book and studied it for a moment before I realized what I was looking at.

It was a charcoal pencil portrait of the woman from the mysterious photo I'd discovered in the attic. Only this time she looked middle-aged rather than young. But I was positive it was the same woman. Despite the lines and other signs of age in this later work, both images portrayed a woman with luxurious hair that fell in deep waves, voluptuous lips, and an identical, and poignant, expression in her wide eyes.

"Who in the world are you?" I asked aloud, as I took a picture of the drawing with my cell phone.

"Excuse me?" Lauren, standing in the open doorway, met my gaze with a lift of her dark eyebrows. "Can I help you with something, Jane?"

"No, no, it's fine." I stood up, shoving my phone into my pocket with one hand and clutching the sketchbook to my chest with the other. "Cam gave me his keys so I could search for something up here."

"I assumed that was the case." Lauren crossed the room, her heels tapping a staccato beat against the hardwood floor. "What were you looking for?"

"Some cookbook that Mateo mentioned the other day," I said. "Cam wanted to know if he'd actually grabbed it, or if it was still here."

"Cookbook? That seems odd. I don't recall a cookbook." Lauren's gaze flitted around the room before she focused back on me. "Did you find anything?"

"No, but I did discover something else." I held out the sketchbook, with the loose drawing laid on top. "I don't know if you've ever seen this before. It's one of the notebooks Patricia Clewe used for her drawings."

"I've seen it." Lauren dropped her gaze, seemingly fascinated with the tips of her shoes. "Cam had me inventory the studio when I first arrived."

"So you've already been treated to the baby Cam pictures?" I asked. "They're really beautiful."

"Yes, they are." Lauren lifted her head, but kept her gaze focused on the view out the window behind me. "Such a shame that Patricia died so young. She was very talented and, from what I've heard, a genuinely lovely person."

"A shame for Cam as well. I can tell she must've really loved him," I said.

"That too." Lauren tossed her head, bouncing her tight black curls. "But what's that drawing on top? I don't remember seeing that one."

"It was stuck inside the sketchbook." I passed Lauren the drawing. "Do you know who this might be?"

"I have no idea." Lauren stared at the sketch, lines creasing her brow. "I don't recognize the subject from any of the family photos I've seen. Perhaps it was one of Patricia's friends?"

"An older friend, then," I said. "This woman looks like she could be in her fifties or sixties."

Lauren shrugged. "Maybe one of her relatives? I really don't know. Since it's a loose drawing, it could've been done before she married. I mean, there doesn't have to be a connection to Aircroft."

But there is, I thought, while admitting that Lauren's words made sense. If I hadn't found the snapshot of this same woman at a much younger age in a box of photographs associated with the Airley family, I would've thought nothing of the sketch. I would have simply assumed it was someone from Patricia Clewe's past, as Lauren did.

But I knew that couldn't be true. Patricia must've met this woman later, after she'd married Albert Clewe. When, for some reason, the mystery girl from the photo in the Airley family collection had returned to Aircroft as an older woman.

But why? I thought, slipping the drawing back between the sketchbook pages. "I think I'd better get to work. My real work, that is. Those materials aren't going to catalog themselves." I pulled the bundle of keys from my pocket and balanced them on top of the sketchbook. "Would you mind putting this back where it belongs and returning these keys to Cam?"

"Sure. I need to stop by his office anyway, to discuss some business matters." Lauren took the sketchbook and keys from my hands. "Anything else?"

A Cryptic Clue

I walked to the door. "Just tell him I'll be working in the library. Oh, and"—I paused in the open doorway to look back at Lauren—"let him know I didn't find anything of significance in the studio."

Even though I did. But I simply hugged this secret to myself as I headed to the library.

Two could play Cam's game.

Chapter
Thirty-Three

I spent Wednesday and Thursday working on the Mary Roberts Rinehart portion of Cam's collection. My work progressed slowly, mainly due to the fact that she'd lived such a fascinating life. I kept stopping to read the materials in full. I knew I should simply skim them, but the information was captivating. I discovered that in addition to writing numerous best-selling books, the most famous of which, *The Circular Staircase*, published in 1908, was a seminal mystery in the American literary canon, she also wrote plays, travelogues, short stories, and articles. The collection even included information on her stint working as a war correspondent during World War I, when she covered the Belgian front for the *Saturday Evening Post*. There were also articles and letters detailing her involvement in the Farrar & Rinehart publishing house, which was founded by her sons.

So much for the retiring wife and mother stereotype of that period, I thought as I marveled at how much creative work Rinehart had produced while being married to a physician and raising three sons. It certainly made me feel like a slacker. Sure, I'd worked full-time as a librarian and raised my daughter as a single mother, but I hadn't created anything to rival Rinehart's output. *Or anything at all, really*, I thought with a frown.

Still, one thing I could do was catalog Cam's collection, helping to preserve and provide access to the materials. Cam had told me that he wanted researchers, writers, and scholars to use the collection once it was processed, which made me feel I was doing valuable work. Maybe I couldn't write something myself, but I could assist others in their scholarly or creative efforts.

Since I ended up staying at Aircroft a little later than usual on Thursday, I decided to pick up some takeout from a farm-to-table restaurant in Bradfordville on my way home. I called ahead, ordering a dinner salad filled with fresh greens and vegetables topped with grilled salmon.

When I walked into the bright and cheery restaurant to collect my food, I was instantly distracted by one of the waitresses. It was Evie Grayson, her long dark hair now slicked back into a tight ponytail. She wore a turquoise T-shirt sporting the restaurant's logo over a pair of black slacks.

My salad could wait. "Hello there," I said as Evie crossed in front of me on her way to the kitchen.

She stopped in mid-stride. "Ms. Hunter, how nice to see you again. Do you need a table? I can alert the hostess."

"No thanks. I'm just picking up some takeout," I said, studying her for a moment. "I would like to talk to you again sometime, though. Primarily to find out how you're doing, but also to see if you can verify some things Rena Allen recently told me."

Evie bit her lower lip and glanced at her wristwatch. "I'm due a break as soon as I process this payment from my last table. Do you mind waiting a few minutes?"

"Not at all. I'll just grab my takeout and meet you outside, near my car. It's a metallic green compact sedan." *With a new side window*, I thought, but didn't share this detail.

"That'd be great. I'll be there in a few." Evie hurried off.

I paid for my salad and carried it outside. After I set the food bag on the passenger seat, I stepped out of the car to wait for Evie. Leaning against the side of my vehicle, I stared up into the canopy of a large maple tree. The tree's turning leaves were layered in a pattern of crimson and green, like a patchwork quilt.

Evie walked out from the back of the small restaurant, zipping her denim jacket against the bite of the autumn wind. "Thanks for waiting," she said as she reached me.

"No problem. My takeout is meant to be eaten cold, so I'm not concerned about the time."

"Unfortunately, I only have a few minutes." A gust of wind flipped Evie's ponytail over her shoulder. "What did you want to ask me?"

"First, I wanted to make sure you don't have any lasting injuries."

Evie's eyes widened in a way that made me suspect she was confused. *Or even*, I thought, *afraid*. "No, what are you . . . What do you mean?" she asked.

"From the incident at the park?" Another blast of cold wind hit us and I pulled the open edges of my jacket together with one hand. "You were struck pretty hard."

"Oh, that." Evie toyed with a few strands of hair that had escaped her ponytail. "Thanks for asking, but I'm fine. I really think it must've been the wind that day. It can blow pretty hard from time to time around here"

"Like now," I said, buttoning my jacket. "Well, I'm glad you're okay, but I do have another question. It has to do with Ashley's old boyfriend, Tristan Blair."

Evie stared over my shoulder, her eyes slightly unfocused. "What about him?"

"Rena Allen seems to think he could've killed Ashley. Maybe during an argument that got out of hand. What are your thoughts on that?"

"But Tristan wasn't at the gala," Evie said in a distracted tone.

"Actually, he was. He told me that himself, and Rena and others have mentioned seeing him there."

Evie's gaze, suddenly clear and alert, focused on my face. "He said that?"

"He did, when I spoke with him at his studio this past Sunday. He said he was invited by a musician friend who was playing at the event."

"Why would Tristan want to attend that gala?" Evie's lips tightened. "I didn't go, why would he?"

Surprised by her obvious discomfort, I thrust my hands into my jacket pockets. "To talk to Ashley. Or so he said."

Evie drew a circle in the loose gravel of the parking lot with the toe of her black leather sneakers. "That doesn't make sense. He was totally done with her, at least as far as I knew."

I pursed my lips. Had Evie and Tristan gotten together after his split with Ashley? It sounded as if that was the case. "Are you saying you didn't know he was attending the fundraiser?"

"I had no idea." Evie flipped her ponytail back over her shoulder. "And we did see each other, after," she added, lowering her gaze so I couldn't read her eyes.

"You saw him later that night? Did you tell the police?"

"No, because I didn't think it was relevant." Evie kicked a piece of gravel. "Tristan didn't tell me he'd been at Aircroft before he met up with me. I just thought he had a gig somewhere and that's why we were getting together so late."

"So he lied."

Evie threw up her head. "No, he didn't. He simply didn't tell me. He doesn't feel compelled to keep me informed of all his movements. Which is fair, since I don't tell him all of mine."

I remembered Tristan flirting with Lauren. *Quite the catch*, I thought, but decided it was none of my business. How Tristan appeared the night of the murder, on the other hand . . . "How did he seem when you met?"

"You mean, was he covered in blood?" Evie met my intense stare with a defiant lift of her chin. "He was not. And he didn't seem the least bit anxious or worried, either. If he'd killed someone that evening, he sure didn't act like it."

"What was he wearing?" I asked, recalling the descriptions of a young man wearing casual black clothing.

"A black T-shirt and jeans, like usual." Evie crossed her arms over her chest. "Now look—I know you're trying to help Cam clear his own name, and that's fine. But leave Tristan out of it. He isn't a killer. Yeah, maybe he can get moody or angry sometimes, but that's pretty normal, especially for someone artistic, don't you think?"

I thought of my daughter. "I suppose. But Rena Allen did mention that he could get physical with Ashley."

Evie threw out a disparaging expression concerning Rena. "That family. Like I said, they're the ones who need to be investigated more closely. They had the motive to kill Ashley, after all. The inheritance, remember?"

I didn't bother to mention Rena's comment about Ashley sharing the money with her family. Evie probably wouldn't believe me, anyway. "You trust Tristan Blair's word over theirs?"

"Absolutely." Evie squared her shoulders. "All the Allens hated Tristan, you know. It's not surprising they'd try to throw the blame on him. That's just typical of their smear tactics. I know Tristan is innocent and don't want him to be accused of something he didn't do."

That you know of, I thought, examining Evie's determined expression. "Then perhaps you should tell the police about your rendezvous after the gala. Let them know that Tristan appeared perfectly normal and had no blood or other marks on him. That might actually help his case."

Evie's dark lashes fluttered. "Would it? I'll have to think about that." She glanced down at her wristwatch. "Oh, wow, I'm late. Sorry, have to run."

She turned and jogged back to the restaurant without offering a goodbye, leaving me puzzling over a few things.

Not the fact that she might be involved with Tristan Blair—I could understand that. As Ashley's friend, she'd probably spent a lot of time around him. Perhaps she'd liked him even then and had decided to comfort him when he and Ashley broke up.

No, it was her obvious dislike of the Allen family that had me confused. If she was one of Ashley's best friends, why would she hate her family?

There are only two reasons, I thought as I climbed into my car to drive home. Perhaps Ashley had also despised them—which supported the idea of a rift in the family that could've led to murder. Maybe Evie had simply accepted, and supported, her friend's feelings.

Or maybe, I thought as I drove away from the restaurant, *despite her claims of friendship, Evie disliked Ashley's family because she'd grown to despise Ashley.*

Chapter
Thirty-Four

On Friday I decided to take a break from cataloging the materials in the library and head up to the attic to continue my inventory of the full collection. Cataloging took a lot more mental effort and after the week I'd had, I just didn't have the concentration to do it well.

Before heading upstairs, I checked in with Lauren, who told me that she and Cam were going to be walking the gardens all morning, making notes on any significant winterizing projects that would need to be contracted out to the estate's landscaping company. Stopping by the kitchen for a cup of coffee, I found Dia and Mateo preparing to take the estate van to a local farmer's market.

"We aren't activating the alarm system in the house, since Cam and Lauren may be in and out," Dia said. "But don't worry. The front gates will be locked. If anyone tries to break into the estate grounds, the perimeter alarms will automatically alert the police."

"Good to know," I told her, laying my cell phone on the counter so I could pour some cream into my coffee.

"We shouldn't be long anyway. The market isn't far," Mateo said, as he slipped on a dark wool jacket.

"I'm sure everything will be fine," I said before wishing Dia and Mateo a pleasant shopping trip.

By midmorning, I'd made my way through several portions of the collection, including the works of Josephine Bell, Margery Allingham, and Phoebe Atwood Taylor, who also wrote as Alice Tilton, when it occurred to me that most of the authors represented were female. I suspected this bias was deliberate on Cam's part. Perhaps he truly wanted to highlight female mystery authors in a research collection he hoped to open to other scholars. *Or maybe*, I thought, *these materials were more easily acquired than first editions and ephemera from more well-documented authors, many of whom are male.*

Whatever the reason, I was happy to see these works from authors who may have been celebrated in their day, but today had been mostly forgotten, preserved for posterity. And study, of course. I knew from my time working in reference that well-documented collections such as this could provide a treasure trove of information for academic scholars and other researchers.

As I logged the information required for the inventory into my spreadsheet, I thought about all the conflicting aspects of the Ashley Allen murder case. It was definitely a puzzle—one whose numerous pieces didn't yet fit together to create a clear picture.

Ashley had failed Mateo and Brendan by promising support for their business endeavors without following through. She'd abandoned both of them, leading to dire consequences—bankruptcy in Mateo's case, and for Brendan, the humiliation of letting down his colleagues.

She'd also dumped Tristan, no doubt hurting his career as well as his heart. Rena had mentioned that Ashley had paid for Tristan's studio space through the end of the year, but I assumed that after their breakup she would've pulled her financial support from him too. So once the year was up, Tristan would've been out on his ear, even if Ashley had still been alive.

Then there was Evie, who displayed signs of a crush on Tristan. Whether or not he reciprocated her feelings, beyond an easy hookup, was hard to say. But she could certainly be covering for him. It wasn't impossible for her to be an accomplice, even if after the fact. She wouldn't be the first person to turn on a friend when a love triangle came into play.

The Allen family, who'd been cut out of a future fortune in favor of Ashley, also could be involved. Although Rena claimed that Ashley had planned to share her grandmother's bequest with the entire family, there was no proof of this promise except Rena's word. And since Rena was one of the beneficiaries, her insistence that Tristan was the murderer might simply be a way to divert suspicion away from herself and her parents.

Of course, there was also Cam. He was the most recent of Ashley's exes and had been seen arguing with her at the gala. He also knew how to move around Aircroft without being seen, and had been observed in the vicinity of the library as the fundraising event ended. Yes, he claimed that he was simply reactivating the security system, but the alarms were off on Monday morning. Which meant either someone else had come behind Cam and deactivated the system, or the thing had never been turned on in the first place. Perhaps Cam had forgotten to activate the system after encountering Ashley again and killing her in a fit of rage. He could've come up with the line about the security system later, simply as an excuse for his presence in the hallway near the murder scene.

I had to admit that, on the surface, it didn't seem Cam had quite as serious a motive as some of the others. But then again, there was that secret Lauren had mentioned. Cam had told Ashley something when he was drunk—a secret that, had she threatened to expose it, could've driven him to kill her.

As this thought swirled through my mind, a loud click resonated throughout the room. I laid down the book I was holding and headed for the door, where the sound had appeared to originate.

Jiggling the doorknob, I realized the door was locked from the outside, using the key I'd carelessly left in the keyhole. Of course, I hadn't expected anyone to lock the door, especially since no one except Cam and I typically accessed the attic.

Although that isn't exactly right. Dia or one of her part-time staff probably come up here to clean. Banging on the thick wooden door panels, I yelled that I was working in the attic and needed to be let out.

There was no response. I shouted again, but hearing no footsteps on the stairs, I assumed whoever had locked the door had already disappeared.

The door was too thick for my fists or kicking feet to make any kind of dent. I stepped back, breathing heavily, and jogged to the desk to look for my cell phone. Even though Mateo and Dia might not have returned from the market yet, Cam and Lauren would either still be in the gardens or, if they'd concluded their survey, back in the house.

But after furiously shifting papers, books, and my laptop, I realized my phone was missing. My shoulders slumped. I must've left the phone in the kitchen when I was preparing my coffee.

Sprinting over to the front dormer window, I snapped up the shade and peered out over the driveway, fountain, and front lawn. The estate van was nowhere to be seen. Of course, that didn't mean that Dia and Mateo were still at the market. They could've parked the van in the garage that flanked one side of the mansion.

I did spy an unfamiliar car parked in the circle. *A visitor?* I wondered, examining the cream-colored vehicle. It was a smaller SUV, the kind one could find all over the roads.

I rapped the window, but unfortunately no one was around to hear me. Dashing to the back dormer window, I tried to lift the sash, to no avail. Layers of white paint had glued the edges of the window to the frame. Frustrated, I rapped this window as well.

Although my vantage point gave me a bird's-eye view of the gardens, I didn't see Cam or Lauren. *Perhaps they've already headed inside*, I thought, clenching my teeth.

Cursing whatever lapse of mental acuity had allowed me to leave my cell phone in the kitchen, I stalked back across the room. Leaning over the desk, with my palms pressed into its pitted wood surface, I pondered my next move.

Lifting my head, my gaze fell on the door sandwiched between the far wall's banks of shelves. It had to lead into the larger portion of the attic, where the flotsam and jetsam of two families had accumulated over the years. Straightening, I circled around the desk and tried the doorknob. Miraculously, it turned, and I shoved the door open, its bottom edge scraping against the uneven floorboards.

I peered into the huge, dimly lit space. It looked like a barn, with rafters soaring above a dusty wooden plank floor. Boxes upon boxes, stacked like hay bales, filled every wall and corner, while larger furniture pieces draped in white cotton looked like ghostly giants gathered for a meeting in the center of the cavernous space.

I sneezed as the dust covering every surface assaulted my nostrils. It was clear that Dia's cleaning regime ended at the doorway that led into this portion of the attic. Not that I blamed her, or the part-time crew she supervised on a weekly basis. I assumed the items stored here had been abandoned and forgotten.

Scrabbling my fingers over the rough boards of the wall beside the door, I finally located a switch. Flicking it turned on a series of bare light bulbs. They dangled from the rafters, casting circles of light that only illuminated small portions of the attic. It was enough light for me to pick my way around the clutter, but it left the rest of the space in eerie shadow.

There must be another staircase at the other end, I thought, basing this assumption on nothing more than hope. I was so fixated on finding another exit that I didn't look down and stumbled over a box blocking my path.

I jerked, banging my elbow into a small box sitting on top of a nearby stack. It toppled off its perch and tumbled to my feet, spilling its contents across the battered wooden floorboards.

Letting loose a string of words that would've earned Tristan Blair's seal of approval, I bent down to scoop up the papers that littered the floor. I intended to simply shove them back into the box until something caught my eye. It was a pile of folded letters, tied up with a faded blue ribbon.

One letter had slid out of the packet. Glancing at the greeting, I noticed it was addressed to "Pat." I assumed that had to refer to Patricia Clewe. Sitting back on the floor without any regard for my beige slacks, I opened the folded paper with care and quickly read through it.

It was short—only a couple of paragraphs. But it was undeniably a love letter. I glanced down at the name scribbled across one bottom corner of the page. *There isn't actually a full signature*, I realized as I held the letter closer to my eyes. *Just a hastily scrawled initial.*

"R. Who's R?" I asked aloud. This letter, dated 1990, could not have been from Patricia's husband, Albert Clewe. I folded the letter and slipped it back into the pile. Holding the ribbon-tied bundle to my chest, I pondered this discovery.

Someone with the first initial "R" had sent Patricia Clewe love letters, even after her marriage. I knew that had to be true, since Cam had been born in 1989.

"Jane," a voice called out from the other room. "Are you okay?"

I rose to my feet, still clutching the letters. "Yes, in here. I was searching for another exit."

Cam stood in the doorway, his slender figure outlined with light from the room behind him. "What happened? I was looking for you and finally thought to check the attic, then found the door locked."

"Someone locked me in," I said. "I have no idea why."

Cam's face appeared pale as milk. "That makes no sense. Are you sure you didn't lock it yourself by mistake?"

"How could I? The key was in the lock, on the other side of the door." I said, using my foot to push the fallen box to one side. I'd have to come back later to return it to its proper place.

But I slipped the packet of letters into the back pocket of my slacks and yanked down my sweater to cover them before I joined Cam in the finished portion of the attic.

Glancing at him after I closed the door behind me, I noticed that Cam's gaze had turned inward, as if he were working through some mental puzzle.

"Well, no harm done, it seems. I'll let you get back to work," he said, handing me the key. "But you might want to keep this on you, rather than in the door, in the future."

I nodded and thanked him as he strode out the door.

Pulling the bundle of letters from my pocket, I considered the fact that its contents were none of my business. Then again, it seemed that fate had tossed it in my path.

And who was I to question fate?

Chapter
Thirty-Five

After dropping off the packet of letters in the library, I headed to the kitchen to look for anything containing caffeine. I wasn't expecting to run into anyone who wasn't resident at Aircroft, but as I stepped into the entry hall, I caught sight of Hannah McKenzie.

"Hello there," I said.

Hannah whirled around, the straps of her oversized canvas tote sliding off her shoulder. "Jane, goodness gracious. You startled me."

I held up my hands. "Sorry. I wasn't really expecting to see you either."

"No, no, forgive me. I just knew Mateo and Dia were in the kitchen, because they told me they were putting away stuff from the market when they buzzed me through the gates a little while ago." As Hannah hoisted the heavy bag back up onto her shoulder, I couldn't help but notice that it was filled with at least one particularly large object that poked against the canvas. She appeared to notice my gaze and stretched her other arm across the bag to hold the straps in place on her shoulder.

"Hello, Hannah," Cam said from the arched opening into the hall leading to his office. "What brings you to Aircroft today?"

Hannah flashed a flustered smile. "My own forgetfulness. I was on my way to the library to return some books"—her fingers tightened on the tote bag's straps—"and thought I'd stop by to see if I could retrieve my lost item."

"What was that?" Cam asked as he strolled across the hall to join us.

The color rose in Hannah's round face. "Just a scarf. I think I left it here when Naomi and I were prepping for the gala."

"And did you find it?" While Cam's tone was perfectly cordial, the gaze he'd fixed on Hannah was intimidatingly intense.

Recalling Evie's comment about not daring to arrive at Aircroft without an invitation, I wondered if Cam was angry Hannah had shown up without warning.

"I did, thank goodness." Hannah turned to me with a smile that appeared as brittle as it was bright. "I'm sure you're wondering why I'd need to make a special visit to retrieve something like that, but it was one of my favorites. My goddaughter actually gave it to me, years ago."

"I understand. It has sentimental value," I said.

"That's it exactly." Hannah pulled the straps of the bag away from her shoulder for a moment.

"That looks heavy," Cam said. "Would you like me to carry it out to your car?"

"That isn't necessary. I'm sure you both have work to do. I'll just be on my way." Hannah took a few steps toward the front doors.

Cam's eyes narrowed. "Alright, I just wanted to offer. But since I was actually taking a stroll to stretch my legs before yet another video chat, I think I'll head back to my office. Good day, Hannah."

"Nice to see you again, Cam," Hannah called out with what I felt was forced cheerfulness.

Cam, who'd already turned away, lifted one hand in a brusque wave before disappearing down the hallway.

Hannah watched him go, then sidled up to me. "Does he seem off to you these days?" she asked in a hushed voice.

"I really have no idea," I replied, not bothering to lower my volume. "I don't know him as well as you do."

Stepping back, Hannah shifted the tote bag to her other shoulder. "It just makes me wonder. He certainly doesn't appear too broken up over Ashley's death."

"Would he show it, even if he was devastated?" I asked, genuinely curious. Despite their longer acquaintance, Hannah seemed to have little comprehension of Cam's personality. "He may simply be grieving in his own way."

"Perhaps. Or maybe he's trying to distance himself because he actually did kill her." Catching my questioning glance, Hannah shrugged. "He was seen near the library after the gala, and like Naomi always says, he knows every secret stair and corridor in this drafty old place."

"He claims he was there to activate the alarm system," I said.

"And that could be true, but it wasn't on the next morning. Dia told me that, not long after the fact."

I frowned. Dia seemed to have told everyone about the deactivated alarms. "I'm sure the police are looking into it. There are other possible suspects, you know."

Hannah's hazel eyes widened. "Absolutely. I didn't mean to imply that Cam was the only one with a motive. There was also Ashley's family."

So she'd heard that rumor as well. Perhaps, as a longtime member of the community, she'd even learned more than Evie had shared with me. I decided to play dumb, hoping to gather more details. "What do you mean?"

"Oh, apparently Stan and Gemma Allen, along with their other daughter, Rena, now stand to inherit a fortune from Stan's mother. They weren't originally going to get anything, you see. It was all going to Ashley. But now that she's no longer with us . . ."

I raised my eyebrows. "They get the entire amount?"

"That's right. Which makes what I saw the night of the gala that much more interesting." Hannah shifted the tote bag back to the original shoulder.

I wondered why she didn't just set the bag on the floor. She was holding onto it as if it contained gold bars, not just some library books and a scarf. "Exactly what did you see?"

"As I told the police—just recently, actually, as this detail had slipped my mind in all the uproar following murder—I noticed that both Gemma and Rena Allen disappeared from the gala for some time. That was when Ashley was nowhere to be seen as well. When I saw Gemma and Rena again, they already had their coats on and seemed in a rush to leave."

"Did they look upset, or anxious, or anything like that?" I asked.

"Not really. It was stranger than that." Hannah took a deep breath, as if recalling this memory required time to collect her thoughts. "They seemed like they were moving . . . well, almost mechanically, I guess. Their expressions were very blank, like they'd distanced themselves from some bad situation. At the time I just wrote it down to exhaustion. Heaven knows, I was feeling rather tired myself."

"But now you think it might've been the horror of killing Ashley? I suppose, especially if unpremeditated, a murder could put one in a state of shock."

"I don't know. I didn't see any blood or anything, but they did have long wool coats on, covering their gowns, and I suppose they could've cleaned up their hands before I saw them." Hannah turned away, her gaze focused on the front doors. "Like I told the police, I have no desire to accuse anyone of anything. I'm just reporting what I observed." She pressed her hand against the tote bag, as if assuring the books were still there. "Sorry, I really should be going. I need to drop these off and run a few other errands today."

"No problem, I should get back to work too," I said. "After I grab a cup of coffee, that is."

"It was good to speak with you again, Jane." Hannah offered me a wan smile before turning and heading for the front doors.

"Have a good day," I called after her.

I waited until she exited before resuming my quest for caffeine. *Although,* I thought as I headed for the kitchen, *Hannah's observations about Gemma and Rena Allen's behavior after the gala might be stimulant enough.*

Chapter Thirty-Six

When I got back to my apartment on Friday evening, I was ready to kick off my shoes and slip into my coziest pair of pajamas while I enjoyed a frozen meal version of shrimp fried rice.

It was definitely not haute cuisine, but then, my outfit was not anything that would've graced the pages of a glamour magazine either. Not that I cared. One of the great bonuses of living alone was that I didn't have to worry about how I looked while lounging at home.

More accurately, I don't have to worry about what anyone else thinks I should look like, I reminded myself. I'd never been obsessed with my appearance, beyond being clean and not so far out of fashion that I was a laughingstock. I preferred comfort to keeping up with the latest trends. But there had been a time in my life when I'd definitely experienced the pressure to look a certain way. *The way he wanted*, I thought, wrinkling my nose as I poured the one glass of wine I allowed myself each day.

It wasn't that I was worried about drinking too much, simply that I'd seen what excess consumption could do to someone's personality. I'd watched it take over someone I'd loved once. It hadn't been a pleasant transformation.

As I walked past the narrow table I'd placed behind my sofa, I paused, once again captivated by the face of the mysterious woman from the photograph I'd discovered in Aircroft's attic and Patricia Clewe's drawing. I'd recently printed the two pictures from my cell phone, planning to show them to Vince. Having left the pictures on the table to remind me to share them with him, I'd since discovered that he and Donna had gone out of town for a few days. Not a fan of clutter, I slid them into a folder I'd left in the table's single drawer.

Settling on my sofa, I prepared to delve into someone else's history. I'd dropped the bundle of ribbon-tied letters from Aircroft on my coffee table as soon as I'd come home, but resisted the urge to read them until after dinner.

I set my wineglass on a side table next to the sofa and grabbed the packet of letters. Since they were likely written in the early 1990s, I didn't worry too much about the fragility of the paper. They weren't from the 1840s to the late 1980s, when the acid in wood pulp–based paper caused print materials to deteriorate rapidly. It was a fact that saddened all librarians who dealt with printed materials created during that time period, since so many books and other documents often crumbled in their hands.

I sat back, tapping the packet of letters against my knee. I found it ironic that Cam had been born in 1989, as that year also saw the birth of the movement to change papermaking production in the United States. In fact, having recently earned my master's degree in library science, I'd been part of the crowd on March seventh of that year, witnessing something called a "Commitment

Day" ceremony at the New York Public Library. The ceremony had honored forty-six authors and forty publishers who'd signed an agreement called the "Declaration of Book Preservation," which marked the beginning of many presses using acid-free paper to publish books and other print documents. It was a development cheered that day by many librarians, including twenty-seven-year-old me and a group of my MLS graduate friends.

Of course, my then fiancé, Gary, had labeled my trip to New York foolish in the extreme, which should've been my first red flag.

But we have to live and learn, I told myself, gently untying the faded blue ribbon binding the letters together. I laid the letters out on the coffee table, hoping they'd been stored in the order in which they'd been received.

Happily, they were in date sequence, starting with the letter from 1990 that I'd read in the attic and continuing until late fall 1992. *That was probably around the time that Patricia Clewe died*, I thought as I picked up the second letter to read its full contents.

There were seven letters in all, each more heartrending than the last. I had to sit back after finishing the last one and sip my wine while I processed what I'd just read.

Patricia Clewe's lover, only identified as "R," had professed his continuing love for her in every missive, but the intensity of his pleas that she leave Albert Clewe and join him had increased exponentially from the first letter to the second to last. However, in the final letter, the tone had changed, passion and desperation giving way to resignation.

I swirled the wine in my glass and stared upward, where a white ceiling fan spun lazily. *Such a tragic story*, I thought. *Two people who truly loved each other, separated because one of them wanted to spare the other from financial ruin.*

It was clear that Patricia had known, even while carrying Cam, that her cancer had returned. I gleaned this from reading between the lines, as well as the fact that she'd forgone treatment while pregnant, only going back to it after Cam was born. I could also surmise that they were extremely expensive treatments for a rare form of cancer that had baffled the doctors at the time.

A few lines from one of the letters kept replaying in my mind—"I don't blame you, Pat. I know my lack of insurance, coupled with yours, would've made your current treatments impossible." So it was money that had separated them; or the lack of it.

Picking up the one envelope included in the packet, I noticed it was addressed to Patricia Clewe at Aircroft. There was no return address. I wondered if Albert Clewe had known that his wife had continued a correspondence with the man she truly loved? It was impossible to tell, but one thing was clear—Albert had known that Cam was not his biological son. "R" made that point clear in several of the letters.

I frowned, trying to puzzle out this odd relationship. There were so many questions in my mind.

How much had Albert Clewe known? Had Patricia conned him into marrying her to provide for both her and her unborn son, or had they made some sort of mutually beneficial deal? Did Albert realize she was ill when they married? Had he actually offered to marry her primarily to provide her with health insurance or otherwise finance her medical treatments? Had he loved her so much that he'd made a vow to take care of her and her son, even when neither one was truly his?

Unfortunately, those were questions I couldn't answer using the text of these documents. I finished off my wine and set the glass on the side table before picking up the final letter again.

In this one, "R" acknowledges that Patricia has made the right choice, giving herself a chance at life while also ensuring that Cam would always be well provided for. He refers to something that Patricia must've said in a letter sent to him, and agrees to stop all contact with her.

And with Cam. "The boy will be better off with Clewe," "R" had written in the last letter. "He can give him the world, while I have nothing to offer."

I sighed and released my hold on the letter, allowing it to flutter onto the coffee table. As it fell, it flipped, landing face down, and I realized there was writing on the back.

Grabbing the letter again, I read the short note jotted across the reverse side of the letter. "No indication of any location found," it said, which didn't offer much in the way of illumination. But it was the handwriting that made me suck in a gulp of air.

I recognized that hand. I'd seen it on several purchase and provenance documents in the mystery book collection. Which meant that although this note wasn't signed, I knew exactly who'd written it.

And was certain, beyond the shadow of a doubt, that Cameron Clewe also knew the truth about his parentage.

Chapter Thirty-Seven

I spent Saturday trying to banish the thoughts of Ashley's murder, Cam's missing father, and the mystery woman in the pictures from my mind. I was partially successful, especially when I was focused on other things, like grocery shopping and trying out a new hair salon for a trim. I even managed to binge watch a new streaming show I'd been saving for a quiet day. Of course, since it was a detective series, I started analyzing my own mysteries again, which meant I didn't sleep as well as I would've liked.

On Sunday afternoon, right before I could call her, Bailey phoned me.

"You always do this," I said. "Call me at the exact same time I'm planning to call you."

"Yeah, I dunno, it's like we're related or something," Bailey said, with that lilt in her voice that could always charm audiences, and me.

"So what's up? Are you relaxing before your performance this evening?"

"Trying to," Bailey said. "Although worrying about my mom being caught up in the middle of a murder investigation has me on edge."

I made a dismissive sound. "I'm perfectly safe. And not a suspect, in case you were concerned about that."

"I wasn't. Figured if you were going to off somebody, a young woman you barely knew wouldn't top your list."

"Very funny," I said dryly, glad Bailey couldn't see my grin. "How's the show going?"

"Great." There was a long pause before Bailey added, "Charlie and I have called it quits, but we're getting along fine."

"Off stage as well as on?" I asked, remembering how madly in love Charlie had appeared to be when I'd last seen the two together.

"Mostly on. I mean, he isn't being vicious or anything in real life either. Just mopey."

"I guess it's difficult to let you go. Which I can understand."

Bailey chuckled. "Really? Seems like I remember you being happy to shove me out the door when I took off on this tour."

"Only because I knew what a fantastic opportunity it was for you," I replied. But there was a kernel of truth in Bailey's humorous statement. Although we loved each other dearly, we often clashed when we spent time living under the same roof. Our personalities were just too different to make a prolonged cohabitation situation work, especially now that Bailey was an adult.

"Yeah, sure, Mom." Bailey cleared her throat. "Oh, by the way, I got my own shock the other day. Dad called."

"Really?" I slumped back again the sofa cushions. "What did he want this time?"

"Tickets, of course. We're heading to Columbus next week, and I guess he must've seen the ads on TV or something."

I worked my jaw to unclench it. "So, looking for free passes? Sounds about right."

"Yeah, and I almost gave them to him too. Mainly because he said he really wanted to see me after the show. Talked about taking me out for drinks . . ."

"Yikes," I said, curling my legs up on the sofa. "That could turn into a disaster. I know he left when you were an infant, but I've warned you about his problems with alcohol."

"I know." Bailey's sigh resonated over the phone. "But I thought I could just see him for an hour and then make a quick exit, claiming exhaustion."

"Which would probably be the truth, after your performance."

"Exactly. So anyway, he did seem sincere about wanting to see me . . ." Bailey's voice trailed off and there was a noticeable pause before she spoke again. "Which made me consider meeting up with him. Until he mentioned who he was bringing along, that is."

"Not that girl who's younger than you are?" I asked, genuinely surprised. Bailey had told me about seeing some photos of a twenty-something hanging all over my ex-husband Gary on his Facebook page. We'd both figured it was one of his short-term flings, but that was over a year ago. Which meant that this girl—whose name was Kendra or Kendell or something—had stuck around. *Better her than me, but I do wonder if she's alright,* I thought, images of Gary's drunken tantrums and bouts of vicious verbal abuse rising, unbidden and unwelcome, in my mind.

"That's the one. Dad said they were living together, and when I asked if he and I could meet without her, he got angry and said I had to make a choice—either join him *and* Kendra after the show, or forget the whole thing." Bailey snorted. "I chose the second option."

"I'm sorry it didn't work out," I said. I wasn't actually sorry, but I'd made it a practice to never keep Bailey from seeing Gary. I'd always hoped they could establish some sort of relationship. Despite his many flaws, he was still her father. Even though he'd been absent for most of her life, I knew they'd met a few times in recent years. It made me nervous, but Bailey had assured me that he'd never been abusive toward her. Still . . . "Did you end up sending him the tickets?"

"Hell no. He can buy them, just like everyone else." Bailey cleared her throat. "Anyway, enough about Dad. That wasn't the main reason I called anyway. I actually wanted to share a little info I picked up from one of my castmates. It concerns your murder, or at least the victim."

I sat up straighter. "Really? What's that?"

"Something to do with Ashley Allen's time at college. I was listening to some media coverage about the murder, and when I heard where Ashley went to school, I asked my understudy if she knew her, 'cause they went to the same university."

"And did she?" I asked, thinking it unlikely since Ashley's college had over twenty thousand students.

"Not personally. But Damaris, my understudy, had a lot to say about the sorority the Allen girl was in. While Damaris was a sophomore, there was a huge scandal that everyone on campus talked about."

"Chi Omega Delta. Ashley Allen was the president," I said.

"Yep, that's the one. Anyway, one of the pledges was badly injured in a horrible hazing incident and another freshman was blamed." Bailey exhaled an audible breath. "It was pretty awful, from what Damaris said. The injured girl was forced to complete a dare—go out on a balcony at the sorority house and balance on a ledge or something like that. The girl was supposedly terrified of heights, according to some other students, so it was a really cruel prank from the start. But she felt she had to do it, or she'd be dropped as a pledge."

"I'm confused," I said. "Weren't they both pledges? Why was the one girl blamed?"

"It was some sort of buddy challenge thing. The pledges were paired up and then each one was supposed to demand a particular action from the other. According to Damaris, most of the girls simply had their partner do slightly humiliating things, like karaoke, or running through the student commons in a bikini. But this girl challenged her partner with a task that was inherently dangerous."

"Did your friend mention the name of the students involved?"

"She didn't know," Bailey replied. "Apparently both girls were seventeen when the incident happened, so the media didn't disclose their names."

"Ah, I see. They were still minors, according to the law." I leaned back and stared up at the ceiling fan. "What about Ashley? Her name must've been released."

"Yeah, she was a senior, so older than the other two. And as the president of the sorority, she made some public statements. Mostly calling the incident a tragic accident. She actually defended the girl who was to blame, claiming that no harm was intended and it was simply a foolish mistake. But the girl was kicked out of the university anyway."

"Wait—she was expelled from college?" My mind raced, processing this news. Was this another possible suspect? I shook my head. No, it wasn't logical. If Ashley Allen had defended the perpetrator, probably in defiance of public opinion, surely the girl would've been grateful, not angry.

"That's what Damaris told me. It was big news on campus. The incident apparently created a protest movement that challenged the legitimacy of the Greek system at the university. The movement eventually blew over, but not before the frats and sororities were forced to make certain changes, especially when it came to pledges and that sort of thing."

"What happened to the student who was injured? She recovered, I hope."

"Mostly. But the girl was an athlete and the fall messed her up to the point where she could never become a professional in her field. She walked again, but she couldn't go back to her sport."

"That is tragic." I'd heard a tremor in Bailey's voice, which didn't surprise me. I knew how deeply she'd empathize with anyone who lost the ability to participate in an activity they loved.

"Yeah. I can't really blame the university for kicking that idiot out. I mean, use some common sense," Bailey said, her tone darkening. "But enough about murder and mayhem. I want to hear more about your new apartment and that interesting-sounding landlord. He's single and your age, right?"

"And has a girlfriend," I said firmly. "Who I happen to like very much."

Bailey sighed. "Alright, Mom, I get it. You aren't interested in romance."

"Not for me, anyway." I lightened my tone. "Now, tell me the latest tales from the stage. Any disasters with props or flying scenery?"

This was the cue for Bailey to launch into a humorous monologue detailing the many mishaps that had happened during performances over the past week. It offered a welcome laugh, and was the perfect way to stop my daughter from asking questions about my personal life.

Chapter
Thirty-Eight

I hoped to find Cam in his office on Monday morning so I could share Bailey's information about the scandal involving Ashley's sorority, but he wasn't in when I stopped by.

Deciding to try to catch him later, I got to work in the library, cataloging more of the Rinehart materials. By midmorning, I was ready for a break and decided, since the weather was good, to take a short walk in the gardens.

It was a gorgeous October day, brisk but not cold. Bright sunshine illuminated the already bare branches of a cluster of ornamental cherry trees. They gleamed like iron filigree against the clear blue sky, while the leaves on the maples that lined one edge of the formal garden fluttered like crimson butterflies.

I thrust my hands into the pockets of my light wool jacket and strode down the path toward the stepped fountain and timber-roofed pavilion. Lauren had assured me that the fountain, and the koi pond it spilled into, were kept heated in the cooler months. Just enough to allow the water to flow, but not so hot that it would adversely affect the fish, who preferred tepid water temperatures.

"Of course, Cam has someone come in to take care of all that," Lauren had told me with a little smile.

I'd smiled too, thinking of Cameron Clewe messing around with a koi pond.

With the temperate weather, the fish were active, swishing their tail fins as they circled the pond. The koi ranged in color from platinum to black, many featuring splotches of russet red or orange. When they noticed my shadow fall over the water, they swam closer, popping their heads up to the surface with their mouths rhythmically opening and closing.

"Sorry, no fish kibble today," I told them, pulling my hands out of my pockets to display my empty palms. Strolling toward the pavilion, I caught the sound of voices.

I bounded up the steps beside the fountain. The voices were coming from the wilder garden behind the pavilion. I was curious to see who it was. Of course, it could simply be a landscaping crew, but one of the louder voices sounded familiar.

It can't be, though, I thought as I crossed to the back edge of the pavilion. *What would Tristan Blair be doing here?*

Gazing out over the back garden, I noticed an evergreen shrub swaying slightly before Tristan burst around the corner of a winding path.

"Call the police if you want," he said. "Have them lock me up for a few pieces of clutter you'll never miss in this gigantic museum of a house."

Cam walked out into the clearing, his posture ramrod straight. His face was an expressionless mask, but his freckles blazed almost as bright as the crimson maple leaves. Dia appeared right behind him, her hands clutched at her waist and her lips visibly trembling.

"As I said, I haven't decided about that yet." Cam's tone was edged with ice.

Thinking I'd better reveal my presence, I coughed. "Sorry," I said, when three pairs of eyes swiveled in my direction. "I was just taking a little break. I don't mean to intrude."

"It's fine. In fact, come down here," Cam said, motioning toward the steps leading off the back of the pavilion. "I could use a witness."

Hurrying down the stairs, I wondered if Cam had somehow found conclusive evidence that Tristan was Ashley's killer. *But no*, I thought. *That can't be right. Tristan mentioned something about items from the mansion. And in any case, what would Dia have to do with anything?*

I approached the three of them, who'd formed a tense tableau, with Cam facing off against Tristan and Dia. "What's going on?"

Cam cast me a look that combined exhaustion with exasperation. "Apparently, my housekeeper has been aiding and abetting a petty thief," he said.

At these words, Dia burst into tears.

"What? Why?" I asked.

"She was simply helping me out 'cause I was in a bad spot." Tristan yanked a clip from his hair, allowing his glossy dark locks to fall to his shoulders. "That's what family does, ya know."

"Family?" My gaze shifted from Dia to Tristan and back again.

"Dia and Tristan are sister and brother. It wasn't obvious because Dia uses her ex-husband's surname, and they don't look alike," Cam said. "I didn't guess it either. It took a little investigating to turn up that interesting fact."

Dia, who was still weeping, didn't respond, but Tristan cast me a laconic smile. "Funny, huh? Yeah, Dia's my big sister. Twelve years older than me, so she was really more like a second mom. Always looking out for her baby bro, too, weren't you, sis?"

Cam tapped his foot against the gravel path three times before speaking again. "I don't know if I'd call enabling your thievery a caring gesture."

"He could've been killed," Dia sputtered. She yanked a tissue from her pocket and wiped her eyes. "He owed money to the wrong people . . ."

"Again, not my problem." Cam's shoulders were so tense that they twitched.

I widened my eyes and met Tristan's sardonic smile. "You mean, like loan sharks?"

"Yeah, a pretty nasty bunch. I shouldn't have gone to them for cash, but I had creditors itching to repossess some of my musical equipment, so what could I do?" Tristan shrugged. "Couldn't depend on Ashley anymore, and Dia here—the only member of my family who still talks to me—well, she isn't that flush with cash herself."

"So she decided to provide you with access to some bits and pieces from Aircroft instead," Cam said. "Stuff you could easily pawn."

"Maybe." Tristan glanced over at his sister. "She let me in the house from time to time, when most of the staff were out or otherwise occupied, or you were holed up in your office," he added, with a tip of his head toward Cam.

"Or when there was a big party going on?" I asked. "You didn't gain entry to the gala because a musician friend invited you to join them backstage. Your sister let you in."

"How was I to know someone would get murdered?" Dia's words ended in a wail. "I had to cover for him after that. I knew he'd dated that Ashley Allen woman. I was afraid he'd be singled out as a suspect."

"Which is why you told me you knew nothing about a young man in black crashing the gala," I said, sharing a look with Cam. "Did you turn off the alarm system as well?"

Dia bobbed her head and dabbed the tissue under her nose. "I'm so sorry," she said, looking at Cam. "I assume you activated the alarms Sunday after the guests left, like you said, 'cause they were on when I checked early the next morning. I turned them off then, but I always do that."

"But you told the police that the system was off when you first checked it Monday morning," I said. "And that was a lie."

"It was, it was." Dia's nervous fingers ripped the tissue into pieces. "I know I shouldn't have done that, but I was afraid that somehow the alarms being on would point the finger at me being involved."

"Because you have the access codes," I said thoughtfully. "But so do Mateo and Lauren. And Cam, of course."

"Yes, but when I heard about the murder, all I was thinking about was my brother." Dia shot Tristan a worried look. "I knew he'd been in the house during the party and just hoped if the police thought the alarm system was off the whole night, they might cast a wider net."

"You hoped they'd wonder if someone from the outside had slipped in and killed Ashley after the gala?" Cam asked, shaking his head. "Your reasoning was flawed, Dia. There were so many people at Aircroft for the party, any one of whom could've been the killer. It would've been easy enough for them to leave with the rest of the crowd, before the alarm system was activated. All you did was contradict my statement, which cast suspicion on me."

"I really am sorry for that," Dia said, a little sob punctuating her words. "But the truth is, I never actually saw Tristan leave."

Her brother spun around to face her. "What? Did you think I killed Ashley?"

"I wasn't sure," Dia said, her voice as thin as rice paper. "I figured if they thought the alarms were turned off, the police wouldn't be as likely to focus on people who had the access codes, like me. I was afraid if they looked closer at me, it might lead them to you. 'Cause I wasn't sure I could hold out during a tough interrogation, Tris."

Tristan exhaled a gusty sigh. "Oh, Dia, you idiot. You probably just made things worse."

"Undoubtedly. But as long as Dia confesses her lie to the police, I think the problem will be solved." Cam clasped his hands behind his back and looked Dia up and down. "You don't have to mention anything about your brother. Just tell them that in the flurry following the murder you confused the days. Admit the alarm system was activated that Sunday evening, as I claimed in my statements. That will be sufficient."

"Wait." I turned to Cam. "You aren't reporting the thefts to the police?"

"No." Cam met my confused gaze with a lift of his eyebrows. "To be honest, I don't want the hassle. The murder is investigation enough. The last thing I need is more detectives prowling around Aircroft."

"Wow, man, that's decent of you," Tristan said, his dark eyes brightening.

"I'm not doing it for your sake." Cam's cold tone wiped the grin from Tristan's face. "After my assessment of the items missing, reporting the thefts just isn't worth the aggravation it would cause *me*. However, if you ever step foot on this property again, I swear I'll bring the full force of the law crashing down on your disreputable head."

Tristan held up his hands, palms out. "No problem. After today, I'm never coming back."

"You'd better not," Cam said, rocking back on his heels. "As for you, Dia, remember our deal."

"What deal?" Tristan shot his sister a sharp glance.

Shaking her head, Dia burst into tears again.

"Alright, both of you—go now. I never want to see either of you ever again," Cam said. "You can help her with her bags, Tristan. She should already be packed."

The expression on Tristan's face grew even more confused.

"I'll explain later," Dia said, before hurrying off in the direction of the house.

After offering Cam a mock salute and me a lopsided smile, Tristan followed her.

Once they disappeared, Cam dropped his arms to his sides and sat on a nearby garden bench. "Stay here," he told me.

I pursed my lips and crossed my arms over my chest.

Looking up at me with a wan smile, he finally added, "Please."

Chapter
Thirty-Nine

"To say I'm confused would be an understatement," I said.

"I suppose that whole encounter was a bit cryptic from your point of view." Cam leaned back against the wooden slats of the bench. "Have a seat and I'll explain."

"Glad to hear any reasons why you'd let Tristan walk," I said, sitting down next to him. "You theorized that Ashley could've been killed during a botched robbery, and not only was Tristan stealing from you, he was also Ashley's ex."

"One of them, anyway." Cam glanced over at me. "Here's the thing—I no longer believe robbery was a motive in Ashley's murder, and I certainly don't think Tristan Blair killed her."

"How can you be so sure?"

"There are certain things that don't add up to him being a killer." Cam swept his hair out of his eyes with one hand. "A thief, yes. Once I discovered the connection between Dia and Tristan through some of my father's old acquaintances, I suspected Tristan was the one involved in pilfering small items from Aircroft. So I set a trap to catch him in the act."

"Using his sister? I assume that's where the deal comes in."

"Right. I confronted Dia and told her that if she would help me expose her brother, I would give her a letter of recommendation for her next job."

"You blackmailed her, you mean."

Cam shrugged. "I suppose. But it was the only leverage I had. I knew she had to go, since I couldn't trust her anymore, but there's a big difference in someone leaving a job 'just because,' especially with a reference in hand, and them being fired."

"You were willing to foist her onto some other unsuspecting household?"

"I think she's been scared straight, as they say." Cam lowered his rose-gold lashes over his eyes. "She knows she could be charged with aiding and abetting, and that her brother could end up in jail. I don't think she'll take any chances."

"Wait a minute." I straightened, shifting my position so I could study his face more easily. "Did you ask if either of them locked me in the attic that day? It would make sense, since Tristan could've had free rein to roam Aircroft and steal more valuable items. Dia would've been aware that you and Lauren were busy outside. She could've easily given Tristan the codes to enter the house once she and Mateo had left for the market."

"I did ask, and Dia denied having anything to do with that incident. I believe, in this case, she was telling the truth."

I slid forward on the bench. "Based on what? There was a car parked outside in the circle when I was locked in the attic. I forgot to mention that."

Cam cast me sharp glance. "Apparently. What type of car was it?"

248

"A cream-colored SUV. Not one of those huge ones, though. A medium-sized vehicle."

Cam didn't immediately respond to this remark. He simply leaped up and began pacing the gravel path in front of the bench. "You're sure it was there when you were locked in the attic?" he finally asked.

"Absolutely. It was definitely there before I wandered into the larger section of the attic, looking for another exit. I didn't actually glance outside to see if it was still there when you arrived to unlock the door. Now I'm wondering if it could've been Tristan's car."

"It could've been, but it wasn't." Cam paused his pacing, tapping the gravel three times again before turning to me. "Which is another reason I'm not concerned about Tristan Blair. He may be a petty thief, but I don't think he's a killer."

"So you aren't going to tell the police anything about these robberies?" I shook my head. "That doesn't seem wise. Surely they should be told. They need to look into Tristan's actions more closely. You may not think he's a murderer, but I'm not convinced."

"Trust me, if I thought he had any involvement in Ashley's death, I wouldn't hesitate to toss him to the wolves." Cam placed his hand on his heart. "I know people think I don't really care that she was murdered, but that isn't true. Even though we'd broken up, we were together for a while. I still want to see her killer brought to justice."

"It's your decision, I suppose. But if the authorities do uncover anything connecting Tristan to the case, and ask me about it, I'm going to tell them the truth. Including spilling the beans about your little deal with Dia."

"Fair enough." Cam wandered over to the back edge of the pavilion and leaned against the brick foundation. "One other thing I will share with you, and the police, is that I now think the library candlestick actually *was* the murder weapon. I wasn't sure at first, but I've changed my mind."

"Any particular reason why?" I asked, rising to my feet and walking over to stand in front of him.

"Several reasons, but I don't have all the facts yet, so I prefer to wait before sharing any of my theories."

"This isn't just some puzzle you're working out in the cozy confines of your sitting room, you know," I said, placing my clenched fists on my hips. "If you truly want Ashley's killer brought to justice, withholding evidence is not the best way to go about it."

"First, you aren't the police," Cam said, his tone much cooler than the fire in his sea-green eyes. "And second, it isn't evidence, simply suppositions. I have ideas, but I need to make sure I'm not accusing anyone unjustly. Having experienced it myself, I'm not in a hurry to inflict that trauma on anyone else."

"I suppose I can't stop you from playing armchair detective," I said.

Cam arched his feathery brows. "Says the pot to the kettle."

I dropped my hands to my sides. "I wouldn't allow a thief to walk free. Especially if there was any possibility he was also a murderer."

"Maybe not, but I think you enjoy amateur sleuthing as much as I do."

Heat rose in my face as I thought about snapping photos of the mystery woman's portraits and my futile attempts to discover who she was. Not to mention reading Patricia Clewe's private letters, which I had not yet returned to the attic. They were still at my apartment, sitting in the sofa table drawer, next to the photos of Aircroft's mystery woman. "Perhaps. But I'm not withholding information in a murder case just so I can be the one to solve it."

Cam stepped away from the wall. Straightening to his full height, he loomed over me. "That isn't my motivation, whatever you may think. I don't want to accuse someone without having all the facts first. But more importantly, there's someone who may or may not be connected to this case who's been dealt a bad enough hand in life already. I refuse to drag their name into the investigation, especially if I'm chasing the wrong suspect."

I stared up into his somber face. The lines bracketing his mouth had deepened and his eyes appeared shadowed by some unspoken unease. "It just seems like you want me to do your legwork, but then aren't inclined to share all your subsequent deductions with me. That is a little off-putting, to say the least."

Cam stared over my shoulder, focusing on something in the distance. "I think I'm entitled to my own secrets."

"Even when they might affect others?" I asked, thinking of the rock being hurled through my car window. *If Cam suspected someone*, I thought, *he should tell me who it is, so I can be wary of that person.*

"Especially then," Cam said, without looking at me.

Chapter Forty

A fter a long pause, during which the wind picked up and scattered some newly dropped leaves over the path, Cam finally said, "I think it's time we both got back to work."

I agreed and left him there, happy to head to the library and the much less volatile portion of my job.

Not that playing Watson to Cam's Sherlock is actually in my job description, I reminded myself as I settled in front of my laptop. But I had to admit we both exhibited the same streak of tenacious curiosity concerning unsolved mysteries. The jury was still out as to whether that was a good thing or not.

I was deep into research, verifying dates and facts related to Rinehart's time reporting at the Belgian Front, when the library door flew open and Kyle Trent stormed into the room.

"Hello," I said, rolling my chair back from the edge of the desk. "If you're looking for Cam, I'm afraid I don't know where he is at the moment."

"I actually want to talk to you," Kyle said, whipping off the wool cap covering his bald head. "Although I'd like to have a few words with Cam later."

"You're in luck then," Cam said from the hallway. "Mateo told me he'd buzzed you through the gates. He said you were here to see Jane and I thought I'd better check on what that was all about."

"I guess talking to you both at once does save some time." Kyle twisted the soft cap between his hands. "And what it's all about is Brendan, and how your nosing about has upset him."

Cam stood in the open doorway with one hand pressed against the doorjamb. "Does Brendan know you're here, playing knight errant?" Cam's voice remained calm, but I noticed him tapping the wooden trim with his forefinger.

One, two, three, I counted. *It's always three.*

"No, he doesn't," Kyle said, shooting Cam a belligerent glance. "He just deals with this sort of thing, even though I know it tears him up inside."

"I'm sorry, what has him so upset?" I asked. "I know I showed up at his studio and one of his colleagues shared a little information about his connection to Ashley Allen . . ."

"Placing him directly in the crosshairs of additional investigation." Kyle pointed a finger at me. "Your visit to the studio apparently convinced Clay Abbott to share more details about Bren's art gallery project with the police. Which made them insistent on questioning Bren again."

"I'm sorry about that. I hoped Clay's information might have the opposite effect. And I certainly didn't accuse Brendan of anything when I spoke to Clay," I said. "To be honest, despite Ashley Allen's reprehensible behavior in terms of the withdrawn offer to fund a gallery, I've never really suspected Brendan of being her killer."

"Nor have I." Cam strolled into the library, crossing to stand in front of one of the bookshelves.

"That may be, but all your digging into his past has dredged up a lot of unpleasant memories," Kyle said, in a slightly molli-fied tone. "Bren went through hell when he was young, simply for being in the wrong place at the wrong time. Sure, he'd fallen in with a bad crowd too, but it all boiled down to youthful mis-takes, born out of his difficult childhood."

"I was told that he'd totally turned his life around since that incident," I said, recalling Vince's words. "And now has an excel-lent reputation in the community."

"Good to know, but a recent reputation doesn't mean much when the police are turning a spotlight on you because you have a record." Kyle's eyes glistened with unshed tears. "Of course, that's only one reason why they've zeroed in on him, but it cer-tainly doesn't help matters. And neither does discovering that people are questioning his colleagues about a failed business deal involving the deceased." Kyle's intense gaze landed on me. "For your information, Brendan shared his relationship with Ashley with the police when they first questioned him, as well as the brief conversation he had with her at the gala, so don't imagine yourself as some genius detective, uncovering damag-ing evidence."

I held up my hands. "I didn't think that, nor did I want to cause any harm."

"At any rate, Jane was working under my orders," Cam said, turning to face Kyle.

"I'm sure she was, which is why I also wanted to talk to you today." Kyle crossed his arms over his chest, the cap dangling from his fingers. "I know you love your puzzles, Cam, but this is messing with someone's life."

"Surely the authorities have realized by now that Brendan had nothing to do with Ashley's murder," I said. This was a bit of fishing. I had no way of knowing if the police were still questioning Brendan or not.

Kyle dropped his arms to his sides. "They have backed off, but who knows. Anyway, even if they leave him alone from now on, the damage is done. This murder investigation has reactivated Bren's PTSD from his youthful dealings with the legal system. You can't really understand something like that unless you've lived it." Kyle shifted his weight from foot to foot. "Or lived with someone who has."

"I'm sorry to hear how badly it's affected him," I said. "I do know how past trauma can affect the present, and I wouldn't wish that on anyone."

From the corner of my eye, I noticed Cam's fingers tighten on the edge of the wooden shelf. "It can be hard to escape," he said.

"It certainly can. Someone who hasn't experienced any real trauma might say 'just move on,' but think about Naomi and Hannah," Kyle said.

I cast Cam a questioning look, but he kept his gaze focused on Kyle. "True enough."

"Well, that's what I came to say. I guess it's all water under the bridge now, but I still wanted you to know how your actions may have driven the police to interrogate Bren a few extra times." Kyle slapped the cap back on his head. "And how that has ratcheted up his anxiety. So maybe lay off the amateur sleuthing in the future.

And if you can't do that"—Kyle tugged down the brim of the cap, shadowing his eyes—"at least keep Brendan out of it."

He turned and stalked out of the library without offering either of us a goodbye.

"It's true that I don't suspect Brendan," I said, after Kyle's footsteps had faded away. "Kyle, on the other hand . . ."

"Has a temper, it's true." Cam walked over to the desk.

I stood to face him. "But I can't quite picture him bashing someone over the head. Too messy. I'd say poison would be his weapon of choice."

"If his actions would only affect him, perhaps," Cam said, tapping the desk twice, and then once more. "But you have to admit he's displayed a fervent desire to protect Brendan. That makes me question whether Kyle would risk any action that might cast suspicion on his partner. Kyle's intelligent enough to know that Brendan would be a person of interest in the death of Ashley Allen, if only due to their failed business venture."

"Good point." I took a deep breath. "Changing the subject and, I suppose, refusing to follow Kyle's advice about our amateur investigation—I should share some news connected to Ashley's time at college." I gestured toward the room's set of armchairs. "Shall we sit?"

Cam nodded and strode over to one of the chairs. "Where did you get this information?"

"From my daughter, of all people," I said, sitting in the chair facing him. "It has to do with Ashley's sorority."

"Chi Omega Delta," Cam said automatically.

I shot him a quizzical look. "You heard that much about Ashley's past, I take it."

"Much to my regret." Cam crossed one leg over the other and leaned back in his chair. "She was obsessed with that sorority. I think she was sorry she had to leave it behind when she graduated."

"Did she ever mention a scandal associated with the sorority?"

Cam tugged the hem of his immaculately tailored chestnut wool slacks down over his thin socks. "No, she never shared anything on that topic."

I stared into his fine-boned face. *He already knows something about this*, I thought, but plowed ahead anyway. "Well, according to Bailey, who heard this from a friend who attended the same university as Ashley, there was a tragic incident involving two freshman pledges to the sorority. Apparently one of them fell from a balcony and was seriously injured, after being dared to walk on a ledge by the other."

"And Ashley was president of the sorority at the time?" Cam asked, his brilliant green eyes narrowing.

"Correct. According to my daughter's friend, Ashley tried to defend the girl who was found to be at fault, saying it was simply bad judgment and a youthful mistake, but the perpetrator of the dare was still kicked out of the sorority, as well as the university."

Cam, resting his elbows on the arms of the chair, entwined his fingers in front of his chest. "I see. Ashley was presented as a sympathetic figure in this story, it seems."

"That's the impression I got from my daughter."

"Interesting." Cam raised his arms, fingers still clasped together, and stretched them over his head. "Please thank Bailey for the information," he said, dropping his arms. "It certainly provides some interesting background on Ashley."

He remembered Bailey's name from just a few mentions. Not sure I like that, I thought as I fixed him with a piercing stare. "But all things considered, it seems this tragedy couldn't have anything to do with Ashley's death. Especially since she wasn't to blame for the incident, and was generous to all involved, the perpetrator as well as the victim."

"It would seem so, wouldn't it?" Cam rose to his feet. "Sorry, but I just realized there's a task I must complete before the day is over. I'll let you get back to work," he added, motioning toward the desk.

"Thanks, I guess," I said as I stood up.

Cam quirked one eyebrow. "I thought you loved your work."

"I do. It's just that it's not always as interesting . . ."

"As playing amateur detective?" Cam flashed a wry smile as he headed for the hall. "I totally understand. My work pales in comparison to that too. Although"—he paused in the doorway and glanced back at me over his shoulder—"I suppose it would be safer if both of us stuck to our day jobs."

"But not nearly as interesting," I replied, earning a thumb's up from Cam before he disappeared.

Chapter
Forty-One

I found it a little harder than usual to climb the steps to my apartment when I arrived home on Monday evening. I chalked this up to the events of the day draining me emotionally, if not physically.

Reaching the landing, I set down my tote bag and fished my keys out of my purse. But I stepped back when my hand touched the door and it swung open. "Vince?" I called out. For a second I thought that he might be fixing something in the apartment, but immediately realized that was impossible. There wasn't a single light on, not even the standing lamp I usually left turned to its lowest setting.

I peered inside but couldn't see anything in the darkness except for shadows and shapes. I squinted. Some of which appeared to be in odd spots.

"Anything wrong, Jane?" a voice called out from below.

I turned to look over the landing railing and noticed Vince pulling a suitcase from the trunk of his car. "I'm not sure. Have you been here today?"

"No, just got back from my weekend trip. Why?"

"My apartment door was open when I arrived a few minutes ago, and I'm sure I locked it when I left this morning," I said.

Vince's eyes widened. "Wait. Don't go inside. Let me drop this suitcase on the porch and make sure my own door's still locked and then I'll come up to check things out."

As I waited for him to join me, I peered into the dimness of my apartment again. There were definitely some things out of place. *A robbery?* I thought, my stomach churning.

"Okay, let's see what's up." Vince reached around the door-jamb to flick on the overhead light fixture. When the space was illuminated, he whistled. "Damn, looks like someone ransacked the place."

"Should we go in?" I asked. "Whoever did this might still be inside."

"Doubtful. They probably scoped out the place ahead of time. Bet they knew your work schedule and were also aware I was out of town." Vince stepped inside the apartment. "But to be on the safe side, let me do a walk through before you enter."

"What? So you can be bashed over the head instead of me? I don't think so," I said, following him.

Since the apartment was so small, it didn't take long to confirm it was empty of any intruders. But whoever had broken in had certainly left a mess. Books and papers were strewn across the floor in the bedroom as well as thrown onto the sofa, some of my clothes were tossed across the bed, and the contents of my pantry had been swept off the shelves. Even my spice rack had been ransacked and the contents of several jars poured into the sink.

But the odd thing was, nothing appeared to be missing.

"It looks like all my jewelry is still here, even the few pieces that were actually gold or silver," I told Vince. "And my electronics. Isn't that the stuff thieves typically grab first?"

"Usually." Vince frowned as his gaze swept over my main living space. "Why would someone go to the trouble to burgle an apartment and take nothing?"

"Maybe they were looking for prescription drugs, which honestly, I don't have." As I turned on the faucet to wash the spilled spices down the drain, the mingled scents of cinnamon, ginger, and turmeric assaulted my nostrils.

"Or maybe they were simply leaving you a message." Vince waved a piece of paper as he walked over to me, his expression uncharacteristically grim.

"What is it?" I took the paper from his outstretched hand.

"A warning, I think. Looks like this wasn't actually a robbery. It was a threat."

The note, which was typed on generic white copy paper, read: *Last chance to stop snooping into matters that are none of your business. Or it might be you who gets turned inside out.* There was no signature.

"Time to call the police," I said.

*   *   *

After the officer took our statements and checked over the apartment, he dropped the note into an evidence bag.

"I don't think it will give us much to go on, but I'll ask our experts to check it out," he said. Urging me to change the lock on my door, which appeared to have been picked rather than forced open, he warned me to take extra precautions and left.

"I'll take care of the lock," Vince said. "I know a guy who does emergency replacements, even after hours. I'll give him a call and have him come over as soon as possible. In the meantime, maybe you'd better come down and stay at my place."

I shook my head. "I've got too much cleaning to do. With the lock being changed this evening and you keeping a lookout, I'm sure I'll be fine. Besides, as you said, it was a warning. If I don't do anything else to tick off the person responsible . . ."

"Who is, don't forget, a murderer." Vince rocked back on his heels and looked me up and down. "Face it, Jane, whoever did this is probably the person who killed Ashley Allen."

"Maybe." I gnawed the inside of my cheek, thinking of Evie and Tristan as well as Kyle and Brendan. "Or someone who's trying to protect the actual killer."

"Either way, they could be dangerous." Concern shadowed Vince's hazel eyes. "I'll make sure the lock is changed. But please give me a call after you get the new key and lock up for the night. I want to check from the outside to make sure it's secured."

"I will, I promise," I told him. "Go back to your house. I'm sure you're tired from your trip and would like to relax for a bit before you deal with the locksmith."

"You don't want me to help you clean up this mess?" Since Vince's tone held more than a tinge of hope, I could tell he'd be happy if I agreed.

"It's really not necessary. You handling the change of the lock will be sufficient," I said, patting his shoulder. "Thanks for coming to my rescue."

A Cryptic Clue

Vince's cheeks reddened. "No problem at all. I'll text you when I have the details from the locksmith," he added, heading for the door. "And I'll sit on the front porch until he arrives."

I thanked him again before he exited the apartment, then turned to survey the damage and determine my plan of attack.

A few hours and a significant amount of scrubbing and tidying later, I finally slumped down onto the sofa, nursing a rather large glass of wine. Turning the television to a program about organic gardening, I allowed my mind to drift back to the note.

It has to be connected to Ashley's murder, doesn't it? But another thought popped into my head—a foolish notion that couldn't possibly be true. There was no way anyone could've known about my discovery of Patricia Clewe's letters, or the photos I'd taken of the portraits of the mystery woman. No one who'd be upset by those actions, anyway. Still . . . I set down my wine glass and leaped to my feet. Circling around to the sofa table, I yanked open the drawer, relieved to find the folder containing the pictures and the packet of letters undisturbed.

I picked up both items and carefully placed them in my tote bag. It was time to share them with Cam. They were mysteries he might know more about. Things that should be discussed before something happened to them.

Or me.

Chapter
Forty-Two

When I spoke with Lauren on Tuesday morning, she informed me that Cam would be busy with conference calls all morning.

"But I can put you on his schedule after lunch," she told me. When I agreed to a two o'clock meeting, she immediately turned away. "Sorry, I can't be late for the first videoconference. I need to take notes." She flashed me a smile and hurried off, her heels tapping against the hardwood floors.

I cataloged all morning, then ate my bagged lunch out in the garden, hoping the lovely surroundings would calm my nerves. After another hour of work, I gathered up my tote bag, and my courage, and headed for the sitting room, where Lauren had scheduled my meeting with Cam.

"You wanted to see me?" he asked when I walked into the room.

I examined him for a moment. He was wearing a tailored charcoal gray suit with a white shirt and a subdued blue-and-gray striped tie. *Probably because of the videoconferences*, I thought as I took a seat in one of the wing-backed armchairs. "Yes. Hopefully this won't take too much time out of your day, but I wanted to share a couple of things I've found—well, stumbled over, really—here in the house." Before setting the tote on the floor beside my chair, I removed the photo folder and packet of letters. I laid the folder in my lap and tucked the letters into the roomy pocket of my cardigan sweater.

"You've been snooping around my home?" Cam, standing near the globe, cast me a sidelong glance.

Since no rancor tainted his tone, I relaxed my grip on the photo folder. "A little. Not on purpose, though. I was looking for other things when I found these items. But I admit to satisfying my curiosity by investigating them a little more thoroughly than I probably should have."

Cam gave the globe a spin. "And these things are what, exactly?"

"A photograph and a drawing, for starters." I held up the folder.

Leaning back against the room's single bookcase, Cam gripped the edge of the lower cabinet with both hands. "Where did you find them?"

"I discovered the snapshot in a shoebox full of photos in the finished portion of the attic, but the drawing was tucked inside one of the sketchbooks in your mother's art studio." I stood and crossed to him, holding out the folder. "I did return the originals. These are copies."

Cam tapped the wood of the cabinet three times before reaching for the folder. He examined the printed pictures, his brows furrowing.

"I thought you might know who she is," I said when Cam snapped the folder shut without volunteering any information.

"I'm afraid not." Cam handed me the folder. "It does appear to be the same woman at different ages, but that's all I can decipher."

"The odd thing is that I found the snapshot of the woman when she was young mixed in with some Airley family photos. Yet there's also the drawing, which must've been done by your mother."

"When the woman was much older," Cam said thoughtfully. "That is strange. I'd say it was one of my mom's relatives, except . . ."

"How would your mother's relative have been connected to the Airleys?" I said, finishing his thought. "That was my question as well."

"Perhaps she was a cousin who visited Aircroft in her later years?" Cam stared up at the coffered ceiling. "My mom could've invited her in and then been struck by the desire to draw her portrait. She does have an arresting face."

"That's possible, I suppose. Although my friend Vince . . ." I paused as Cam lowered his gaze to stare at me. "Actually, he's my landlord, but we've become friends. Anyway, he's a retired newspaperman who's done a great deal of research on the Airley family."

"Vincent Fisher. I know him." Cam's eyes narrowed. "He's asked for access to the photos and documents the Airley family left at the house several times. My father always refused his requests, and I've continued that practice."

"He really means no harm. He's mainly interested in the mystery surrounding Calvin Airley's death. It has nothing to do with your family," I said, pressing the folder to my chest like a shield.

"That may be true, but I don't like reporters rummaging through my home." Cam hooked a thumb through the knot of his tie to loosen it. "But now that the damage is done, what does he have to say about this mystery woman?"

"Nothing," I said. "He doesn't recognize her either and is baffled by why her picture would turn up in a stash of Airley family photos."

"Interesting." Cam slipped the loosened tie over his head and stuffed it in his jacket pocket. "It is a fascinating mystery, and I suppose one you'd like to investigate further?"

"If you don't mind."

Cam shrugged. "That's fine. I'd like to know who she is as well. Obviously, my mom thought she was interesting enough to sketch, which does intrigue me."

I laid the folder on the top of the bookcase cabinet. "There is one other thing."

"And what might that be?" Cam asked, unfastening his collar and top shirt buttons.

"When I was locked in the other day, I decided to search for another exit in the main part of the attic." I slipped the packet of letters from my pocket. "I stumbled over one box and another box spilled and . . . well, these fell out."

Cam stared at the letters, his eyes widening and breath quickening as if I were gripping a cobra. "You read them?"

"Yes. I know I probably shouldn't have, but one letter had fallen from the packet and when I noticed what it was"—I cleared my throat—"I allowed my curiosity to get the better of me, I'm afraid."

Striding past me, Cam stopped to grip the back of one of the armchairs. "So you know."

"As do you," I said, speaking to his rigid back. "I saw your note on the back of one of the letters."

"Of course you did." Cam leaned into the chair, his head lowered. "You seem to have an uncanny ability to ferret out secrets, Jane."

"This was simply a case of dumb luck."

"Or fate." Cam straightened and turned to look at me. "It all made sense, once I discovered those letters. Why my father, who was a good man and always took excellent care of me, still couldn't find it in his heart to love me."

"Did you ever talk to him about it?" I asked, leaning my hip against the bookcase to help support my wobbly legs.

"Unfortunately, no. I didn't find those letters until after he'd passed." Cam's face had paled until his freckles stood out in high relief.

"He never told you the truth?"

Cam shook his head. "I suspect my mother asked him not to. He truly loved her, you know. I could tell, simply by observing the look in his eyes when he spoke her name." His lips tightened. "It wasn't a look I ever recall seeing when he was around me."

"But he left you his entire fortune. He must've cared for you." I realized how feeble my words sounded in the face of Cam's obvious distress, but couldn't think of anything else to say.

"Again, I believe he was doing what my mother would've wanted." Cam stared at some point over my shoulder. "Don't get me wrong, my father was never cruel to me, in either words or actions. And he obviously always provided me with the best of everything—top-notch nannies, an excellent education, and all that."

"But he couldn't give you his love," I said, as Cam finally met my sympathetic gaze.

"No. But to be fair, he wasn't a man who loved easily. He was gregarious and charming and had many friends. But it was all superficial. I believe he was very lonely, underneath all the bluster and banter. I don't think he ever loved anyone, except my mom." Cam's fingers beat a waltz tempo tattoo against his upper thigh. "I never hated him, you know. There wasn't enough of a connection between us to engender a strong emotion like hate."

I swallowed back a comment, not sure I could express my thoughts without also expressing the anger I suddenly felt toward Albert Clewe. My daughter had never really known her father, who'd vanished from our lives after the divorce, so in that way she was a little like Cam. But she certainly hadn't been raised in the lap of luxury. And, as a single mother struggling to work enough hours to support both of us, perhaps I sometimes hadn't been as present as I should have been. But there was one thing I knew that Bailey had always had that Cam had apparently lacked—a parent's unconditional love.

"Did you ever try to locate your biological father?" I asked, when I could finally speak without swearing.

"To no avail." Cam stepped away from the chair, once again turning his back to me. "Despite my access to unlimited financial resources, it seems he is nowhere to be found."

"Your mother did ask him to cease all contact," I said.

"She did, but a father"—Cam's hands, hanging by his sides, clenched into fists—"a real father, would've come back for me. Or at least made some sort of connection, especially after my stepfather died."

"To play devil's advocate, your father could be dead as well," I said gently.

"True. I really have no way of knowing that." Cam released his fingers, flexing them.

Three times, I thought, my chest tightening. "It must be difficult for you, not knowing."

"It is, but I can't complain, can I?" Cam's voice cracked on the last word. "Here I am, a healthy, wealthy, well-educated owner of a magnificent estate and multiple businesses. What do I have to complain about?"

Laying the packet of letters on top of the photo folder, I took a few steps toward him. "Absolutely true. But I've learned something over the years. Something that perhaps you haven't yet realized."

"And what might that be?" Cam asked, in a strained tone.

"That suffering is individual, and not necessarily mitigated by circumstances," I said, moving closer to him. "You see, I've felt the same way as you do. I spent years dismissing my own pain because it really wasn't that bad. Or at least, that's what I told myself. After all, I may have been trapped in a toxic relationship for a while, but I hadn't suffered as much as so many other people. I'd never been hit, much less beaten, so how could I complain? My mental anguish couldn't really compare to what others had gone through." I stepped close enough to lay a hand on Cam's rigid shoulder. "And then I learned that wasn't the point."

While Cam didn't respond, he also didn't shake off my hand.

"The thing is, we have to acknowledge our pain, especially if it has burned a hole through our heart. Even while recognizing that others may have it worse, we must also give ourselves a little grace. If we've truly suffered, that agony is real and not something to gloss over or dismiss. We deserve a little kindness, especially from ourselves." I dropped my hand. "Whatever you may think, what I'm telling you is that you deserve such kindness, Cam. Your suffering is real. Your pain is valid."

Cam said nothing. With his back still to me, he simply reached behind him with his right hand.

I gripped his trembling fingers.

We stood like that, hands tightly clasped, for at least a minute. In the silence, I heard Cam take a deep breath before he released my fingers and strode out of the room.

Chapter
Forty-Three

It wasn't until I got home on Tuesday that I realized I hadn't mentioned my apartment break-in to Cam. But I decided it didn't really matter. The police were on the case—no need to concern my boss with yet another unsolved mystery. Besides, this wasn't really new, groundbreaking information. Cam knew from the car incident that someone was trying to frighten me away from the investigation.

When I stopped by the kitchen on Wednesday morning to grab my usual cup of coffee, Mateo was busy creating a marinade for the salmon he obviously planned to cook for dinner.

"How are you doing?" I asked him, wondering if he was feeling overworked due to Dia's sudden absence.

"I'm fine." Mateo whirred the food processor as I filled my mug. "But I'm glad you stopped by, Jane. I've been wanting to confess something to you." He poured the marinade over a slab of fish in a glass casserole dish. "It has to do with that day that Ms. Wilt almost fell down the stairs."

I stirred some cream into my coffee. "In terms of the reason why you were actually upstairs that day?"

Mateo nodded. "I didn't go up to the second floor to search for a cookbook."

"I'd already guessed that. Especially since the art studio is usually kept locked. It struck me as odd for you to have a key to that room."

"That was a pretty stupid white lie." Mateo stretched a piece of plastic wrap over the casserole dish. "But I had to think of something quick and remembered Cam once mentioning that some cookbooks might've been shelved in the studio."

"Why were you up there, then?" I asked, after taking a sip of my coffee. "And why the need to lie? Surely no one would care if you were strolling through the house. You do live as well as work here."

"Normally, no. But I was actually"—Mateo cleared his throat—"following someone."

I cradled my mug between my hands and considered his words. "Wait—did you already suspect Dia of something?"

Mateo slid the covered casserole into a large refrigerator before turning back to face me. "There were things missing. I didn't typically mess with that stuff, but I knew how many place settings we had of the silver and how much Waterford crystal was kept in storage. When I was preparing for the gala, it seemed like there was less of those things than there should've been. Then I remembered that guy Dia would sometimes allow in the house."

"Her brother, Tristan Blair."

"Right, but I didn't know they were related at the time." Mateo strolled over to the percolator to pour himself a cup of coffee. "Dia claimed he was some sort of repairman, which I thought was strange, since he didn't seem like the type. He did carry a large satchel that he said was for his tools, but . . ."

"He was using it to carry off the items he stole," I said.

"That's my theory." Mateo blew on his coffee. "I was especially suspicious after I caught a glimpse of the same supposed repairman at the gala. I figured there was no way someone was coming to fix something that late. But I was really busy that night, so I didn't raise any alarms about it." Mateo frowned. "Wish I had."

"You followed Dia upstairs that day to see if you could catch her in the act of stealing?" I asked.

"I know that sounds weird, but she'd taken a large canvas tote with her when she went upstairs to clean, along with her regular cleaning caddy. I couldn't help but wonder if she was part of a theft ring, along with the dark-haired guy. But I didn't want to come right out and accuse her." Mateo took a long swallow of his coffee. "I liked Dia. She was easy to work with and never tried to second-guess my menu choices, like some housekeepers do. If she was innocent, I didn't want to cast any suspicion on her."

"You didn't notice her taking anything, I suppose."

"No. And I didn't see the dark-haired guy around after the gala, either. At least, not until this past Monday." Mateo stared at me, his dark eyes radiating curiosity. "That was right before Dia left without a word."

He probably hoped that I'd enlighten him about the reason for Dia's exit, but I wasn't about to satisfy his curiosity. Saying too much might jeopardize the deals Cam had made with Dia and Tristan. "Speaking of Ms. Wilt's almost-accident, did you happen to see anyone near the top of the stairs when she claimed to have been pushed?"

"I did not." Mateo set his coffee cup in the sink and crossed to the island. "Honestly, I believe she simply tripped or slipped. This old house can be drafty, so maybe she felt a breeze and thought someone touched her back." He leaned forward, gazing right into my eyes. "Or perhaps she simply lied because she didn't want anyone to label her as old and feeble. From the little I've seen of her, I've realized she's determined to present herself as strong and capable. Wouldn't even let me help with her bags."

"I remember you mentioning something about that," I said, my thoughts swirling around the idea of Naomi lying about being pushed. It didn't make a lot of sense, but then, Mateo might be right about her being obsessed about her personal dignity.

"Well, I'd better get to work. After grabbing one more for the road," I said, heading to the counter to refill my mug.

"You know I didn't murder Ashley Allen, right?" Mateo asked.

He'd caught me off guard. I spilled a little cream on the counter. "I'm not sure I can know that," I said, as he grabbed a kitchen towel. "You did have a motive."

"The restaurant thing?" Mateo snapped the towel through the air. "Nonsense. Sure, I was furious with Ashley for backing out of our deal. But I have this job now, which includes room and board. It's allowing me to save money pretty quickly. In a few years I can start up my restaurant without a backer, which will be much better in the long run."

I studied his face for a moment. He wasn't blinking excessively or displaying any other tics that could signal deception, but then again, I was no body language expert. "I admit you aren't on the top of my suspect list." I held out my hand for the towel.

"Don't worry about that, I'll clean it up." Mateo draped the towel over his shoulder. "Ashley Allen wasn't my favorite person, that's for sure. But I didn't want her dead."

"Noted," I said, picking up my mug and heading for the door.

"By the way, I'll be off Friday," Mateo called after me. "So you might want to grab a coffee on the way in."

I thanked him and waved my free hand over my head in a casual goodbye. On the off chance that Mateo *was* a killer, it seemed prudent to stay on his good side.

* * *

The rest of the week passed quietly. Not hearing anything from the police concerning my break-in, I decided that the new lock, and a little more vigilance, would have to suffice. At work, both Cam and I were so busy that we didn't even cross paths, although he did send me a text confirming Rena's story about Ashley sharing her inheritance.

One of my father's old acquaintances works for the law firm that handles the Allen family's affairs, he wrote. *They told me Ashley had discussed splitting her grandmother's estate with the rest of the family. It was common knowledge at the firm.*

I tapped a pen against my chin. If Ashley had planned to give her parents and Rena a portion of her inheritance, there was no motive for them to murder her. Or none that made sense, anyway.

A Cryptic Clue

It whittled down the suspect list, although I still had my doubts about Tristan, as well as Kyle Trent. *Or even Brendan, I suppose, although he doesn't seem like the killing type. Then there's still Mateo, despite his disclaimers. And a ballroom full of people,* I reminded myself. *Who knows what other enemies Ashley may have made over the years?*

I no longer suspected Cam but had to admit I wasn't sure whether that was based on logic or my desire to see him cleared.

After lunch on Thursday, Lauren stopped by the library to let me know that she wouldn't be at work the next day. "I'm taking a long weekend," she said, adjusting the hand-painted folk-art brooch she'd pinned to the lapel of her ivory jacket. "My friend who was in the accident has a birthday this weekend, and I want to help her celebrate. But if something comes up, don't hesitate to call me." She offered me a wry smile. "I know Mateo's going to be off too. That will leave you on your own."

"I assume Cam will be here," I said.

Lauren rolled her eyes. "He will, but he can get a little . . . overwhelmed if things go wrong, like the power going out or one of the appliances breaking down or anything similar. So just call me if you need help."

"Will do," I told her, fervently hoping I wouldn't have to do any such thing.

Chapter
Forty-Four

I managed to remember to pick up a large cup of coffee on my way to Aircroft, mainly because I happened to look over at the passenger seat and noticed my insulated lunch bag sitting next to my tote. I'd brought food and drink with me so I wouldn't have to use the kitchen at Aircroft. It made me nervous to use the equipment without Mateo or Lauren present—I had visions of breaking some expensive appliance or misplacing a valuable piece of cutlery.

Once I'd settled in the library and started cataloging, the hours passed swiftly. It was only the sound of footsteps in the hallway that made me glance at the clock and realize it was noon.

"Hello, Jane," Cam said, poking his head around the open door. "Mind if I interrupt you for a minute?"

"Of course not. I was going to take a break anyway." I stood and stretched my arms over my head before shaking out my hands.

"Too much time sitting at the computer," Cam said. "I have that issue as well. Working from home is great, but it's easy to become too sedentary."

"I should force myself to get up more, but I'm often so involved in what I'm doing I forget," I admitted. "How are you today?"

"Good. I've actually come to a realization about Ashley's murder that I wanted to share with you . . ." He paused, his brow furrowing, as more footsteps rang out from the hallway.

"Who could that be?" I asked. "I thought Lauren and Mateo were both out today."

"They are." Cam pressed a finger to his lips. "And I'm not expecting anyone else," he added, sotto voce.

"Ah, there you are." Naomi Wilt strolled into the library, sweeping her long crimson wool cape back over one shoulder. "I told Hannah we'd probably find you here."

Hannah made a less grand entrance. In fact, she appeared to be trailing Naomi with reluctance. Her head was down, and a wide-brimmed felt hat shadowed her face.

Cam backed up until his upper thighs pressed against the desk. "What brings you here today?"

When I circled around the desk to join him, I noticed Cam clutching the edge of the desk as well as the rhythmic tapping of his forefinger against the wooden trim. "Hello," I said to both women. Neither acknowledged me

"I thought we might need to chat about a few things," Naomi said. Under the crimson cloak, she was wearing a black turtleneck and slacks. The combination contrasted vividly with her white hair and pale complexion.

"Gala related," Hannah said, her voice so low it was difficult to understand her. "Financial accounting and such."

"I see." Cam shot me a confusing sidelong glance. It almost looked like a warning. "But I don't remember noticing any appointments on my calendar today."

"We didn't actually make one," Naomi said. "The truth is, I spoke with Lauren earlier this week, mentioning we might stop by sometime over the weekend and she very kindly supplied me with the entry codes to the gates and the house." She lifted one black-gloved hand. "I hope you won't be angry with her about that. She's been allowed to do it before, she said, for your friends."

"Yes, for my friends." Cam released his grip on the desk and straightened to his full height. "Naturally, she had no way of knowing that you two might no longer be listed in that category."

I shot him an astonished look. "What do you mean?"

"Just that Hannah and Naomi may have a more devious agenda than simply discussing financial aspects of the gala. Isn't that right, Hannah?" Cam's freckles blazed against his paper-white face.

"What's Hannah got to do with anything?" I stared at both women. Naomi stood, regal and still as a statue, but Hannah was shuffling one booted foot against the hardwood floor.

"Why don't you tell her?" Cam suggested. "Explain to Jane why you locked her in the attic that day."

I took a step forward, stopping when Cam grabbed my hand. "Excuse me?"

"Hannah drives a cream-colored SUV, don't you, Hannah?" Cam cast me a quick glance. "It was obviously parked outside before she told me she'd arrived to look for her missing scarf. Remember, Jane—you saw it in the driveway right after you were locked in the attic."

"So what?" Hannah whipped off her hat. Crushing it between her hands, she glared at Cam. "That doesn't mean anything. It took a while to search this big old house."

"But you weren't actually looking for a scarf, were you?" Cam squeezed my fingers before releasing my hand. "You were at Aircroft to retrieve something else."

Hannah shoved the hat into the pocket of her beige and brown houndstooth coat. "I have no idea what you're talking about."

"Really? I remember that large canvas tote you were carrying that day. It appeared to be full of bulky objects . . ."

"Books," Hannah said, casting a wild look at Naomi, who simply tightened her ruby-tinted lips.

"Partially, I'm sure. But I think you stuffed something else in there as well. Which was why you reacted so negatively when I offered to carry the bag to your car." Cam's voice was calm, but I observed a nervous tic twitching his left eye.

"I really don't understand why you're pursuing this line of questioning, Cam," Naomi said, with a lift of her chin.

Cam shot her a sharp look. "Don't you? At any rate, the point I'm trying to make is that I know Hannah was actually at Aircroft that day on a special mission. She conveniently chose a day when Dia and Mateo usually went to the market, and she'd discovered, in talking to Lauren about stopping by, that Lauren and I would be out in the gardens. So she just had to make sure that Jane, who, as she'd also found out from Lauren, was working in the attic that day, wouldn't interfere with her quest."

"You locked me in?" I asked, fixing Hannah with an intense stare.

Fiddling with a button on her coat, she nodded. "I knew someone would find you eventually. I didn't mean to hurt you. I just wanted you out of the way."

"But why?" I turned to Cam. "What's this all about?"

"Hannah was looking for an item that had been stashed somewhere at Aircroft after the gala," Cam said. "A candlestick, I believe."

I gasped. "The one taken from the library?"

Cam squared his shoulders. "The murder weapon."

Glancing from Hannah to Cam and back again, I blinked rapidly. "But that means"—I clutched my shoulders with both hands, as if that would offer some protection—"Hannah, please tell me you didn't murder Ashley Allen."

Hannah's anguished expression almost confirmed my suspicion. Until, that is, Naomi slipped her gloved hand out of the pocket of her finely tailored slacks and the overhead light glinted off the metal barrel of a small revolver.

"She didn't," Naomi said, her voice as calm as if she was discussing the weather. "I did."

Chapter
Forty-Five

"Naomi," Hannah wailed. "You promised we were going to play this cool. Simply find out what they know and leave."

"Change of plans." Naomi gestured toward Cam and me with the gun. "Toss your cell phones over here, if you have them on you."

I reached behind me to grab my phone off the desk and threw it across the room.

"I said *to me*, but I suppose that will do." Naomi aimed the revolver at Cam's chest. "Now you, please."

Cam held up his hands. "I left it in the office. Search me if you like."

"I think I'll have Jane do that," Naomi said, her pale eyes narrowing.

Apologizing under my breath, I patted down Cam's trouser pockets. "He's telling the truth. He doesn't have a phone on him."

"Why are you doing this, Naomi?" Hannah's voice trembled like dead leaves in autumn. "There's no coming back from this. Let's just go."

"It wouldn't help. Because our brilliant young friend Cam has already figured it all out, haven't you, Cam?"

"I think so," he replied.

I side-eyed him. "Then please explain, because I'm totally clueless."

Cam stepped back and leaned against the desk again, this time half sitting, with his long legs stretched out for balance. "I'll tell you what I've deduced, and Naomi can correct me if I get any facts wrong."

"I'm sure you won't," Naomi said, sarcasm dripping from her tone. "I should've known you might puzzle it all out, given your fascination with mysteries."

"Actually"—Cam cast me a warm, if slightly tremulous, smile—"I had a good deal of help. From Jane, among others. She provided me with several pieces of the puzzle. I just had to fit them together."

"A match made in heaven," Naomi said, shooting me a snide look.

"Maybe. Anyway, after looking at all the facts, I realized there was only one possible solution to this mystery, and what it actually all came down to was love."

"Now I'm even more confused," I said as a sob erupted from Hannah's throat.

"Naomi's love for her granddaughter," Cam said. "A girl who was blamed for something she was forced to do, and has suffered ever since."

"Her life was destroyed!" As the words burst from Naomi's lips, her carefully maintained composure slipped. Anger transformed her face into a macabre mask.

"I'm not disputing that. What Ashley did was unconsciona-ble." Cam looked over at me. "This involves that hazing incident at Chi Omega Delta that your daughter told you about."

"It was your granddaughter who was injured?" I asked Naomi, sympathy tinging my tone.

"No. She was the one blamed," Cam said, before Naomi could answer. "The girl who was tossed out of the sorority and the university because she supposedly forced another pledge to undertake a dangerous stunt."

"Oh." My mind raced as I assembled these new facts into a coherent picture. "Ashley Allen was the president of the sorority at the time."

"And seemed to defend Naomi's granddaughter, whose name is Selena Wilt, by the way. Of course, that was in public. I sus-pect things were different behind the scenes." Cam gripped the edge of the desk until his knuckles blanched. "Ashley was the one who set up that dare, wasn't she? And pushed Selena to egg the other girl on. Then she disavowed all knowledge of the incident after the fact."

"Ashley Allen ordered my granddaughter to challenge the other pledge to walk on that ledge. She told Selena she'd never be accepted into the sorority unless she complied." Naomi's shoulders twitched but the hand holding the revolver remained rock steady. "Then, after the accident, Ashley refused to take any responsibility."

"She lied." The words burst from Hannah's trembling lips. "She told Selena—my goddaughter, who I've always loved dearly—that no one would accept the real story. She was Ashley Allen, presi-dent of the sorority and member of a wealthy and powerful family. Who'd believe little nobody Selena Wilt over her?"

"But what about the girl who was injured?" I asked. "Surely she could've told everyone the truth."

Hannah lowered her gaze. "She didn't know. Ashley convinced her that Selena was behind the dare, so once again it was Selena's word against Ashley's. The injured girl even considered bringing a civil suit against Selena, but she called it off when Selena had a bad breakdown and ended up in the hospital."

"She was a decent sort, really," Naomi said. "I've just always wished she could've known the truth—that it was Ashley who was really to blame, not my Selena."

"So Ashley supporting Selena in public was simply a way to protect herself?" I shook my head. "I can understand your anger over that."

"You don't understand anything." Naomi practically spat out the words. "Selena was never the same after that accident. She'd always struggled with depression, but had been able to manage it with therapy. By the time she went to college, her parents and I felt that she had finally conquered the darkness. I know she was so thrilled to be doing well at the university and seemed so happy. Getting into a popular sorority was the cherry on top. But then everything fell apart."

"Because of Ashley Allen," I said, recognizing the depth of Naomi's hatred. *I might have felt the same*, I thought, *if someone had done such a thing to Bailey.*

"Once she had to leave the university, Selena fell into a terrible depression." Hannah cast a concerned glance at her friend. "She saw therapists and was taking medication, but nothing seemed to help."

"She felt guilt." Naomi drew in a deep breath. "Deep, debilitating guilt over what had happened to the girl who fell off the balcony. That guilt compounded her chronic mental health problems."

"Which caused her to spiral into psychosis," Cam said. "I found out where she is now."

"The psychiatric hospital?" Naomi's light blue eyes glittered like fractured ice. "As I said, her life has been ruined. And Ashley Allen was to blame."

"It might not be forever," I said, earning a warning glance from Cam. "People do recover, you know."

Naomi gripped the revolver with both hands and pointed it directly at me. "Perhaps. But why should Selena suffer at all? She really did nothing wrong, yet she bore the brunt of another person's bad decisions. Do you think that was fair?"

"No, not at all. But killing someone . . . ," I said, before Cam pressed his foot over my instep.

"It was wrong of Ashley to force Selena to carry out that dare, and then basically blackmail her into staying silent about the truth," he said. "But why not simply take her to court? A civil case might have garnered Selena some monetary compensation, at least."

Naomi audibly sniffed. "Money? Is that all you can think of? I suppose that makes sense. It's all you have, isn't it, Cam? Wealth and property. But alas, no real family, or any close loved ones. Because if you did, you'd understand why monetary compensation never entered my mind."

I slid close enough to Cam that our arms brushed. "That's hardly fair. I'm sure Cam can comprehend why you'd hate

Ashley. But I don't think either of us can quite understand why you'd want to kill her."

Footsteps tapping the hall floorboards caused both Hannah and Naomi to spin around. I shared a look with Cam. "If both of us tackle her . . . ," I murmured.

He straightened, stepping away from the desk. But we paused our forward movement when another woman burst through the doorway.

It was Evie Grayson, breathing heavily.

"Thank heavens I arrived in time," she said.

Chapter
Forty-Six

"What are you doing here?" Naomi asked in an icy tone. Evie, jerking her head back when she noticed the gun, took a deep breath. "Hannah sent me a text. She said you were going to Aircroft to find out what Mr. Clewe might know." She turned her wide-eyed gaze on Cam. "Too much, I guess."

"I'm afraid so," Naomi said. "Toss your cell phone over here, Evie, that's a good girl."

Evie complied, but her expression told me she was not on board with whatever Naomi had in mind. "This is craziness, Ms. Wilt. How is any of this helping Selena?"

"It's justice," Naomi replied.

"But Mr. Clewe and Ms. Hunter had nothing to do with what happened to Selena." Evie planted her feet in a fighter's stance. "They're totally innocent."

"They know too much," Naomi said grimly.

Hannah choked back another sob.

"You were Selena's friend, not Ashley's." Cam caught Evie's concerned gaze and held it. "I discovered a connection between you two through some old online posts."

"I met Selena in kindergarten," Evie used both hands to shove her thick hair away from her face. "We were best friends through high school, and stayed in touch later, although we didn't see each other as often."

"You got close to Ashley to help Selena," I said.

Evie bobbed her head. "That's right. I wanted to see if I could get her to confess what she'd done to Selena."

"And did she?" I asked, while Naomi motioned for Evie to join Cam and me at the desk.

"No, I'm afraid not." Evie, standing next to me, shifted her gaze to Naomi. "I was the one who found out the truth in the first place. I was visiting Selena in the psychiatric hospital when she broke down and shared the entire story—how Ashley had forced her to push the other pledge to walk the balcony ledge, and how, after the accident, Ashley had convinced her to remain silent." Evie shook her head. "Selena was so riddled with guilt, she couldn't think straight. She honestly believed that changing her story from what she'd originally told the police would land her in jail."

"That's what Ashley told her, to manipulate her," Naomi said.

"Yes, it is. But it was Selena's own delusions that allowed Ashley's words to take root in her brain. Her own fears are what forced her to remain silent." Evie's lips quivered. "Right after she finally told me the real story, I ran into Ms. Wilt, who I knew from when Selena and I were kids."

"And you told her everything," Cam said.

Evie sighed. "I'm sorry for that now, but at the time I thought she had a right to know."

"Which I did." Naomi rolled her shoulders without lowering the gun.

"I just didn't realize how far she'd take things," Evie said, casting me an apologetic look.

"The scene in the park, that was all a ruse," I said. "No one tried to attack you."

Evie lowered her dark lashes over her eyes. "It was Ms. Wilt's idea. She wanted to set up scenarios that would cast doubt on various people who'd attended the gala, as well as possibly strangers."

"Just like your almost-fall on the stairs," Cam said, addressing Naomi. "That was staged too, I assume."

"Of course." There was more than a trace of smugness in Naomi's expression. "I knew about Brendan and Mateo's past issues with Ashley, and of course there were your recent arguments and break-up, Cam. Since so many possible killers were all serendipitously in the house at the time, I thought it was a good chance to cast a net of suspicion over you all."

"Very clever," Cam said, his tone dry as burnt toast.

I reached out and found Evie's hand. Clasping her trembling fingers, I said, "You enlisted Hannah and Evie's assistance because you knew how much they loved Selena, and you hoped they'd be willing to aid in covering up your crime."

"Which they were." Naomi shot a swift glance at a weeping Hannah before fixing her gaze on Evie. "I sent Hannah to retrieve the candlestick, which I'd hidden after killing Ashley, and convinced Evie to help me scare you off."

"By hurling a rock through my car window?" When she tried to pull away, I tightened my grip on Evie's fingers. "Who trashed my apartment?"

"That was me," Naomi said. "No one paid any attention to an old woman fiddling around with a door lock or going in and out of an apartment. It wasn't like I was someone suspicious, like that Tristan Blair character."

Evie yanked her hand free. "Tristan isn't a thief!"

"I'm afraid he actually is," Cam said, casting Evie a sympathetic glance. "But he isn't a killer."

"Ashley treated him like crap, just like she did Selena." Evie's tone may have been belligerent, but her slumped shoulders and downcast eyes told me she knew Tristan had brought some of his troubles on himself.

"No doubt." Cam took a step forward, causing Naomi to point the gun directly at his chest. "What I want to know is, did you plan it? Did you go to the gala intending to kill Ashley?"

Naomi grimaced. "No, of course not. I knew she'd be there, and did hope to confront her. When I realized that you two had argued, I decided to take advantage of that fact. I assumed she might want to patch things up, considering your finer qualities"—Naomi's sarcastic grin displayed her small white teeth—"such as your good looks and wealth. So I sent a message through a waiter, saying that you wanted to meet with her in the library. She fell for that like the flighty little fool she was."

"Naomi only meant to talk to her," Hannah said. She blew her nose into the wad of tissues she'd pulled from her coat pocket. "She just wanted Ashley to confess the truth. And agree to go public and clear Selena's name."

"Which, naturally, she refused to do," Cam said.

Anger flared in Naomi's eyes. "She laughed at me. Stood there, in her skimpy silver dress and tossed that ridiculous mane of hair of hers and laughed, while my darling Selena was fading away in an asylum. Sweet Selena, who was willing to take all the blame for something Ashley Allen coerced her to do." Naomi lowered the hand holding the revolver. "When I heard that laughter, I felt something wash over me, red-hot as lava. Without thinking, I reached for the first thing that came to hand and smashed it down over her stupid, narcissistic head."

"The candlestick," Hannah said, her lashes fluttering. "It was a lot heavier than Naomi thought. She didn't mean to kill anyone."

Naomi absently patted her friend's shoulder with her free hand. "Oh tosh, Hannah, stop trying to protect me. No, I didn't plan to kill her. And I know her death doesn't really help Selena. But confronted by that harpy's total indifference and that laugh . . . Well, I just snapped." Naomi's bright eyes grew clouded. "I knew, in the instant I struck the first blow, that I'd destroyed any chance of clearing Selena's name. That fed my anger, making me lose all sense, and I hit Ashley again. In that moment I no longer cared about anything except revenge. All I wanted was for Ashley to feel pain, like my granddaughter had. So when Ashley crumpled to the floor and I saw all the blood pooling around her head, I was happy. Happier than I'd been in several years. I may not have planned to kill her, but once it was done, I felt no guilt. I still don't," she added, her expression daring the rest of us to challenge this assertion.

"You must've gotten blood on your clothes," Cam said quietly.

"That was the advantage of staying at Aircroft. I could hurry up the back stairs and get to my room before anyone saw me. Carrying the candlestick with me, of course." Naomi turned her head toward Hannah. "Hannah noticed the condition of my clothes and my odd demeanor as soon as she came upstairs looking for me. She was shocked, but immediately agreed to support whatever tale I was planning to tell the police."

"It's not like I'm okay with murder," Hannah said, with a sniffle. "But it was an accident, you know?"

I met her pleading gaze with a shake of my head. "I'm not so sure about that. But I suppose I can understand protecting your friend, especially since you love Selena as well. I think maybe, deep down, you too may have seen it as justice?"

Hannah didn't reply but I could read the acceptance of this judgment in her eyes.

"Now what?" Cam asked. "You're facing a roomful of people who know the truth, Naomi. Do you think you can somehow talk all of us into staying quiet?" He took a few steps forward, until he was only a few paces away from Naomi. "Or are you planning to silence us all?"

A little squeak escaped Hannah's lips. "No more killing," she whimpered. "No more."

Naomi raised the revolver. "Maybe just one more."

Chapter
Forty-Seven

A cting on instinct, I dashed forward, but Cam threw out his arm to keep me from stepping in front of him.

"Don't worry, Jane. I know things have gone too far. There is no way for me to move beyond this now." Naomi pulled her arm back, twisting her hand until the barrel of the revolver was pressed to her breast. "I can only go away."

Hannah shrieked and Evie shouted "No!" while Cam simply held out his hand.

"There's no need for that," he said. "Give me the gun, Naomi."

She pursed her perfectly tinted lips. "And go to jail for the rest of my life? No thank you."

"If you confess that you only hit Ashley because you snapped during a heated argument, it won't be seen as premeditated murder," Cam said. "It would be second degree at worst."

"And I can back you up." Both Hannah's hands and voice were shaking. "We talked right after it happened and I can testify to your state of mind and validate the fact that you didn't attend the gala with the intent to harm anyone."

"But you see, that's the problem. I would rather not involve you or Evie in any of the legalities," Naomi said.

Evie moved to stand beside me. "It's okay. I'm willing to admit my part in the cover-up and subsequent deception, and the threats against Ms. Hunter. If that means jail time, I'll take my punishment."

"Me too," Hannah said, before blowing her nose again.

"But I'd rather you not go down with me." Naomi glanced over at Hannah. "Especially not you, my dear friend. I know you protected me out of love—for me as well as Selena. If I remove myself from the equation and everyone here agrees to tell the authorities that I acted alone"—she swept a commanding gaze over the rest of us—"then you two can walk free."

"What about Selena?" Evie asked, in a remarkably calm tone. "Think about how your suicide will affect her. She's bound to realize you attacked Ashley because of what Ashley did to her, and then if you kill yourself . . . Well, she'll just feel more guilt than she already does."

This statement appeared to penetrate Naomi's stoic armor. "Then you must make her understand it wasn't her fault," she told Evie.

"How am I supposed to do that?" Evie cast a swift glance at the door.

Is she waiting for someone? I wondered. *Did she tell Tristan to join her here, as backup?*

"You'll think of something," Naomi said, positioning the gun so it pointed directly over her heart.

"Naomi, listen to me." Keeping his hands hanging loosely at his sides, Cam took a step closer. "There's no need to take such drastic action. I know you feel that everything has been shattered, and there's no hope in your future. But it isn't true."

Naomi focused on Cam, her pale eyes glittering like diamonds. "What would you know about despair? You've always had everything so easy. Yes, I know your mother died when you were just a toddler, but then you had nannies and tutors fawning over you. You were given a superior education, and your place among the elite was always guaranteed. This estate and basically the whole world was handed to you on a silver platter. What do you know of hardships or suffering?"

Cam's entire body stiffened, but to my surprise when he spoke again his voice was cool and calm. "A great deal more than you think. Yes, I have money and property. And I've been told I'm not bad to look at. Not to mention I've always enjoyed good health. But there are things you don't know. Things that almost no one knows." He sent me a sidelong glance. "Jane has learned some of it, so she can verify the truth."

"The truth of what?" Naomi asked.

"My own struggles. How I've had to deal with darkness, and even despair, just like you granddaughter. Just like you, Naomi."

"You've never felt anything like the betrayal and anger I've experienced," Naomi said, her tone barbed as a serrated knife.

Cam shook his head. "I have, I just never let anyone know it. You see, despite what the world thinks, Albert Clewe was not my biological father."

Hannah squeaked as Naomi's finger slid off the trigger of the revolver.

"I didn't learn this fact until after he died." Cam's fingers drummed against his thigh. "He never told me the truth. Which was, I think you'll agree, a fairly massive betrayal. It did explain a lot, though. Like why he never loved me. Oh, he made sure I always had everything I needed. Every *thing*," he repeated, staring directly into Naomi's eyes. "There were plenty of *things*. Just no real affection, much less love."

"I had no idea," Hannah murmured.

"No one did," Cam said, offering her a quick glance before focusing back on Naomi. "My stepfather made sure of that. And then, of course, there's my biological dad, whose name I don't know. The truth is, I don't even know if he is dead or alive. I've tried to find him, but so far it seems he vanished off the face of the earth as soon as my mother died."

Looking over at Cam, I realized from his clenched jaw that he was battling a tidal wave of emotion.

"You think this sad tale will sway me?" Naomi asked. "It is unfortunate, but all Albert's subterfuge hardly rises to the level of betrayal that Selena, and by proxy I, experienced."

"Again, you're mistaken." Cam moved one more step closer to Naomi. "What if I told you that just yesterday I discovered proof that my stepfather told my biological dad that I had died not long after my mom? Would that satisfy your criteria? Would it be betrayal enough?"

Clenching my fists, I swallowed back a swear word. As much as Cam had shared with me, he'd still held something back. *The final plunge of the knife.*

Naomi wavered slightly. As her knees appeared to buckle, Cam rushed to her. "We all experience pain and suffering," he said, laying his fingers over the hand that gripped the gun. "A rather wise person brought that to my attention recently."

A Cryptic Clue

Evie and I hurried forward, flanking Naomi and holding her up by slipping our hands under her armpits as Cam gently removed the revolver from her fingers.

Sirens wailed. I looked to Evie from behind Naomi's slumped shoulders. "The police?"

Evie nodded. "I called them right before I entered the house. I was worried something bad might happen." She glanced over at Hannah. "Leave now if you want to avoid arrest."

"I'm not going anywhere. We walked into this together, we'll face the consequences together." Hannah strode forward and tapped my shoulder. "I'll take over here. You'd better go and see to Cam."

As she replaced my support of Naomi, I glanced at the desk, where Cam had retreated with the gun. He deposited the revolver on the desktop before collapsing into the chair.

Thundering footsteps echoed down the hall. *The cavalry has arrived*, I thought as the police burst onto the scene.

Chapter
Forty-Eight

After Naomi, Hannah, and Evie were escorted off the premises by the police, Cam and I were questioned, separated so we could recount the incident from our own points of view. I ended up in the music room while Cam was interviewed somewhere else, leaving the library swarmed by detectives again.

The police talked to me for some time. Before they eventually left, they obtained my assurance that I wouldn't leave the area for at least a week. Having been through this scenario after discovering Ashley's body, I'd expected that requirement. They'd undoubtedly want to call me in for more questioning. Not a pleasant prospect, but necessary.

Once I was alone, I went in search of Cam, finally discovering him in the sitting room. He was hunched over in one of the armchairs, staring at his recovered cell phone. I paused in the doorway. He swore as his fingers scrabbled over the phone.

"Need help?" I asked, strolling into the room.

Cam dropped the phone into his lap and looked up at me. "I was trying to send a text to Lauren, letting her know what happened before she sees it on the news." He held up his hands, which were visibly shaking. "But it seems my fingers aren't working right now."

Judiciously deciding not to make any comment about his concern for Lauren's feelings—a level of social awareness I was frankly surprised to see him demonstrate—I pulled out my own phone. "I can send her a message if you like."

"Thanks, that would be helpful." After a couple of fumbling attempts, Cam managed to shove his phone into one pocket of his beige wool slacks.

"You were very calm before," I said as I typed a brief text and sent it to Lauren. "And very brave."

Cam swept back the auburn hair that had tumbled over his brow. "Not really. I went into some sort of fugue state, I think. I do that sometimes, when events become overwhelming."

"It worked, all the same. Telling that story about your past seemed to make Naomi think twice about pulling the trigger." I sat down in the facing armchair. "I was actually shocked to hear you confess the truth. I know how careful you've been to keep it under wraps."

"It seemed like the best way to try to relate to Naomi." Cam leaned his head against the tall back of the chair. "I'm not an expert at determining such things, but I knew she'd be interested in anything to do with my past, since it's something I've never talked much about."

"It was a smart move. I imagine such a huge revelation caught her attention, as it would anyone's. Lauren was even worried that you might've had a motive because you'd confessed a secret to Ashley while you were drunk. She didn't know what your secret was, but I assume it was the truth about your father. Or fathers, I suppose I should say."

Pain flickered in Cam's gray-green eyes. "Lauren actually thought I could've murdered Ashley?"

Interesting, I thought, studying his wan face for a moment. *He doesn't like the idea that Lauren would have anything less than a high opinion of him.* "I don't think she really believed you would. It was just a random thought she expressed to me once."

Cam, his shoulders sagging, didn't immediately reply. He gripped the arms of the chair with both hands and stared up at the ceiling.

"You knew Naomi killed Ashley before they arrived today, didn't you?" I asked.

"Yes, but I'd just clicked all the pieces together fairly recently. It was the only thing that made sense, based on facts you'd discovered as well as my own investigation. I was planning to go to the police later today to lay out my theory." Cam lowered his gaze and cast me a wry smile. "I wasn't convinced that they'd believe me, but I thought it might at least compel them to question Naomi and Hannah more thoroughly."

"And you believed both women would crack if presented with all the evidence?"

Cam nodded. "As they did today." In the pause that followed, Cam began tapping the chair arms. "I'm sorry you were involved in today's events, Jane. That was never my intention. I had no idea that Naomi would show up here. I suppose I should've gone to the authorities sooner, but I truly wanted to be sure of all my facts before I accused anyone. Especially"—he grimaced—"old friends."

"I know it's a shock, but I guess I can kind of understand why she hated Ashley so much." I shrugged. "I was thinking about my own daughter, and how I'd feel if someone had treated her the way Ashley treated Selena."

"Naomi could've gone after her legally, though, like I suggested. She could've sued Ashley in a civil case."

"She would've needed solid proof."

"Evie Grayson could've provided some of that." Cam leaned forward, gripping his knees with both hands. "It's too bad Evie got mixed up in this. She seems like a loyal and intelligent young woman. I hate the idea of her wasting away in prison."

I arched my eyebrows. "If only there was someone who could afford to pay for a top-notch lawyer to handle her case."

Cam sat back, a faint smile curving his lips. "Touché. I hadn't considered that option."

I bit back a smart retort, choosing the high road instead. "You could actually help all of them, I imagine."

"I can, and will." Cam examined me for a moment. "But right now, I'd like to get out of here."

"Do you want to head back to your office?" I asked, rising to my feet. "I totally understand. I'm sure that space holds less stressful memories. As for me, I'd like to go home, if you don't mind."

Cam stood to face me. "Of course you can leave, if you wish. And no, I don't want to go to my office. I actually don't want to be in this house. I'd really like to leave for a few hours."

I widened my eyes. "Wait—you want to leave Aircroft?"

Appearing slightly sheepish, Cam nodded.

"Where do you want to go?"

He lifted his hands. "I have no idea."

Taking a deep breath, I looked him over, noticing the exhaustion that had overtaken both his face and body. "Well, there's my apartment." I offered him a warm smile. "It's about as far from Aircroft as you can get."

"Sounds good," Cam said.

Chapter
Forty-Nine

I f Vince found it odd that a silver Porsche parked behind my car, and a tall young man wearing a chocolate-brown cashmere sweater over tailored slacks climbed out of the expensive car, he gave no sign.

He knows who it is, I realized. *He's done enough research on Aircroft to recognize Cam.* But despite his overriding interest in the estate and its history, Vince didn't try to make contact. *He might have a reporter's instincts, but he has a gentleman's good manners*, I thought, giving him a wave as Cam and I ascended the stairs.

When we entered my apartment, Cam looked around the compact space with obvious interest.

"It's small," I said.

"It's cozy. I like it," he replied.

I gestured toward the sofa. "Have a seat. I'll get us something to drink. What would you like? I have coffee, tea, cranberry juice, and some white wine. And water, of course," I added as I headed for the refrigerator.

"Water is fine." Cam sat on the sofa, his gaze sweeping over the bookcases. "Nice selection of books."

"Are you surprised?" I asked, carrying two tumblers of water over to the sofa. I handed him one and set the other on the side table placed next to my single armchair.

"Not really. I figured you'd have an excellent book collection." Cam sipped his water, his focus switching to the armchair as I sat down. "Forgive me if I seem inquisitive about my surroundings. I haven't visited anyone else's home in a long time."

"I gathered that. How are you feeling right now?"

"Nervous," he admitted, before taking another gulp of water. "But I'm still glad to be away from the estate, if only for a little while."

"You should get out more often." I leaned back against the chair cushions.

"I should. I know I should. It just makes me anxious." Cam set his tumbler on a cork coaster on the coffee table. "Even more anxious than usual, I guess I should say."

"Have you ever undergone therapy?" I asked, figuring we were past any need for me to tiptoe around such topics.

Cam's lashes fluttered. "No. I suppose I should try that too. It just wasn't something my father—I mean my stepfather, of course—believed in."

Placing my elbow on the arm of my chair, I rested my chin on my fist. "Not sure you owe him enough loyalty to continue following all his dictates, especially in that area."

"I'm sure you're right." Cam stretched his legs out over my brightly patterned rug. "You know, Jane, I've actually discovered something surprising recently, in the midst of our amateur investigation."

"Oh, what's that?"

Cam cast me an intent look. "How satisfying it is to help solve mysteries, not just due to the achievement of piecing together the puzzle, but also because it can resolve long-simmering issues for other people."

"That is a good feeling," I said, eyeing him with interest. I wasn't sure where this conversation was headed, but I was definitely intrigued.

"I've also realized that I'm sorry Naomi didn't come to me before she killed Ashley. To ask for my help in getting justice for her granddaughter, I mean."

"Ask for your help?" I arched my eyebrows. "Do you think a lot of people would feel comfortable doing that?"

Cam straightened and squared his shoulders. "No. Which is a shame, isn't it? I have the resources to aid others in their quest for justice. Maybe I should do something with that."

"Become a more professional amateur sleuth, you mean?"

"Yes." Cam's face lit up, as if the idea had flipped a switch energizing his entire body. "I have the intelligence, and logic, to puzzle things out. There are a lot of powerful connections I could leverage too. And, of course, I have the money to pay for informants or outside investigators."

"Are you thinking about digging into cold cases?" I asked. "Because you have some of those at Aircroft, you know."

Cam glanced over at me. "You mean the mystery woman in the drawing and photograph? Or the case involving Calvin Aircroft's death?"

"Both, actually." I dropped my hand and leaned forward, gripping the arm of my chair. "Maybe you could even allow

Vince Fisher to help with that one? He's already done a ton of research."

Cam sat back, crossing his arms over his chest. "Perhaps. It could be interesting."

"And then there is the cold case you've already tried to solve," I said, not flinching when Cam shot me a sharp look. "I'm talking about discovering what happened to your biological father." I paused for a beat before adding, "He could still be alive."

After taking a deep breath, Cam grabbed his tumbler and drank down the rest of the water. "You're right," he said, plunking down the glass. "I should continue that search. But I might need help."

"Sure, like you said—outside investigators and such."

"No, I mean someone I really trust." Cam shifted his position so he could look at me more directly. "Like you, Jane."

I lifted my hands. "I'm just your cataloger."

"Are you, though?" Cam asked, with a twitch of his lips. "I would be happy to pay you a higher salary if you'd be willing to help me with some sleuthing work."

"You want me to become your sidekick?" I asked, with an answering smile.

"Partner, I think." Cam crossed his arms behind his head so he could cup the back of his head with his hands. "We could investigate those cold cases you mentioned, and also maybe take on a few investigations for other people. Discreetly, of course. We wouldn't be working with law enforcement, so we'd have to step carefully."

I rose to my feet. "Maybe focus on cases where justice didn't seem likely to be served?"

"Exactly," Cam said.

Studying him for a moment, it struck me that he appeared calmer than I'd ever seen him. "I wouldn't be opposed to such a plan."

"Good." Cam lowered his arms, stretching them out to rest on top of the sofa. "I do like your apartment. It has a special sort of charm. Like you, Jane."

I opened my mouth but snapped it shut again before I expressed any shock over that remark. "Well, one of the charms a hostess is supposed to possess is to provide her guests with sustenance. I don't have much in my pantry or fridge right now, but I'm pretty adept at ordering takeout. What do you say?"

"I say that sounds like the best idea I've heard in a long, long time," Cam replied.

"How about pizza?" I asked, as I headed over to peruse the menu I'd tacked to my refrigerator with an "I Love Reading" magnet. Not sure how particular Cam would be, I added, "Just tell me what toppings you prefer."

Cam turned his head to meet my questioning gaze. "Let's live dangerously. Ask for absolutely everything."

"You got it," I replied. "Everything it is."

I caught the flash of his brilliant smile right before he looked away.

Acknowledgments

B ooks require a dedicated team to bring them to life. The author may be the primary creator, but there are many others whose contributions are essential. For helping to bring this book into being, I'd like to sincerely thank the following people:

My agent, Frances Black of Literary Counsel.

My editor at Crooked Lane Books, Faith Black Ross.

The Crooked Lane Books team, especially Madeline Rathle, Dulce Botello, and Rebecca Nelson.

My friends and my family, especially my late mother, Barbara K. Lemp, who always supported my writing journey and was a devoted fan of my books.

My husband, Kevin, and my son, Thomas, who gracefully deal with me spending so many hours locked away in my office.

My fellow authors, many of whom have become friends as well as colleagues.

Bookstores and libraries—who not only support my work, but also provide me with so many great books to read.

The bloggers, podcasters, YouTubers, and reviewers who have mentioned, reviewed, and promoted my books.

And, as always, my lovely readers!